# PRAISE FOR
## *MY KIND OF CRAZY*

"I had so much fun reading this book. Great characters you instantly care for, and a lot of heart."

—Adi Alsaid, author of *Never Always Sometimes*
and *Let's Get Lost*

"A witty, charming, and thoroughly entertaining debut that celebrates the bit of crazy in all of us."

—Jessica Brody, author of *A Week of Mondays*
and *52 Reasons to Hate My Father*

"Readers will fall in love with Robin Reul's unique and deliciously flawed characters on page one. *My Kind of Crazy* is for everyone who felt they never fit in and weren't sure that they wanted to."

—Eileen Cook, author of *With Malice*
and *What Would Emma Do?*

"Hank Kirby will steal your heart, Peyton Breedlove will set it on fire, and then together they'll mend the pieces."

—Shaun Hutchinson, author of
*We Are the Ants* and *FML*

# MY KIND OF CRAZY

# ROBIN REUL

sourcebooks
fire

Published by Sourcebooks Fire, an imprint of Sourcebooks, Inc.
P.O. Box 4410, Naperville, Illinois 60567-4410
(630) 961-3900
Fax: (630) 961-2168
www.sourcebooks.com

Library of Congress Cataloging-in-Publication data is on file with the
publisher.

Printed and bound in the United States of America.
VP 10 9 8 7 6 5 4 3 2 1

FOR MOM AND DAD,
INFINITY AND INFINITY.

FOR MY FAMILY,
WHO NEVER STOPPED
BELIEVING.
YOU'RE MY KIND
OF CRAZY.

# 1

SO HERE'S THE THING. IT'S NOT LIKE I WOKE UP
this morning and said, "Hey, I think I'll light the hundred-year-
old eastern red cedar tree in front of Amanda Carlisle's house on
fire today." Because I don't know about you, but when I wake up,
my mind doesn't go straight to arson. Honestly, the first thing
I focus on is how fast I can get from my room to the bathroom
without my dad's girlfriend, Monica, trying to chat me up while
I'm awkwardly standing there in my boxers.

I'd read online that how you ask a girl to prom can completely
make or break a guy's chances. I wanted to do something special
that Amanda would never forget. Apparently it worked, just not
the way I intended. "Use sparklers to spell out PROM," the article
on the Internet said. There was even a picture with them all lit up
on the ground. Totally idiotproof.

I snuck into her yard like a ninja under the cover of darkness
and tried to jam the sparklers into her lawn, but the soil was hard
and unyielding. I looked around, desperate, and then I spied a

nice, soft patch of mulch underneath the cedar tree near the side of her yard. It was perfect, and the sparklers slid in easily. A few minutes later, I had them all lined up just like I'd seen in the picture. Once they were lit, I yelled, "Amanda!" I actually had to call out twice because she didn't hear me the first time. Then she came to the window and gazed down as the sparklers fizzled down to the ground and—*boom!*

Turns out it was fresh pine mulch underneath that cedar. Pine trees produce turpentine, so I might as well have lit those sparklers in a pool of gasoline, considering how quickly the mulch caught fire.

I didn't know what to do, so I ran. Which is why I'm now hiding behind a bush across the street in her neighbor's yard. This is definitely going down in history as the most epic promposal fail ever. And then, as if things couldn't get more catastrophic, they do.

Baseball is practically a religion where I live in Massachusetts's South Coast. People take their Red Sox pretty seriously, and the diehards decorate their trees with red and blue streamers every season in a show of support. The Carlisles are no exception. And it doesn't take long for the flames to catch and race the length of those ribbons into the dry branches above.

From where I'm crouched down, I have a perfect view of

the Carlisle house. I can see Amanda's eyes widen and her jaw drop open as she observes the quickly escalating situation in her yard. She pulls away from the window—I'm guessing to call the fire department. We should probably talk about prom some other time.

With things clearly going south, I do what any sensible person would do: I get the hell out of there. Of course, a sensible person wouldn't have put sparklers in a pile of fresh mulch directly under a highly flammable tree. Hindsight is twenty-twenty.

So in the most casual way possible, I hook my backpack— which is loaded with empty sparkler boxes—over my shoulders, hop on my bike, and pedal away from the scene at what I hope passes for a normal speed. Cool as a cucumber, that's me.

I reason for a brief moment that perhaps Amanda didn't actually see me there. Even if she did, she doesn't know me all that well so she might not recognize me. I am wearing black jeans, and my Batman hoodie conceals my medium-length, stick-straight brown hair, so I am sort of camouflaged. Not to mention that those flames were pretty distracting.

The fire station is about five streets away, near the library. I start to worry that the firemen won't get there fast enough and Amanda's whole house will burn down. I know I'm a lame-ass chickenshit for hightailing out of there, but the last thing I need is Dad on my case for something else. As far as he's concerned, I can't do much right. I would like to say he's just being an asshole, but lately I've been wondering if he's onto something.

I consider turning around and heading back to Amanda's, which would be the right thing to do, but I swear I'm about to piss myself with fear so I pedal faster, listening for the sounds of approaching police sirens. For good measure, I jerk my bike off the main road, cutting through the back alleys toward home.

By the time my key is in the door, I'm sweating like a whore in church and feel like I'm going to puke. I have two objectives: avoid all human contact and get to my room as quickly as possible.

Naturally, this does not happen. Dad is sitting downstairs, nursing a beer and watching a baseball game on TV. He's wearing his stained lucky Red Sox shirt that he never washes because that would bring bad luck. His eyes are puffy and his face hasn't seen a razor in days. It's sad to see him like this. He's actually a pretty handsome guy. Even when my mom was alive, I noticed other women checking him out. If I'd been paying a little more attention, I might have noticed he was checking them out too. It wasn't until Mom was gone that I think he realized how much he loved her.

Normally when I come home, Dad acknowledges me with little more than a wave and a grunt, his eyes glued to his precious Sox, but lucky for me, tonight he decides to strike up a conversation.

"Hey! Hank! Just in time. Sox're killing 'em. Top of the ninth." He raises his bottle and tips it toward me as if he's toasting me.

"Nice," I tell him, but I can't think about baseball right now. The only balls I can concentrate on are my own as I wonder how I'm going to grow a pair and deal with this mess.

Dad yells at the umpire on the screen. When he was younger, Dad was a hell of a ballplayer with dreams of playing for the Sox. He was offered a spot in the minor leagues out of high school, met my mom, fell in love, and the future looked bright. Four years went by, and he never got picked up for the majors. Then he tore his ACL and that was that. Game over. Time for Plan B.

"Monica made some kind of enchilada casserole. I think there's some left. You could warm it up."

That sounds dangerous. She means well, but Monica might possibly be the worst cook on the entire planet. It's not that my mom was some great cook, but in comparison she was Betty frickin' Crocker.

Dad takes a swig of his beer and then places it on the coffee table beside an empty. The condensation will leave a wet ring on the wood. All our furniture is covered with them, like a dog pissing to mark his territory or something. That's one of the few things I remember my mother hassling Dad about the day she and my older brother, Mickey, died, even though that was nearly six years ago. "Use a coaster, Larry!" It was her mantra.

"I'm not all that hungry." It isn't even a lie. I'm pretty sure that if I eat anything, it will come hurtling back up at light speed.

"Not like you to pass up the Sox or a meal." The role of concerned parent fits him like a cheap suit. He gives me a once-over, clearly judging my pale, skinny frame. I'm no wimp. Just because I'm not bench-pressing with a bunch of jockstraps at the gym doesn't mean I can't lift four forty-pound bags of dog food at my job at the Shop 'n Save without breaking a sweat.

I'd much rather be up in my room working on the latest installment of my comic *Freeze Frame*. Add that to the list of disappointments life has dealt my dad. The only thing worse than losing his wife and superjock son and being left with me would be if I were a girl.

"I'm good. Maybe later. I gotta take a shower and study for a bio test tomorrow. Plus, I have to work tonight. They're doing inventory so I'll be back late…" I drift off, hoping he'll lose interest and I can make an escape.

"Yeah, well, you'll have to wait a few minutes. Monica's upstairs using the shower."

Initially, I wondered what the hell someone like Monica was doing with a guy like my dad. She's twenty-six, only nine years older than I am, and she's a dancer. Not ballet or Broadway or some fancy crap, but off the highway at Mo's Boobie Barn. She says it's only temporary to help her pay her way through beauty school, but I guess it goes without saying where they met.

According to Monica, he showed up at the club one night and they spent some "private time" in the back. Somewhere along the line, he lost his shit and broke down crying, and they ended up spending the rest of the night just talking. They've been seeing each other ever since. Monica moved in nearly a year ago, so it seems pretty serious. From what I can tell, she loves that he sees her as more than what she does for a living, and she has a soft spot for men she thinks she can save. I'm hoping she can.

The opposing team strikes out, and the crowd goes bananas. The TV switches to a commercial and a newscaster saying, "Coming up on the news at eleven, sparklers lead to a fire in a local neighborhood igniting controversy: prank or arson?"

I try to act casual as they flash live video of Amanda's charred front yard. Must be a slow night for them to pick up the story that quickly. I swallow hard.

Dad stares at the TV and shakes his head. "Jesus, what goddamn moron would do something like that? Sparklers on a lawn?"

*This moron.* "Crazy."

"At least it sounds like nobody got hurt." He belches and wipes his mouth with the edge of his fist.

"Well, that's what matters, right?" And then I do that thing I do when I'm nervous or trying to cover something up but hope that nobody will notice. I get total diarrhea of the mouth. "Who knows why anyone does anything really. Maybe the person had a reason. Someone doesn't just light sparklers on a lawn for no reason, right?"

The game comes back on and instantly he's gone, his attention riveted like a dog's to a squirrel. Someone hits a homer out of the park on his first at bat and Dad is up out of his seat cheering, so I make my exit.

I sprint up the stairs and pass the bathroom door, which is cracked open precisely enough for me to make out a sliver of Monica's pale-white skin as she wraps herself in a terry-cloth towel. My hand is reaching for my bedroom doorknob when suddenly the bathroom door opens. She smiles as if I've been lurking.

Which I haven't.

I mean, it was only for like a second.

She runs her fingers through her long, brown, wet-from-the-shower hair. Her skin glistens with moisture.

"Oh, hey, Hank," she says. I try to act like it's completely normal to stand in the hallway chatting up my dad's girlfriend who is only wearing a towel.

"Oh, hi. I…um…have to study for a test." I readjust my backpack strap. "Gotta maintain that GPA."

She fiddles with the edge of her towel. "Hey, what'd the girl say?"

"What girl?"

"The other night you told me you were goin' to ask some girl to prom this week. How'd that go? Did she say yes?"

*Shit. Fuck. Shit.*

My mouth hangs open for a second as I regroup and collect my thoughts. Monica had asked me if I was going to prom while I was cleaning up after dinner. Fortunately, I hadn't told her any details, only that I had someone in mind to ask.

"Uh, it went fine, I guess."

"Fine? So she said yes?" Her face lights up like she is genuinely happy for me.

"Um, not exactly. I'm not really sure." Her towel slips a little, but I pretend not to notice.

"How can you not be sure? You either asked her or you didn't. Did she say she had to think about it? Because any girl who says she has to think about it is probably waitin' for some other guy to ask her, and you've become her backup plan while she buys some time."

I nod, perhaps a little too vigorously. "Right. You are so right. Great advice. I will definitely keep that in mind."

"Never settle, Hank. You're a great guy. And you're adorable. Any girl would be lucky to go with you."

"Adorable" is a word that I generally reserve for teddy bears and kittens, but I'll take it. The smell of soap and Suave Ocean Breeze shampoo hits my nose as she pulls me close for a hug, and I start to feel awkward. Now I really have to get in my room fast, or else this could get highly embarrassing. So I pull away and hurriedly push open my door, shouting, "Thanks! See ya!" and give her a thumbs-up as I swing it closed.

*Holy Mother of God.*

Once I'm in, I throw my backpack on the bed and tear it open, pulling out the empty sparkler boxes. I've got to hide them somewhere until Thursday, which is trash pickup, because I can't risk leaving them in the garbage can. Murphy's Law says that if I do, this will be the week a freak band of raccoons decides to rummage through our garbage or some homeless guy goes diving for recyclables. I've got enough fish to fry without Harry the Hobo getting interviewed on the eleven o'clock news about the "suspicious packages" he found when he was playing amateur archaeologist for old Pepsi cans.

I quickly inventory my boxes. And then I panic. There should be seven of them. Eight sparklers came in a package, and the website specifically recommended seven boxes. But there are only six boxes here. My bag was zipped, which means I dropped one of them somewhere in front of Amanda Carlisle's house. And unless it burned up in the fire, it's lying there covered in my fingerprints and practically wrapped with a bow for someone to find.

I've done a lot of dumbass things in my life, but this is pretty much the capper. I break into a sweat all over again. If someone had found the box and connected it to me, the police would have already shown up at my door, right?

I count the boxes again but there are still only six. Which means I have no choice.

I have to go back to Amanda's house.

# 2

ALL I WANT TO DO IS FIND THAT MISSING SPARKLER
box, but I can't go now because the fire department will still be
there. They'll probably have the road blocked off, and my snooping
around would be totally obvious. I have to be at Shop 'n Save
in an hour anyway. I'm picking up someone else's shift to do
inventory because it pays double time, so I'll be there from 10:00
until 2:00 a.m. I decide to sneak by Amanda's on my way home.
If it's not already too late, it's my best shot at saving my ass.

It's frickin' freezing at 2:00 a.m., especially when you're riding
a bike. Not to mention that it's also dark as hell except for the
occasional pools of light from the street lamps. I roll up in front
of the Carlisle house, which still has police tape cordoning off the
singed area of the lawn. Otherwise, it's pretty quiet.

I lay my bike gently on the pavement and tiptoe toward the
spot I used as my staging area. I turn on the flashlight app on my
phone and cast it in a low-lying arc, but there's no empty sparkler
box. Which means I'm pretty much screwed because the police

probably found it and took it for evidence. And if I'm incarcer-
ated, I'm guessing there is no way in hell Amanda Carlisle will
go with me to prom.

"Looking for something?"

I practically jump out of my skin. I straighten up and shine
my phone into the eyes of a girl with the craziest hair I've ever
seen, causing her to squint and angle away from me, holding
her hand up as a shield.

"Can you quit that, please? What are you trying to do,
blind me?"

"Sorry," I say and click off the light.

She looks vaguely familiar, though I can't put a finger on
why. And despite the fact that it's almost two thirty in the
morning, she is not wearing pajamas. In fact, she has on a pair
of jeans and an old Pink Floyd shirt that is about two sizes too
big for her. In the moonlight I can make out the graffitied,
white rubber tips of her Converse. Her long, curly brown
hair sticks out at all sorts of defiant angles, and she peeks at
me with the bluest eyes I've ever seen from underneath her
unruly bangs.

"You're not going to find what you're looking for," she
tells me.

"How do you know what I'm looking for?" I ask. "And

why are you walking around the neighborhood at two thirty in the morning?"

"Hmmm, I could ask you the same questions," she says and puts a finger thoughtfully to her chin.

"I lost something. I think I might've left it here." I shoot another glance around, trying to play it cool.

"What'd you lose? Maybe I can help you."

She takes a step toward me, and I reflexively step away from her. "Why are you here?" I ask again.

"I was heading out for a jog."

I look her over suspiciously. "At this hour? You're wearing jeans."

"I didn't know there was a dress code. Look, do you want my help or not?"

"Not. I'm good. Enjoy your run. Thanks though." I give her a little wave, hoping she will take the hint and be on her way, but instead she crosses her arms and stares at me.

"You're Hank Kirby, right?"

My back stiffens. "How do you know my name?"

"I know who you are. I've seen you around." She smiles. "I've been waiting for you to come back."

This girl is starting to creep me the hell out.

"What do you mean 'come back'?" I ask nervously. What

if she's a serial killer? What if she's about to chop me into
bits, divide me into a bunch of garbage bags, and toss me in
the county dump alongside a bunch of rotting produce and
stained, saggy mattresses? I can't die a virgin.

She reaches behind her and I panic. This is it. She's going
for her knife. I start to back away, but she's looking at me with
this confused expression. When her hand comes around, she's
not holding a knife at all.

She's holding a box of sparklers.

My box of sparklers.

She's seen me. She must know what happened, that I'm
responsible. I'm totally screwed. *Oh God. Who has she told?*

"Impressive," she says as she places the box in my hand. I
quickly shove it into my back pocket and pull my sweatshirt
over it to make sure it's completely hidden from view. "Too bad
it didn't burn the place down. That would have been beautiful.
Lord knows I've thought about it a thousand times myself."

Now I'm the one looking at her like she's whack-a-doodle.
"What are you talking about? I didn't try to burn down her
house. I was trying to ask her to prom. Jesus. You didn't tell
anyone that, did you? Does anybody know you found this?"

"Prom? That's disappointing. And also slightly pathetic,"
she says with a smirk and scoops that mane of hers up into a

ponytail, twisting a hair band around so it looks as if a small poodle is hanging off the back of her head. "And no, I didn't tell anyone. Your secret is safe with me."

I don't know who this chick is or what her deal is, but I do know that hanging around chitchatting in front of Amanda Carlisle's house at 2:30 a.m. with an empty box of sparklers in my back pocket is probably not a stellar idea. I dart past her, pick up my bike, and swing my leg over it, angling myself in the direction of home. "Well, thanks. I better get going. See ya."

She shakes her head and bites at her lip. "Don't you even want to know my name?"

I shoot a glance down the road. A pair of headlights appears in the distance. Time to go. "Uh…sure."

"It's Peyton."

"Yeah, well, I'll see ya 'round, Peyton," I say and push off. I don't wait for her to say good-bye, and halfway home I start to feel like a jerk about that. I mean, the girl saved my ass. She could have handed that box over to the police, or even to Amanda Carlisle.

The more distance I put between us, the more questions I have. Who the hell is this girl and how does she know my name? Why did she save my box of sparklers? And how do I find her again? I have no idea what she wants from me.

It's like my entire life flipped upside down when she gave me that box. Suddenly, my fate is in this chick's hands. Why did she protect me like that? And what if she decides to stop?

For the third time in six hours, I flip my bike around and pedal furiously toward Amanda Carlisle's house. If I don't find Peyton, I'm gonna spend the foreseeable future worried that she might share what she knows.

Amanda's street is empty, with no sign that we were ever here. I know I didn't imagine Peyton because the corners of that box dig into my spine as I pedal, but there's not as much as a light on in a neighboring house, not a single jogger in sight. I'm pretty certain her jogging story was a load of crap, but just to be safe I pedal up and down a few streets on the chance that I'll see her.

*Zip. Nada.*

I better get my ass back before Dad wakes up for his shift and discovers I'm gone. I race home and stash the empty sparkler box with the others behind my bin of old comic books underneath my bed, then grab an Avengers T-shirt and faded pair of jeans that are lying on the floor. I sniff to see if they're tolerable, since I haven't done laundry in a while. Not too ripe.

I'm about to head downstairs when I realize that being up and ready might arouse suspicion, especially if I stumble in while Dad is nursing his morning coffee, adding the shot of whiskey that he thinks no one notices. Of course, if he'd seen me sneaking in, he probably would have assumed I was out somewhere getting laid. That would make him happy, no doubt. Then again, we'd lose half of our source of conversation: him asking me if I'm getting any, me telling him "not that I'm aware of," him giving me the list of why I'm repellent to the opposite sex.

Better to crawl back under the covers and wait it out. I try to close my eyes, but my brain is racing, processing everything that's happened since last night.

As soon as the clock turns to seven, I'm out of bed like a shot, flying down the stairs two at a time and out the door, letting the screen door slam with a *fwap!* behind me. I have to find Peyton. I pedal to school like my life depends on it, and for all I know, it does.

# 3

THE FIRST THING I SEE AS I LOCK MY BIKE AT SCHOOL
is a cop car parked out front. Although this is not a highly unusual
occurrence at Kennedy High, I'd be lying if I didn't say a little bile
is rising in my throat. No one's in the car, which means the cops
must be inside talking to someone in the office.

Or searching a locker.

Or waiting for someone.

Or waiting for someone so that they can search their locker.

Beads of sweat sprout on my upper lip alongside the stubble. I
mentally inventory my locker, trying to remember if I have as much
as a wadded-up piece of paper with the name Amanda Carlisle
written on it, let alone anything that would tie me to the events of
the previous evening. But all I can come up with are a stinky pair of
gym shorts and a Snickers bar so old it could chip a tooth.

I walk to my locker, whistling to show how totally relaxed and
at ease I am with the world. I'm fiddling with my lock when I hear
Amanda approach with her gaggle of girlfriends, who listen with

rapt attention as she recounts how she defied death. I pretend to focus on my lock with all the concentration of a safecracker, careful not to look directly at her. In my peripheral vision, I can see her hair is loose and wavy today, her blond bangs swept to one side. Her lips are painted bubble-gum pink to match her cardigan. If her jeans were any tighter, she'd need a crowbar to get out of them.

She stops at her locker, which is in the next bank over. The girls fan out around her as she spins the dial and puts her books away. I hear her tell them, "The cops said whoever did it was trying to spell something, like a message. I swear to you, when I looked out, I saw someone standing there. These eyes looked up at me, but not in a creepy way, and then there was just this wall of flames."

"Whoa." Becca Henry's eyes widen and her mouth hangs open.

"The thing is, I don't think he was trying to hurt anybody. I believe that message was for me. I mean, right before it happened, I heard him *call my name*."

"I've got chills," Hannah Wolf says as she runs her fingers up and down her arms.

If I were a cartoon and Amanda looked over at me right now, she would see my heart practically beating out of my chest. I glance at her. She's smiling and eating up the attention, as several of her friends make swoony noises. I decide to reorganize my locker so that I can keep listening.

"That's so romantic. Who do you think it was?" Jenny O'Leary asks.

Amanda shrugs. "I don't know. But I'm dying to find out."

Hannah grabs Amanda's arm and bounces on the balls of her feet as she says in a loud whisper, "O-M-G! Maybe it was Clay Kimball!"

Clay is a douche-bag jock on the baseball team who thinks that being able to hit a ball with a large stick entitles him to be a jerk. For reasons that remain a mystery, women seem to find this attractive.

"No, Clay's too tall and built. This guy was shorter and skinnier."

"He was a midget?" Jenny crinkles her nose.

*Jesus, I'm five foot ten. It's not like I'm a pygmy.*

"No, not exactly. Just…not tall. And his eyes were sort of beady, but that could have been from the heat of the flames. He might have been squinting."

They all nod in agreement. I cringe and bite down on my tongue to keep from responding. Then Amanda closes her locker and adds in an extra-dramatic voice, "What if he's totally hot and he's scared to talk to me now that my house nearly burned down and I almost died?"

More like part of her lawn and a tree caught fire—and the firemen were right on it—but the girl certainly knows how to tell a compelling story. Her power of exaggeration only adds to her charm, and I smile to myself, knowing she's talking about me, which is six kinds of crazy, even if she did just describe me as short and unathletic with beady eyes.

The girls collectively suck in their breath, and Hannah tells her, "If it's meant to be, he'll find you. He obviously went to a lot of trouble to get your attention, so he's not going to simply disappear, right? Not if he really loves you."

*Love? Who said anything about love?*

"You think so?"

"Of course!" Jenny squeals with absolute authority. "But are you mad about what happened? I mean, like you said, he could have killed you."

Amanda shakes her head, hugging her notebook to her chest. "No. I just want to know who he is and what he wanted to say last night."

Becca nods and tilts her head, letting out a wistful sigh. "It's so totally romantic, like a Cinderella story. I wish stuff like that happened to me."

Now *this* is the reaction I was hoping for when I started researching promposals online. It's the perfect opener. I get a blast of courage and I turn to Amanda. My mouth is open, ready to tell her everything and hoping we can both laugh about it, but the words hang there in my throat. This is a terrible idea.

Hannah glares at me, her eyes forming little slits. "Can we help you?" Now all of them are staring at me.

"Uh…" I panic and say the first thing that comes to mind. "Do you have a pen?"

Amanda smiles at me and extracts a blue pen that is wedged in the spiral of one of her notebooks. "You can keep it," she says.

"Thanks," I say. They're all looking at me, seemingly waiting for me to say something else since I'm still standing there. I clear my throat, which makes me cough. And once I start coughing, I can't stop. And then they're all laughing and walking away, weaving through the crowd to first period while I'm practically bringing up a lung. *Smooth, genius.*

✳

By noon, I realize that I flew out of the house without grabbing a lunch, and I haven't eaten since this time yesterday. All I have is fifty-two cents rattling around in my pocket. My stomach makes a deep, hollow, growly sound. I hover at the entrance to the cafeteria, hoping I will see someone I know to borrow a few bucks.

A moment or two after the bell, Nick Giuliani approaches, his black, greasy hair slicked back, loping along in his untied Dr. Martens. His red flannel shirt flaps open as he walks. His jeans hang just low enough on his hips that you can see the waistband of his black plaid boxers. Most kids are scared of him because, rumor has it, his dad has Mafia connections. It could also be because Nick has a lazy eye. When it's really bad, he wears an eye patch, which makes him look like a pirate of the frickin' Caribbean. They say that makes him a good lookout when his dad has business going down, because his eye's always moving around.

Nick doesn't scare me. In fact, he's pretty funny once you get him going, and he's always got great stories. For the most part, like me, he keeps to himself, but sometimes we hang out after school and grab a burger or go to the comic shop and look at the new issues. He's pretty cool, even if he does like DC better than Marvel.

"Yo, Hank. What's up, my man?" His right eye is looking at me, but his left eye wanders off to take in the quad.

I look him square in his good eye. "Hey, Nick. I forgot

to bring a lunch today. You got an extra couple of bucks? I'll owe ya."

"You're in luck. Today was payday, and my old man gave me a bonus." He grins and smooths his slick hair back with one hand, then peels a couple of dollars off a wad from his back pocket and hands them to me.

"Thanks, Nick. I'll pay you back tomorrow. I promise."

"With interest," he says as he folds a bill in half and starts using it to pick between his two front teeth. I freeze. He cracks up and gives me a slap on the back as his left eye rotates back into position. "I'm just jokin'."

The lunch lady gives me an extra scoop of mac and cheese. It's my favorite, even though it's the industrial version of that bright-orange crap that comes from a box and probably makes your intestines glow in the dark. I settle in with Nick at a table in the corner of the cafeteria, off the radar from where the jocks and popular kids hold court. I'm popping open my container of chocolate milk and sliding in the straw when I see her.

Actually, the first thing I see is her hair. It's a wild mane of curls like early this morning, but now she's added a red bow on the side. It looks as if it's hanging on to that nest for dear life. The Pink Floyd shirt is gone, replaced by a black vintage Stones T-shirt and a pair of faded jeans with holes in the knees. She's drawn a happy face on both exposed kneecaps, which is ironic because her mouth is turned down in an Eeyore frown. She's holding her tray and scanning the room, and the second she locks eyes with mine, she pivots and starts walking toward our table.

Wordlessly, she sits down next to me as if she's been invited, which causes Nick to raise an eyebrow at me. I shrug. She busies herself buttering her roll by tearing it in half, wiping the patty across the center, then crushing the two halves together and smearing them back and forth to spread the butter out evenly. Next she turns her attention to her fruit cocktail. She picks out every single grape with her spoon and lays them in a neat arc on the side of her tray.

She rakes her fork through the mac and cheese, breaking up the congealed layer of cheese on the top, which in my opinion is the best part. She shakes her milk back and forth vigorously, then peels open the top and sticks in her straw. Bending the tip to meet her lips, she takes a sip and then looks up at us.

"What do you have against grapes?" Nick asks, fascinated.

"They're disgusting. I don't eat anything that has skin of any kind." She stabs her fork into a wedge of cantaloupe and pops the melon into her mouth.

"That cantaloupe had skin," Nick shoots back and openly stares at her.

"Yes, but the skin is removed to get to the fruit. When you eat a fruit with its skin, it's been touched, peed on by rodents and insects, stored in dirty trucks and warehouses. I can't possibly expect it to have been washed properly before it lands on my plate."

Nick presses her further. "What about strawberries?"

She shakes her head. "Nope."

"Awwww, c'mon. Most people like strawberries," he says and glances at me for support. "You like strawberries, Hank?"

"I do." I take a bite of my mac and cheese and chase it with a swig of chocolate milk.

"I guess I'm not most people," she says.

That seems to satisfy Nick. He looks amused. "I've seen you before."

"That would stand to reason. I go to school here."

Nick takes a bite of his roll and says with his mouth full of food, "What's your name?"

"Peyton." She stabs another piece of fruit and then dips it in the mac and cheese. I guess it could be gross, but in a way it makes sense. It's like fondue or something.

"You got a last name, Peyton?"

She points her fork at him and says, "Breedlove. Why, are you taking attendance later?"

Nick raises both hands in surrender. "Do you know this girl, Hank?"

"Of course he does," she answers before I can even open my mouth.

I'm scared she'll tell Nick how we know each other so I quickly say, "Yeah. This is Peyton. She's cool."

She puts her fork down, turns to me as if Nick isn't even there, and says, "I was wondering if you wanted to hang out after school today, Hank."

She seems serious. I honestly don't know what to say. Until this morning, I'd never seen Peyton Breedlove, and now here she is again, sitting next to me with some serious blackmail material, and I'm wondering what would happen if I said no. I'm too scared to find out. "Sure."

"Perfect. I'll meet you at my house."

Nick is full-on staring at me now because he's never seen me with a girl before, and naturally the one he sees now bears a strong resemblance to a walking Chia head. He wiggles his eyebrows. It looks like two fuzzy black caterpillars are doing push-ups.

"Um…I don't know where you live," I say with a nervous laugh, then shrug at Nick, as if to say, "This girl is mad as a hatter." His eyes shift to her like he's watching a tennis match.

"I can't eat this." She drops her fork and sighs, then stands up holding her tray, stepping over the sides of the metal lunch-table seats and angling toward the trash can to dump the contents. "I'll see you around three thirtyish." Her mouth curls into a smile, and her ice-blue eyes lock with mine. "I have faith in you."

Nick watches her walk off, shaking his head and muttering, "Interesting, interesting."

He doesn't know the half of it.

# 4

IT'S A LOT OF RESPONSIBILITY WHEN SOMEONE puts faith in you.

Looking for Peyton's house is like trying to find a straight guy at a Lady Gaga concert. I pretty much zigzag my way through every street in a five-block radius of where Amanda lives, hoping there's a house with a sign that says "Crazy lives here." It's not like I can ask anyone, because I'm pretty sure no one knows who the hell she is. It's like she appeared out of nowhere. In fact, if Nick hadn't been sitting across from me today and witnessed the whole lunch episode, I would wonder if anyone else could see her.

I decide my best bet is to retrace my steps from early this morning, so I start to pedal to Amanda Carlisle's house. Everything appears pretty normal—people out walking their dogs, mowing the lawn. No sign of Peyton. As I get within a couple of blocks of Amanda's house, I notice the damnedest thing on the side of the road: matchsticks. Not the kind that come in a little book. I'm talking about the matches that are about two inches long, made of tan-colored wood with a red tip, and come in a box. The tips are spent though, so whoever left them lit them first. There's one about every ten feet, like a trail of bread crumbs.

I follow the trail, and as I do, the matchsticks get closer and closer together. They appear to be leading to Amanda Carlisle's house. Is this someone's idea of a sick joke? The smell of burned tree still lingers in the air and grows more pronounced as I draw closer. Then, just before I reach Amanda's house, the matchsticks form a figure-eight pattern in the middle of the road and cross the street toward a giant bush, where they end abruptly.

It's the bush I hid behind the night of the fire. I skid my bike to a stop.

Hidden by the overgrown bush and set back from the road is a house that seems to fit the neighborhood well enough, though the yard is not tended with the same care. The patchy crabgrass is only partially mowed in an erratic zigzag pattern, like someone got bored and gave up midway. The only real greenery is weeds that have stubbornly sprung up between the rocks in the planter beds. The dusty-blue ranch-style house is still sporting Christmas lights despite it being mid-April, and the blinds are all closed. An old beater sits in the oil-stained driveway, and to the side of it, a wooden fence bows forward, looking like one good windstorm could bring it down.

Apparently, the Breedloves are *those* neighbors. Everything about this place needs a hug, and that's how I know—even before I see her—that I've found the right house.

"Nice job, Sherlock. I told you I had faith in you," Peyton says, stepping out from behind the bush.

"What's with the matchsticks? You probably shouldn't leave them lying around here. Just a hunch, but someone might think you're responsible for what happened across the street." I lean down and collect a few, then hold them out to her like a bouquet.

"Well, we both know that I'm not, don't we? Though I admit that I admire your style." She throws a nasty glance at her house and then back at me. "Besides, I was wearing gloves, so they'd have his fingerprints on them, not mine. I'm no fool."

"Whose fingerprints?"

"My mom's boyfriend, Pete." She says the words like they're poison. "Or, as I like to call him, Pete the Deadbeat. At least he's better than Dave the Dealer or Steve the Sociopath, but only by a small margin. My mother has outstanding taste in men." She takes the matches from me, shoving them in the back pocket of her jeans. I'm still processing that last comment, which she's shared as casually as a preference for Coke over Pepsi, when she says, "C'mon. I want to show you something."

I start to roll my bike, but she grabs the handlebars. "No, leave this here. It won't get stolen. I promise."

"You're just saying that because it's orange," I joke. I let go, and she steers it into the bushes where it is perfectly concealed from view. Then she motions for me to follow her around the side of the house, putting her finger to her lips as she tiptoes past the window. I can hear the faint strains of a television inside.

"He's glued to the couch watching some home improvement show. Trust me, he doesn't like interruptions," she whispers.

She leads me around to the backyard, which isn't much more attractive than the front. On one end, there is a massive hole. She sees me looking at it and tells me, "Pete decided we needed a pool so he could skateboard in it. Dug it himself last summer, after watching how to do it on TV. Got about halfway through and gave up on the idea, which came as no surprise. My mom is pissed because this place is a rental, so it pretty much guarantees her deposit's history. I think it's a great place to hide his body."

Her face is so serious that I can't tell she's making a joke until her mouth curls into a smile. "Kidding."

I let out a nervous laugh. "Of course. I knew that," I say, even though I'm not entirely convinced.

We pass a semicircle of broken lounge chairs and a table piled high with boards and rusted tools—evidence of other projects gone by the wayside. She leads me to the far corner of the yard, obscured from view of the main house by another abandoned pile of plywood, to a stone fire pit, like for roasting hot dogs or marshmallows. It's loaded with ash and debris, and when the breeze kicks up, little particles fly in the air like those white thingies from dandelions.

"I know this seems small time, but I wanted to show you my spot." Her whole face lights up with pride. "I mean, it doesn't compare to what you did, but it can still be pretty satisfying." She takes a deep breath and then puffs out her cheeks as she exhales slowly. "Anyhow, I've never shown it to anyone. I mean, not anyone who would understand."

I look at the pit, then at her, and I shake my head. "I'm sorry. I'm not quite sure I know what you're talking about."

She laughs and I laugh, almost as if we're sharing some inside joke but only one of us knows what's funny. And it isn't me.

Then I start to worry. Because maybe if this girl thinks I get something and it becomes clear that I don't, she could go completely batshit crazy on me. Who would even know where I was? I'm pretty sure Pete the Deadbeat isn't going to have my back. So I swallow hard and decide to play along.

"Yeah, that's cool," I say and dig my hands into my pockets, then take them out again for good measure in case I need to defend myself. "So…show me how it works."

She grins like the Cheshire cat. "I thought you'd never ask."

Next thing I know, she's pulling this blue tarp off a big plastic container near the fire pit. She pries off the lid, and I honestly don't know what to expect when I peer in. For all I know, this is where she keeps pieces of her victims or a pet python or some other weird shit. What I don't expect to see is a bunch of naked Barbies. The container's half filled with them. I try my hardest to look unfazed, but this shit keeps getting weirder and weirder.

She kneels down excitedly and riffles through them. "At first I started with pieces of paper. I'd write down the names of people who pissed me off and then set fire to them, but this is so much better. Who gets under your skin? Just completely goes out of their way to make your life a living hell?"

I smile. "That's a no-brainer. Kyle Jonas."

Kyle Jonas is this total dick in my English class who's had it out for me ever since elementary school. In tenth grade, he put a smear of chocolate pudding on my seat, and then he and his equally dickish friends howled with laughter as I proceeded to sit in it. The chair was dark brown so I couldn't see it. I had to walk around looking like I'd crapped in my pants for three periods before I could escape to the locker room and change into my gym shorts. Two years later, and he still thinks the "can't hold it" jokes he makes at my expense are hi-frickin'-larious.

She smirks. "That guy's an ass. Watch and see how much better you're gonna feel."

She paws through the Barbies until she extracts a male one that bears an uncanny resemblance to Kyle with perfectly combed brown hair and a chiseled chin. She holds it up victoriously, then grabs a black Sharpie from inside the bin and scrawls "Kyle" across its chest before handing it to me.

I look at the naked doll, unsure what I'm supposed to do with it, but Peyton's already throwing balls of newspaper on the fire pit and a few pieces of old plywood. She sprays some fuel on top and sets it all on fire. The flames dance at the edges of the paper, slowly eating at the corners until the fire finds the dry lumber. The wood starts to pop and crack. I can feel the heat coming off it, and the breeze blows the smoke toward me, which makes me sneeze.

I have no idea what the hell is going on.

I stand to the side as Peyton pokes at the fire with a metal rod. It's like she's in a trance. She never takes her eyes off the flames. She turns to me. "Go ahead. Throw it in."

"The Barbie?" I ask.

She locks gazes with me and says, "It's not a Barbie. It's Kyle Jonas."

"Kyle Jonas," I repeat. "Right."

I take a step toward the fire. She grabs my hand.

"Wait! Close your eyes. As you throw it in, tell yourself that you're taking back the power. That Kyle Jonas can never hurt you again."

She releases my hand and nods in encouragement. I take that as my cue to chuck Ken, a.k.a. Kyle Jonas, into the pit. I gotta admit that I am a little freaked out, but at the same time, I'm slightly intrigued as Ken nose-dives into the flames.

The flames attack the doll instantly, blackening and distorting its plastic features, and causing its arms and legs to melt and mutate at weird angles. After a few more moments, it becomes unrecognizable as what it once was.

Finally I say, "Is this some weird voodoo shit? Because I gotta be honest. I'm not really down with black magic."

She scoffs. "No, of course not. Voodoo is like people running around with bloody, headless chickens, saying incantations and speaking in tongues."

I hesitate. "Well, I'm not sure I get it is all."

Peyton's brow creases, and she is clearly disappointed by

my comment. She chews at her lip, then says, "It's…it's like they transform from being beautiful to ugly and distorted. There's a different kind of beauty in that, I think. Everything beautiful can be ugly, and everything ugly can be beautiful. It's all perspective. But it's like you're the artist with the brush, and everything else is your canvas. I don't know—I thought you might understand that."

She grabs a nearby bucket filled with water and douses the flames with a hiss. As the fire gives way to smoke, she shakes her head. "I'm sorry. I never should have shown you."

I see the tears building up in the corners of her eyes as she works to clean up while I stand there awkwardly, rocking back and forth on my heels, trying to figure out the right thing to say. I settle on, "No, it's cool. I get what you mean: the whole brush-and-canvas thing. That felt pretty good."

She stabs at the contents of the fire pit with the poker, tamping down the ash. "You're just saying that."

Peyton is the one person who knows I'm responsible for what happened last night. She could blow my life up in two seconds if she wanted to. I can't afford to piss her off. Plus, for some reason I can't put my finger on, I feel sorry for her. So I opt to follow that old saying: keep your friends close and your enemies closer. It's not like Peyton's an enemy, but she's not exactly a friend. I don't know what she is yet, so I merely nod and say, "No, seriously. I felt like I had the upper hand for once. Like I was in control and that douche bag was at my mercy for a change."

She dabs the corners of her eyes, then sniffles. "Really?"

"Absolutely." While this seems to calm her, I'm still a little nervous about this whole situation and I start to ramble. "In fact, if you hadn't put that out, I probably could have come up with at least a dozen more names we could throw into the fire. And that's without including the football team or the lacrosse team or any other team. Because you know what 'team' spells backward? Meat. And that's all they are. A bunch of meatheads."

"Actually, 'team' spelled backward is 'maet.'" She exaggerates the sounds as if she's trying to speak with some lame southern accent.

I shrug. "Yeah, well, spelling was never my strong suit."

She smiles and says quietly, "I knew you were special, Hank Kirby."

And then a voice rips through the yard like a needle scratching across a record. "Peyton! Where are you? I know you're out here because I can smell the damn smoke! You better put that out, or I'm gonna tell your mother you're starting up with that crap again."

"Shit," Peyton whispers, her hands balling into fists.

I'm guessing it's Pete, lured away from his home improvement show by the acrid smell of burning Barbie. Peyton shoves me back and motions for me to squat by the Barbie bin as she throws the tarp back over it. In a low voice, she says, "Just hide here. He won't come out this far. He never does. Wait until after we go inside, then sneak around the side of the house."

"What's the big deal? Why can't I just leave with you?"

Her eyes widen and she squeezes my hand. "Please. Just do it. I don't want him to see you. It will only cause problems. Do this for me, okay? I'll see you tomorrow."

"Pey-ton? I'm not in the mood for hide-and-seek. Where the hell are you?" Pete's voice has more urgency this time, and although he can't see me, I spy him stumbling across the yard in a stained wifebeater tank. His feet are bare, and when he steps on something in the dirt, he rages and screams her name again, as if blaming her for his injury.

"Are you gonna be okay?"

"I'll be fine. I'll see you tomorrow." The crazy look in her eyes has been replaced by fear, and my stomach lurches as she runs off. Pete greets her by grabbing her arm with enough force that her body rocks to keep upright.

As he drags her toward the house, I can hear him berating

her though I can't make out exactly what he's saying. But even from here, I can tell her spirit is broken in this guy's presence. She curls into herself, following his lead and never once turning back in my direction.

I wait in the corner of the yard until I'm sure they've gone inside and then cautiously make my way to the side of the house. I am tempted to pause by the open window and listen, just to make sure Peyton is okay, but I don't hear anything, not even the faint drone of the television we heard on the way in.

I run and pull my bike out of the bushes, then pedal away as fast as I can, past the trail of burned matchsticks and all the people leading normal lives, completely unaware that right down the street some seriously messed-up stuff is going on. I've finally met someone whose life is potentially more craptastic than mine. Who knew that was even possible?

I suppose on some level I should feel relieved, but I don't. I just feel sad. As much as I wish I could forget this entire day, I can't stop thinking about her all the way home and wondering what her story is.

# 5

I ROLL INTO THE DRIVEWAY JUST AS MONICA IS heading to her car—going to work I'm assuming, based on her outfit. She's wearing a pair of denim shorts so revealing that half her ass is hanging out, and her white T-shirt is so tight and see-through that the outlines of her nipples are like two brown berries. The top's cropped just below her boobs, revealing a bejeweled belly button ring. The ensemble's a little distracting.

"Hey, Hank."

I try to keep my eyes focused on her face. "Hey."

She stops midway down the drive and frantically roots through her purse. She holds up a pair of red tassels like a victory prize. "Thank God! I thought I lost these. Gotta give 'em what they like, right? These always translate into big tips."

"Right." *Jesus.* Does anyone else have conversations like this with their father's girlfriend? I'm pretty sure the answer is no.

She tilts her head and studies me, cracking her gum loudly. "You okay? You seem kinda out of it."

"I have a lot on my mind, that's all. School and stuff. It's cool." I shake my head to brush my bangs out of my eyes. A part of me wants to tell her about Peyton, about what I saw at her house, and ask Monica what she thinks, but she's already fiddling the key into the lock of her piece-of-crap 1992 Dodge Shadow.

The door gives way with a loud groan, and she climbs into the driver's seat, then pumps the gas pedal a few times before turning the key so the engine will catch and start. She always talks to it, patting the dashboard with a soothing "C'mon sweetie. You can do it," as if that will help. With a roar, the engine engages. She smiles at me.

"Hey, listen. I know being a teenager completely blows. And with your mom gone and your dad not being the easiest person to talk to, you can totally talk to me."

"Thanks." I really want to, but I don't know how to bring this up. It's not the sort of thing you just blurt out.

"You know what I think? I think you need a little excitement. A guy your age—you need to blow off some steam. I could probably sneak you in to one of the shows and have one of the girls give you a private dance. I mean, unless that would be weird for you since I work there and all." She cracks her gum loudly again, and I'm thinking her working at Mo's Boobie Barn would be the least bizarre part of that scenario.

"Yeah, probably," I tell her and shift my weight between my feet.

"Well, think about it. Just don't tell your dad. It'll be our little secret." She holds her index finger to her lips. "Everybody doesn't have to know everything about everybody's personal business, right?"

I nod. I like Monica. There's something about her that I feel like I can trust. She understands that people have secrets. She gets that things don't always make sense and people have to compromise to get by.

My mind is swimming with images of everything I just saw at Peyton's: the messed-up yard, the burning Barbies, Peyton's mom's drunk boyfriend grabbing her like that. If I don't say something I'm going to explode.

"So…can I ask you something?"

"Sure, anything." She angles her rearview mirror, checks her teeth for lipstick, and rubs blush on her cheeks.

"What if you saw something that didn't seem right? Like, someone could be in danger, but you don't know the whole story. Do you tell someone?"

"Well, I think the first thing you have to do is find out the whole story. Can you ask this person what's goin' on?"

I shake my head and dig my hands in my pockets. "I don't

actually know her that well. Plus, I don't know if she'd even want to tell me."

"What kind of danger exactly? Is someone trying to kill her? Is she suicidal?" Monica raises her eyebrows and her mouth hangs open a little.

"Nothing like that, just… I don't know. Forget it. It's probably nothing. Like I said, I don't know the whole story, and the truth is I don't want to get involved. But…this person involved me, so now I don't know what I'm supposed to do."

"Look, sometimes shit goes down between other people and the best thing you can do is stay clear. It can get messy. Trust me, I know from personal experience. I didn't leave home and become an exotic dancer because it was my life's dream or somethin'. But one day, I'm gonna finish gettin' my cosmetology license and have my own salon and leave dancin' behind. Sometimes life delivers more than you can handle, but survival is a strong instinct."

"Right. So since we're basically strangers, I can walk away and not feel like a total douche, right?"

"Only you can answer that, Hank. I'm a fan of stayin' out of other people's shit. You are less likely to create expectations. And people never live up to those. So if you don't know this girl and you don't really care, then I say step off. Otherwise, you could be signin' up for a whole lotta drama."

I nod as she winks at me and kicks the car into reverse. The gravel crunches under her wheels as she backs down the driveway, shooting pebbles in all directions. She sticks her hand out the window and shakes one of her red nipple tassels in the air, waving good-bye as she drives down the street.

Dad's still not home so I grab a soda from the fridge and head upstairs. I lie back on my bed to read the Shakespeare crap that's due tomorrow in English, but my mind keeps drifting to this afternoon.

Picturing Peyton's face when her mom's boyfriend came outside.

The way Pete talked to her.

The way she's put on this big, mouthy show whenever I've seen her, but clammed right up around him.

Wondering what happened when he dragged her inside.

I don't want to think about Peyton. I don't want to get in the middle of some crazy girl's life and problems—I have enough of my own—but a nagging voice in my head tells me I should. That it's the right thing to do. I just have to figure out exactly *what* I should do. So I reassure myself that there's time to let it marinate and come up with a plan, that she's not going anywhere anytime soon. But ironically, she does.

# 6

PEYTON IS NOT AT SCHOOL THE NEXT DAY. OR
the day after that.

In fact, she's not there for the rest of the week, and life is practically normal. She's not showing up unexpectedly at my lunch table or lurking in the hallways or anything. It's like she's disappeared into thin air. While a part of me wonders where she is, I'm also relieved. I can finally breathe without worrying if my life is about to be turned upside down any second.

I'm in such a good mood that I don't even mind when Kyle Jonas cracks yet another one-liner at my expense during gym. I just chuckle along with him and tell him he's hilarious, which seems to rattle him. He waves his hand dismissively and takes off with his knucklehead simian buddies. Of course he takes his frustration out on me for the next half hour by throwing the dodgeball at me extra hard and always aiming for my balls. Fortunately, I'm quick on my feet.

"You have a serious death wish, man," Nick tells me on our way to the locker room. His gym uniform is so oversize it makes him look even skinnier than he is, if that's possible.

I wipe the sweat off my upper lip with the bottom of my gray school-issue tee and say, "I'm sick of putting up with that assclown."

"He's a *fessacchione*. Before you graduate you should find some way to get back at him." Nick's eyes light up, and he grins from ear to ear. "You could leave a pile of dead fish on the front seat of his car on a hot day. I saw that in a movie once."

I laugh at the mental image. It's glorious. "That would be pretty amazing except for the fact that the guy has a convertible, so it would never smell."

"Trust me, you'd smell that shit two states over. Let me know if you're ever interested. My dad's friend owns a fish market. I could get you a good deal."

"Thanks. I'll keep that in mind."

We reach our lockers, and as we spin the dials on our combination locks, Nick asks me, "So did you hear about Amanda Carlisle?"

My mood perks up at the mention of her name. "No, what about her?"

"You know how some loser tried to burn down her house but she's convinced it was all some romantic gesture?" He snickers.

I feel my cheeks get hot and redden. "Yeah. What a moron. The guy I mean. Not Amanda. But go on, what about her?"

Nick glances around, then leans in, speaking in a low voice. I can still smell the salami sandwich he ate at lunch on his breath. "Turns out she's wicked serious about wanting to find out who this 'mystery guy' is. She's talking about setting up a website so guys can fill out an anonymous survey of questions only the person who did it would know how to answer."

I try to act casual even though my mind is racing. I stuff my gym shirt into my locker and slide my red Flash tee over my head. "Seriously? That's whack."

His eye drifts to the side as he says, "All the girls are going bonkers over how sweet it is. Meanwhile, it's pretty much open season for the guys. If you can guess the right answers, you have a shot at Amanda Carlisle. So every idiot and his brother is going for it. Hell, I'm even considering taking the survey."

I try to process what he's saying. "Hold up. People are essentially making up a load-of-crap story and entering a contest so they can go on a date with Amanda?"

"Yup. Wild, huh?" He pulls his shirt over his head and I can see the outline of his rib cage, along with a shiny, jagged scar on the side of his stomach. Rumor has it he was stabbed in a knife fight. I quickly avert my eyes before he catches me staring.

I pull on my jeans. "The thing is, anyone who claims to be 'the guy' has pretty much confessed to nearly burning down her frickin' house. While Amanda may be willing to overlook that, I'm guessing Mr. Carlisle won't. And probably not their insurance company either. Not exactly the way to score points at the beginning of a relationship, if you know what I mean."

"She promises total immunity, though you raise a good point." Nick's brow furrows as he considers all this, and then he shrugs. "She's smokin' hot. It might be worth the risk."

I'm still skeptical, but of course I'm interested. I stack the pros of winning a date with Amanda against the cons of how much trouble my confession could potentially bring. "So what happens if you answer all the questions right? I mean, twenty guys could luck out and guess the right answers. How does she know who's the real one?"

"I don't know. Maybe she has a bonus question."

"And then what? She goes out with the guy?"

"Get this: sounds like she said she would take him to prom."

Prom.

With Amanda Carlisle.

It might still happen after all. But this is too easy. I mean, I know all the answers. I was there. It sounds so simple and straightforward, but there's gotta be a catch. Despite her offer of immunity, what if this is all some elaborate plan to catch the poor dumb bastard (me) and then humiliate and punish him publicly? And what if Amanda finds out it was me and bursts out laughing and refuses to go through with it? She doesn't seem like the type who would do that though. I think that's why I got the nerve to ask her in the first place.

Any time I've ever talked to her, Amanda has always been polite and friendly. Of course, it's never a deep conversation or anything; more like she says, "Do you know what time it is?" and I say, "Two fifteen." One time she asked me, "Do you want to sign my petition to get the school cafeteria to start carrying gluten-free entrees?" and I said, "Sure," even though I didn't have the slightest clue what gluten was. It seemed important to her so I went with it.

I got the idea to invite her to prom two weeks ago when both our lab partners didn't show up and Mr. Seitz put us together. She basically sat back and let me dissect our whole frog, but she kept thanking me, saying I was so sweet for understanding that she could never harm a fish, no matter how big or small. She was so emotional about it that I didn't have the heart to tell her a frog is actually an amphibian. Even the formaldehyde couldn't mask how good she smelled—like baby powder and jasmine flowers all mixed up.

While I was doing our lab work, Amanda made small talk and asked me if I was going to prom. I said I wasn't sure, and she said she didn't know if she was going either. No one had asked her yet. It was almost like she was hinting.

Granted, I knew inviting her was a stretch, but it felt like we'd had a moment. Sometimes in life you have to go for what you want. It's pretty freeing, actually. In the best-case scenario, things work out. And in the worst-case scenario, you set the girl's lawn on fire and make the evening news.

I'm not much of a religious guy, but I gotta say that hearing about Amanda's website feels like somebody upstairs is giving me a do-over, the chance to make things right. At the same time, I'm sure he (or she) is laughing his (or her) ass off, amused at how I get myself into these situations.

"Earth to Hank!" Nick's waving his hand in front of my face. I snap back to reality.

"Sorry, man. I completely spaced out. What did you say?"

"I said the downside of winning is I'd actually have to go to prom." We close our lockers and head out of the gym toward the quad. "Hey, you wanna go to Ziggy's and grab a burger after school?"

Ziggy's is this amazing hole-in-the-wall hamburger joint in town that makes the most incredible kick-ass chili cheese fries.

But they are known for their How High burger. It's two patties topped with mozzarella sticks, jalapeño poppers, a fried egg, potato chips, bacon, lettuce, tomato, pickles, and secret sauce. If you can eat the whole thing, they take your picture and put it on the wall. Nick and I have made a pact to do this someday.

"I can't. Gotta work. Rain check?"

"No problem. Another time. Maybe you could invite your friend."

"What friend?" I'm thrown for a minute because he's pretty much the only person that I talk to.

"That chick with the frizzy hair who hates grapes."

"Peyton?"

"Yeah, Peyton." He clears his throat and bobs his head. "She seems pretty cool."

"I haven't seen her."

"Well, when you do, tell her I said hi." The corners of his mouth tease at a smile, and I can't help it. I burst out laughing.

"You like Peyton?" It comes out like an accusation, and I instantly regret it because his face becomes stony and one eye locks onto me while the other glares menacingly over my shoulder.

"Why'd you say it like that? What's wrong with her?"

I start to tell him and then snap my mouth shut like a fish.

I can't. It would mean unraveling the whole story of how we met and everything that I know about her, and how she told me she'd never shown anyone any of that stuff before, like she trusted me. Even though it was weird, there was definitely something cool about how she opened up to me.

The fear in her eyes the other afternoon flashes in my mind. I don't think I'll ever be able to forget it. My stomach churns every time I think of it, and I silently wonder if she's okay. As much as I want to talk to Nick about it, that doesn't seem right. I can't explain it, but I feel oddly protective of her.

"Nothing. She's all right," I counter quickly. "I'll tell her the next time I see her."

"Excellent." Nick nods.

And then I find myself saying, "I might swing by her house later on my way to work. You know, check in and see what's up. I'm passing right by there anyhow."

So much for not getting involved.

# 7

MY BIKE PRACTICALLY GLIDES TO PEYTON'S ON autopilot, navigating the now-familiar potholes and curves. My shift at Shop 'n Save starts in a little over an hour so I'm dressed for work in my uniform, a bright banana-yellow polo. Nothing says "blend in and be low key" like a guy wearing a blinding polo and riding a bike through a neighborhood he doesn't live in. I'm practically a beacon.

I'd be lying if I said I wasn't nervous. Okay, a lot nervous. I don't want that Pete guy to see me and get Peyton in trouble. He didn't strike me as the kind of person who would invite me in for a glass of milk and freshly baked cookies. Probably not even a warm beer and some stale peanuts.

But something keeps tugging at me, needing to know that she's all right. I don't actually have to talk to her. I could just sneak up to the house and assess the situation. Once I'm certain that she's fine, I can take off. She doesn't have to know I was ever there. No harm, no foul.

Technically, I wouldn't be getting involved; it would be more like satisfying my curiosity. Nothing wrong with that.

When I get within sight of Peyton's house, I jump off my bike and walk it to the giant bush, engaging the kickstand and propping it up on the street side. I'll only be here a few minutes at best.

Clouds have rolled in during my ride over, and the temperature has started to drop. It looks like it could rain. I silently curse for forgetting to bring my sweatshirt because I can feel the bumps popping up on my bare arms like chicken skin. I rub my hands up and down them for warmth, then carefully poke my head around the bush.

It's as quiet as the first time I was here. The house is still shut up tight with the blinds drawn. The only thing that's different is that the driveway is empty, with black, shimmery orbs where the dying Subaru had been parked. I'm guessing this means that Pete's not home.

I take a deep breath, scoot across the driveway, and sink beneath the window in the side yard. It's open, same as it was when Peyton snuck me around back.

I should probably just leave right now.

Instead, I stand up slowly, aligning myself with the side of the window frame, and turn my head so that I can peer in. This window is right above the kitchen sink, which is stacked with dishes. A fly settles on the edge of a food-encrusted plate, then buzzes through an archway into what appears to be the living room. It's hard to tell, what with the blinds being drawn and the house being dark like the inside of a cave.

I hear a noise inside as if someone is coming. I try to control my breathing so I'll remain undetected. That's when she walks into the kitchen.

She's carrying a garbage bag that clinks and rattles as she moves. With a disgusted look, Peyton plucks an empty beer bottle from the counter where it stands next to a frozen dinner tray and dumps it into the bag. It clatters against the others.

She appears even more unkempt than usual. Her hair is pulled back in a weak attempt at a bun, but loose strands stick out all around her face, and her collarbone protrudes from her oversize, faded Led Zeppelin tee. She turns toward me and is reaching for another beer bottle on the counter when our eyes connect. She sucks in her breath, startled, as the bottle in her hand crashes to the floor.

"Sorry about that," I say as I move to the center of the window.

"Hank? What are you doing here?" Her tone is frantic, and she glances nervously at a clock on the wall. She kneels, disappearing from my view below the counter, presumably to collect the pieces of broken glass.

I keep my voice low. "I just wanted to see what's up. You haven't been at school in a while."

"You came to check on me?" She seems surprised.

"Is that okay?"

She finishes picking up the last of the broken glass and ties the bag closed. "I guess."

"So you gonna tell me where you've been?" I ask, taking in her disaster of a kitchen.

"I wasn't feeling well. Plus, I had stuff to do. My mom gets pissed if I fall behind on the cleaning," she says, glancing at the clock again, then back at me. Now I know something's up.

"Are you sure you're okay? Because from what I can see, I'm pretty certain this house hasn't been thoroughly cleaned since the last presidential administration."

Her face softens. "I'm fine. I just took a few days off. No big deal. But thanks for checking on me."

"Well, after what happened when I was last here, I didn't know what to think. Things got sort of weird, you know?"

She nods, then tucks a strand of hair behind her ear and smirks. "Yeah, Pete's kind of an asshole. He acts like a hall monitor so he can keep in my mother's good graces and she doesn't kick him the hell out." She bites at her lip nervously and shoots a third glance at the clock. "You want to come in for a few minutes? He won't be back for a bit. He went to the package store two towns over. Says it's cheaper than the local one where the fascist owners are ripping him off."

"He sounds like a real winner."

"You have no idea." We both laugh and it lightens the mood a little. She rolls her eyes as she motions toward the sliding door. "I'll meet you around back."

I walk around the corner of the house, and she's waiting with the door open. I step inside, and the first thing that hits me is the smell—like stale cigarettes and beer. It hangs in the air like anti–air freshener. Everything is mismatched and in need of repair: the stained orange couch that clashes with the deep-red walls, the bookcase with a collapsed shelf, the dining room table piled high with wallpaper sample books. It makes my house look like it should be in *Better Homes and Gardens*. Taking it all in at once definitely causes sensory overload. She catches me staring.

"Another one of Pete's projects. One day he announced he wanted to re-wallpaper the whole house. We're not even allowed to paint. They've been sitting there ever since." She points to the sample books and pushes at the edge of one to reveal a dust-free triangle of table underneath.

"Why does she stay with this guy?"

"A warm body is better than no body, I guess. He moved in two weeks after she met him. At least he had a job then. Three weeks later, he told his boss to go screw himself. He's been unemployed ever since and sits on the couch all day watching TV. My mom keeps assuring me that he'll be back on his feet soon, that he just needs 'time to sort things out.'" She makes air quotes around the last part. "Meanwhile, it's been a year. People can do some pretty stupid things when they're into someone. Though I guess I don't need to tell you that," she says as she leads me down the hall.

"Yeah, thanks," I say, taking in the oddball assortment of faded family pictures as we walk. An elementary school photo of Peyton with her two front teeth missing; a fading picture of a baby sitting on a woman's lap at a piano. The woman looks like an older version of Peyton with the same ice-blue eyes. I'm guessing it must be her mother. In many of the photos, holes have been cut where a man's head would be, though his body has been left in the picture.

Peyton pushes open a door at the very end of the hall. "Let's stay in my room. My mother has this lame rule that I'm not allowed to have people over when she's not home. I can crack my blinds to see when Pete's coming, and you can crawl out my window."

"You have this all figured out. You sneak many guys in here?" I'm anxious about Pete returning, but my curiosity about seeing her room and desire to keep talking to her override it.

"Hordes." She stands in the doorway, waiting for me to enter. I refrain from telling her this is the first time I've set foot in a girl's room because I know if I say the words out loud they'll sound even more pathetic than they do in my head.

Peyton's room is covered floor to ceiling in posters of rock bands from the seventies and eighties. She has old forty-fives dangling on fishing wire from the ceiling. I reach for one and spin it around in my hand. It's a Paul Simon single, "Kodachrome." Next to that is Bowie's "Changes" and Queen's "Bohemian Rhapsody." On the far wall by her bed are black-and-white photos that have been pushpinned to the wall.

"Whoa. This is really cool," I say, trying to take in all the details.

"What'd you expect? Pink walls and a fluffy bedspread with unicorns and rainbows? Five Seconds of Summer posters?"

"Did you take these?" I ask, pointing to the photos. They're all of ordinary people doing everyday things: a homeless guy pushing a shopping cart with his belongings down the street; a child playing in a sandbox at the park; an old couple sitting on a bench; a woman talking on her cell phone with her hand to her mouth, on the verge of tears.

"Yeah."

I walk toward them to look closer. "They're awesome."

"Thanks. I like capturing random moments. There's such honesty in them, like you're stripping away all the bullshit and what's left is real and raw. It's a total dream, but it would be really cool to work for, like, *National Geographic*. Or to have an exhibition in a gallery. Of course, that'll never happen."

"You don't know that." I point to the forty-fives. "Where'd you get all these?"

"I'm super into music." She gazes at them wistfully and bites her lip. "They're all I have left of my dad."

"Did he die or something?" I tap the edge of a forty-five with my finger and make it spin in circles. "My mom died when I was twelve. My older brother too. Car accident." I've told the story so many times that I've nailed the SparksNotes version.

"Wow. I'm sorry."

I shrug. "Thanks."

She reaches for a pack of matches on her nightstand and lights one, letting it burn down dangerously close to her fingers before blowing it out. She tosses it in a cup and lights another. She does it over and over, as if it's some sort of nervous habit or meditation. "Mine might as well be dead. He left a long time ago. I think he lives in California. Or maybe it's Arizona. I can't remember which. It's somewhere with a lot of sun."

"You don't talk to him?"

"No. But it's okay," she says nonchalantly and hugs her knees to her chest, making room for me on the bed, but I opt to stand.

"How is that okay?"

"Because he wanted a different life. I get it. I wouldn't mind that myself most days. I understand why he left. They were kids. He was a musician and a free spirit. My mom was sixteen when she dropped out of high school to become the lead singer in his band. If her parents weren't ready to disown her for that, then she got pregnant with me. He stuck around for the first couple of years, but then he took off. My mom got me and his record collection. He got freedom and a fresh start."

"So is your mom still a singer?"

Peyton shakes her head. "Nah. That dream pretty much went out the door with him, which is sad because she has an amazing voice. Now she works three crappy jobs just to keep things going. She's, like, never here."

I know what that feels like. The difference is that although her situation may be less than ideal and she may not see her mother a lot, at least hers still exists. "That's too bad."

"I guess." She lights another match and stares at the flame, then adds it to the growing collection. "When I was little, my mom sang to me all the time. But the older I got, the more she resented me. I was the one standing in the way of her having any sort of a life. All these responsibilities, you know? She gets into bad relationships. I feel sorry for her. I know it's hard for her, but I don't know how to help."

I'm surprised she's telling me all this stuff so casually, as if we're good friends. The weird part is, I'm interested. "I take it you guys aren't close."

"Truthfully, the only time we get along is when she's between boyfriends, which is rare. Even then, she treats me more like a sister than a daughter. And each time she gets dumped or fired, she wants us to move. It's like she can't stand being in one place too long. Reminds her of how she couldn't make it work. She tells me that the minute you start to get attached is the perfect time to let go."

"Interesting philosophy."

"I don't know. Seems like it would be smarter to put energy into trying not to mess things up in the first place. Oh well. Life isn't perfect, right?" She peeks between the slats of the blinds.

I change the topic, hoping to lighten the mood a little. I

gesture to her posters. "Has anyone ever told you that you have the musical taste of someone in their midforties?"

"I take that as a compliment. These are real bands. They made real music that endured. There isn't much today that you'll hear twenty or thirty years from now except as a pop culture joke."

"So I guess it's safe to say you're not a Directioner?" I turn to smile at her as she twists the bottom of her Zeppelin tee, causing it to ride up and expose a purplish bruise on her side. She self-consciously adjusts it, avoiding my stare.

"You sure have a lot of band shirts."

She pulls her shoulders back, arching her back defensively. "You sure have a lot of superhero tees."

I laugh. "Touché."

"So what's the deal?"

"With the shirts?" I dig my hands in my pockets. "I guess superheroes are my thing. I collect old comics and I draw one too. I call it *Freeze Frame*. It's about this dude who has the ability to freeze time and go back to change fate."

"That's cool."

"Yeah, my brother got me into comics when I was a little kid. He used to love superheroes. Used to watch all the movies over and over 'til the damn DVD player broke." I smile at the memory. Dad had been about to pop a vein, but Mickey knew how to talk him down. Mickey could do no wrong. And now that he's dead, he's practically a saint.

I go on. "Anyhow, superheroes tend to be regular guys who have experienced some freak accident or trauma that results in them developing extraordinary powers or abilities. They take all the crap in life and find a way to turn it around for good. When my life gets insane, I try to imagine I could be like that."

Peyton laughs, and I feel my cheeks flush. I have no idea why I shared that with her. I've never told anyone that, and it certainly wasn't meant to be amusing. "I'm sorry," she says and waves her hand.

"Why is that funny?"

"It wasn't really… I was just picturing you in a full-on super-hero costume."

"I don't want to *dress* like one," I snap. "You know, you do all kinds of weird shit and then I tell you something personal, and you make me feel like an idiot."

She can tell I'm genuinely pissed and stops laughing. Her face becomes lined with worry, like she's afraid I'm going to leave. "No, seriously, I'm sorry. I shouldn't have laughed."

I shift my weight from one foot to the other and shake

my bangs off my face with a jerk of my head. "Oh, before I forget…uh, Nick Giuliani says hi."

She wrinkles her nose. "The dude with the freaky eyes who called me out on my grapes?"

Now I'm the one laughing. "Yeah."

"I heard his dad killed someone."

I shrug. "You hear a lot of things about Nick."

"Well, what do *you* think? Do *you* think his dad killed someone?"

"I don't know. I doubt it."

"Doesn't it make you wonder? I mean, are you scared to be alone with him? Think he'd knife you when you're not looking?"

"Nah. I figure he's got his secrets, and I've got mine. He's a pretty cool guy if you get to know him."

She considers this for a moment. "Maybe I'll ask him next time I see him."

Bad idea. Aside from the fact that the question would probably upset him, I wouldn't want Nick thinking I was spreading rumors. "Whoa. You can't just walk up to someone and ask if their dad offed somebody."

"Why not?"

"Well, it's rude. Nick's my friend. People say a lot of crap about him, but that doesn't mean any of it's true. They don't even know him. Not everybody is comfortable putting their cards on the table." I cross my arms.

"Fair enough. Everyone is hiding something though. There's the story we tell ourselves and the story we tell everyone else." She blows out the match and strikes another. I can't act like I don't notice much longer, because it's starting to make me feel uncomfortable.

"Hey, what's with the matches?"

"I like doing it. Does it make you nervous?"

"It just seems a little dangerous."

"That's what makes it so satisfying." She puts the matchbook on her nightstand. "Why did you come here, Hank?"

The truth is that I don't know. I'm kind of scared for her to tell me what's really going on because I'm not sure I'll know how to handle that information. But I do know one thing: the minute this girl walked into my life, something shifted. As strange and messed up as she is, there's something about Peyton Breedlove that's more honest and real than anyone I've ever known.

Before I get a chance to answer, we both hear the high-pitched squeal of worn-down brake pads as the Subaru pulls into the driveway. Peyton's eyes get wide as saucers. "Shit, that's Pete."

She struggles to raise her window but it doesn't budge. "It sticks sometimes." She motions me over, and I stand next to her to help. It finally yields, sliding up with a loud screech. A blast of cool air hits me in the face. There's no screen, so I'm guessing this is not the first time it's been used to sneak out. "I'm going to go out and distract him. You wait until he's inside, then climb out and run."

"Got it." I position myself, ready to make my escape. My heart starts beating fast, just like it did the other night when I was worried I'd get caught at Amanda's house.

She heads to the door. Before she opens it, she turns to me and says, "Hank?"

"Yeah?"

"Thanks."

"Anytime."

The look in her eyes tells me that coming here tonight really means a lot to her, and I know that I can't walk away this time the way I might have before. Moreover, I don't want to.

She slips out the door, closing it with a click behind her. I wait until I hear her opening the front door and talking to Pete. He says, "Someone left a bike in front of the house. You know anything about that?" but I don't stick around for Peyton's response. I shimmy out the window and drop low to

the ground. When I'm sure the coast is clear, I book it back to
the bush and my bike.

Naturally, Amanda Carlisle is at her mailbox, flipping
through the envelopes one by one. When she catches sight of
me running out of Peyton's yard like I'm being chased by a pack
of wolves, she regards me curiously. Then she breaks out in a
big grin.

"Hey, I know you. Aren't you in my bio class? You were my
lab partner a few weeks ago, right?"

I freeze like a deer caught in headlights. I turn to her and
smile, trying to act nonchalant, but my adrenaline is pumping.
Of course she chooses to strike up a conversation as I'm trying
to get the hell out of here. Story of my life.

"Hey, what's up?" I casually lean against my bike, which
causes it to pitch over with a loud crash. At least that makes
her laugh. I fumble to right the bike, and she's already halfway
across the street by the time I regain my composure.

"What's your name again?"

"Hank. Hank Kirby." I shoot a quick glance toward Peyton's
house, hoping Pete won't come outside to see what the racket
is about.

"Right. Do you live over this way?" She eyes my highly
fashionable Shop 'n Save polo.

"I…uh…I was just bringing Peyton some groceries," I lie.

"On your bike?"

"She needed some stuff. You know, milk and bread and… um…toilet paper." *A million items in the supermarket and I have to mention toilet paper. Jesus.*

"You're friends with her?" Amanda's face crinkles like she's smelled something foul.

"Uh…kinda. I know her from school." I don't know why I get so nervous around Amanda. It's like I go into hyperdrive, especially my mouth. "It's not like we hang out or anything. I see her and we say hi and stuff, but we're not close. She hasn't been at school though, so I figured I'd bring her work by because, you know, if I was out sick, I'd want someone to bring me my work so I didn't fall behind." It's like a bullshit burrito: bullshit sprinkled in cheese, wrapped in a layer of more bullshit.

Amanda looks confused. "I thought you said you were bringing her groceries."

"Oh yeah, I brought her groceries *and* homework." *Dumbass.*

"That's very nice of you," Amanda says and runs her finger absently over her bottom lip. I'm mesmerized. "I didn't think she had any friends." She peers past me at Peyton's house, then leans in a little, cupping her hand around her mouth, and says in a loud whisper, "She's kind of weird. Truthfully, she scares me a little. I swear, strange stuff happens over there. Yelling, loud noises, smoke—even at all hours of the night. Everyone wishes they'd move. They're bringing down the whole neighborhood."

I don't know what to say and I can't bring myself to make eye contact with her, so I glance back toward Peyton's house. "It's a nice neighborhood."

Amanda continues as if she didn't hear me. "Plus, I never see her parents. Which explains why the house has become such an eyesore. Seriously, how hard is it to mow a lawn once in a while? My parents say the guy who owns the place will rent to anyone as long as the check clears the bank."

Her mention of the lawn makes me think of accidentally scorching hers, and I reflexively shoot a glance at it.

She giggles conspiratorially and I swear she's flirting with me, so I play along. I don't want to screw up this moment. I'm having a bona fide conversation with Amanda Carlisle. This doesn't happen every day. Not in my world.

"Yeah, it's pretty much a train wreck over there."

I feel my insides twist. It's the truth, but saying it so casually feels like I'm throwing Peyton under the bus. I try to ignore my conscience and focus on Amanda—the dimple in her left cheek when she smiles, the little flecks of gold in her blue eyes when the light hits them just right, the winding trail of freckles down her neck leading underneath her sweater. I wonder how many more are hiding under there.

Right then, the universe puts an abrupt end to my fantasy. The sky opens and it starts raining so hard I swear Noah is gonna gather animals for the ark. Amanda holds her mail over her head to shield her hair and says, "I better get inside. Hope you don't have a long ride home!"

The fact that she's worried about me, even a little, makes me smile. There is a clap of thunder and I raise my voice because it's so loud. "I'm actually headed to work. I'll be all right. It's only a few blocks. I don't mind the rain."

"Okay then." She grins and starts up her driveway, then pivots on her heel and says, "Sorry if I upset you by saying something mean about your friend. I was just being honest."

She runs toward her house as I call after her, "It's all good. Like I said, Peyton and I aren't really friends."

Amanda gives me a wave before she disappears inside.

Standing there in the downpour, I feel the rush of talking with Amanda disappear as quickly as it came. I am a royal asshole for betraying Peyton not once, but twice. I'm soaking wet and the insides of my shoes squish water when I walk, but I tell myself that I deserve to miserable. What I did? I'm no better than Kyle, saying crap to sound cool at another person's expense.

I swing one leg over my bike and am set to pedal toward Shop 'n Save when I hear a bang from the direction of Peyton's house. It's the sound of a window being slammed shut. More specifically, Peyton's window.

*Shit, fuck, shit.*

How much of the conversation did she hear?

# 8

I GET MY ANSWER LATER THAT NIGHT.

I'm lying in bed looking through an old Captain America comic that I got about a year ago, trying to chill out. It's an old one from 1987 called *Captain America No More!* in which the Red Skull devises a plan to destroy Captain America, but ultimately his plans are revealed and order is restored. The comic book isn't worth jack, particularly in this condition, but it's one of my favorites, mainly because Dad bought it for me.

The night I got it stays with me because Dad and I don't generally hang out. Things have been pretty messed up between us since I was a kid, even before Mom and Mickey died, and I've felt like an inconvenience for the better part of a decade. I'd always envied the closeness he and Mickey shared and wished he and I could be like that. That we'd have something more in common than our shared DNA.

It's not like Dad has never tried. It's just always been on his terms. Back when Mickey and I were kids, my parents would save up all year, and every August they would pack us in the car for the long drive to Boston to catch a Sox game at Fenway. My dad had an old Chevy that had no air-conditioning and was prone to overheat, so it was always an adventure. And on the ride, Dad and Mickey would be shooting off all kinds of stats from the season: RBIs, home runs, batting averages, that sort of crap.

We had the cheapest seats, way in the outfield, but I never cared because I was more interested in doodling on my concession-stand napkin than watching the actual game. I mostly liked how we were all together and it felt like we were a family. Then, when I was ten, I screwed everything up.

The truth is, I didn't really like baseball that much, which was sacrilege in my house. My father was convinced that if I played Little League, I would turn into an all-star like him and my brother. It didn't matter that I had zero interest or ability and would rather take art classes; Dad was determined that I follow in his footsteps. He coached my team every year. I went along with it because I wanted to make him happy, but I was miserable.

One day, I saw a poster at the comic book store about a showing of Steve Ditko's original sketches from early Spider-Man comics at a gallery in Boston, and he was supposed to be there in a rare public appearance with Stan Lee. Even though I knew it meant missing the last game of my team's season and that my dad letting me go was probably a total long shot, I begged him to take me. He laughed it off as if it were trivial, just a bunch of drawings. I was so upset that I told him I thought baseball was boring as shit, that I didn't want to play anymore and he couldn't make me. He was so furious that his jaw clenched and a vein bulged in his forehead as he yelled at me that I didn't make the rules. So at the game, bottom of the ninth inning, bases loaded, score tied, with everything riding on my at-bat, I decided to show him who's boss.

When the pitcher threw the ball, I didn't swing. I could see my father out of the corner of my eye, yelling at me to hit the ball. He was on his feet, pulling his baseball cap on and off his head, practically having a frickin' coronary. With each of the next two balls, he kept yelling, asking me if I was a moron, then reprimanded me in front of the crowd, but I didn't move a muscle. I stood my ground. I had to show him I wasn't—and would never be—like him and Mickey.

While I felt like a jerk for throwing the game and letting down the team, I was tired of my dad trying to mold me in his image. I felt proud of myself for standing up to him. But happiness was fleeting, because when the game ended, the entire team—including my dad—completely iced me out. I'd humiliated him publicly. I'd pushed things too far with him, and I tried to apologize the entire ride home, but he didn't want to hear it.

There were no more family trips to Fenway after that. He'd still go, of course, but he'd only take Mickey. Mom loved baseball, but Dad was adamant that I not "subject myself to that boring-as-shit game," and Mom worried about leaving me alone, so she stayed home with me. I could see in her eyes how disappointed she was to miss it, which made me feel worse. I tried explaining to him that I didn't really feel that way, that I had just been upset, but it didn't matter. The damage was done. And after Mickey died, Dad stopped going altogether.

Most days Dad makes it clear that sharing a house doesn't mean we have to share a conversation. So last year when he invited me out for a pizza and we found ourselves at the comic store, it was kind of a big deal. That night, Monica was working, there was no game on, and Dad wanted company. Sure, he spent most of the evening draining a pitcher of beer, ranting about how the Pats weren't gonna be able to take it all the way to the Super Bowl, and checking out the boobs on our waitress, but it was progress. He didn't ask me a single question about myself, but I was glad to be there with him. He's pretty much all I've got.

On the way home, we passed Metropolis Comics. They were getting ready to close, and Victor, the old guy who owns the place, waved at me as we walked by.

"Who the hell is that?" my dad asked with a belch.

I waved back. "That's Victor."

My dad leaned in to me and grabbed the inside of my arm near the elbow, steadying himself. "He a friend of yours?"

"Kinda."

He snickered and added, "Ain't he a little old for you, Hank? What's a guy his age interested in some young kid for?"

"Dad, he owns the comic book store. I come here a lot. He knows me." *Probably better than you do*, I'd thought.

Dad stopped in his tracks and eyed the neon sign as if he was noticing the store for the first time. "Metropolis Comics, eh? I used to like comics when I was a kid. Who's your favorite?"

I tried to play it cool. "That's a tough call. So many great ones, but I'm going to have to go with the Silver Surfer."

He raised his eyebrows. "Yeah? That the guy on a skateboard?"

"Surfboard, actually. That's why they call him the Silver Surfer." Dad had shared so little of himself with me, and now that we were finally speaking the same language, I didn't want to mess it up. "Who was *your* favorite?" I asked him.

"Jeez, it was so long ago. I was about your age, maybe younger." Dad shook his head.

I tried to imagine my dad as a teenager. I saw a photo once a long time ago. He actually looked a lot like I do now. It's as if his life was divided into before and after Mom and Mickey died. Everything that came before was put in a box and closed up tight like the door to Mickey's room. It's different for me. I like to think about my mom and brother, to imagine the things they'd say or do if they were still here. It comforts me in a way I can't fully explain. But for Dad, I guess the memories are too painful to revisit.

"I used to love the classics. You know: Hulk, Wolverine, Iron Man, Spider-Man."

"So you're a Marvel guy then?" *Who knew?*

"Absolutely. Superman and Batman were all right, but DC lost me with Aquaman. I always thought, how can you take someone seriously who rides a sea horse?"

We shared a laugh, and I felt excited, hopeful. Neither of us was yelling. We were having fun. I wondered what he'd think about *Freeze Frame*. I'd never shown it to him, but for the first time, I thought that maybe I could. I'd always been too worried he'd discount it the way he had the drawings I'd made as a kid.

"You like Captain America? That guy was wicked cool."

"I do. He's one of my favorites." He grinned and slapped me on the back, saying, "Let me buy you a Captain America comic."

"That would be awesome!" It was big. I remember thinking that maybe, *maybe* he'd forgiven me a little bit. I wasn't even nervous that he'd upset a display or talk too loudly.

We spent about a half hour there, sifting through comics together and talking. Ultimately, the one he bought me set him back about fourteen bucks. I wondered if he'd even remember it in the morning. More likely, he'd wonder where his money went and assume I'd stolen it. It wouldn't have been the first time.

But whenever I read *Captain America No More!*—tonight being no exception—it makes me remember what a great night that was, and how much I want Dad and me to be like that more of the time. So far, that hasn't happened.

I reach the last page of the comic and am carefully putting it back into its protective plastic sleeve when I hear the sharp crack of something hitting my window. It sounds like the little pebbles from the driveway. I look out, but I don't see anything. As I lie down and reposition the pillow behind my head, I hear it again.

*Clack! Plink!*

This time I put down my comic, open my window, and

stick my head outside. The moon slices through the trees, casting long shadows in the side yard. A stray cat sprints across the grass to the shelter of some nearby bushes, but that's about it.

It's close to midnight, but I decide to go against the warning of every horror movie I've ever seen and head downstairs to check things out. As usual, Dad is passed out in front of the TV, a half-empty bottle of beer nestled in the crook of his arm. His head is slumped over his chest, causing him to snore like a jackhammer with each breath.

I carefully remove the bottle and place it on the coffee table next to two other empties and the remains of what appear to have been bean dip and a bag of Fritos. *Late-night snack of champions.* I think Dad drinks more when Monica's not around to slow him down.

I flip on the porch light. Then as quietly as I can, I open the front door, hoping the hinges won't squeak too loudly. The screen makes a yawning creak as it resists my push, but Dad's out cold and doesn't seem to hear it over whatever crappy rerun is blaring on the TV. I tiptoe outside and down the steps. It's long since stopped raining and the sky is clear, but the ground is still wet and the air is heavy with a damp chill.

I survey the perimeter of the property for potential serial

killers, but everything is still. It's only when I walk around to the side yard below my window that I step on something that makes me yowl.

I squint and kneel for a closer look. Yep, it's as I suspected: the charred remains of a male Barbie. I can't see the original hair color because the plastic's blackened and melted into a twisted lump, though the doll's feet have miraculously retained their shape. I can't read the writing on its chest because it has been obliterated by flame, but if I had to bet on it, I'm pretty sure I'd know what it would say. The message couldn't be clearer.

"Peyton?" I half yell, half whisper, hoping she'll pop out from behind a bush like she usually does.

There's no way she could have hightailed it out of here that quickly, and the urgency to find her overshadows the fact that I am not wearing any shoes. I hop down the gravel driveway, turning in circles, looking for any sign of her.

"*Peyton?*"

No response. The only sounds are the leaves rustling when the breeze kicks through the trees and a dog barking somewhere up the road. I call her name again and am about to give up and head back inside when I catch movement by my neighbor's trash cans. Tomorrow's garbage pickup, which means it's as likely to be a raccoon as it is Peyton, but I decide to take my chances. It's clear she's angry and isn't coming out if she's hiding, so I say my piece.

"Peyton, I get that you're pissed at me. What I did was shitty. I don't know why I said what I said. Seeing Amanda threw me off. She was talking to me, which rarely happens, and I got carried away. I wasn't thinking."

The breeze picks up again and I bear-hug myself, because even though the calendar says it's early May, someone forgot to tell the weather this week. My toes are starting to go numb. How long does it take for frostbite to set in?

I address the trash cans again. "I'm an asshole, Peyton. You didn't deserve that. The truth is, it's been a long time since anyone was nice to me. You could have busted me right from the start. But you didn't, and even though you might do and say some freaky shit, I think you're pretty cool. I shouldn't have taken advantage of your trust like that." I sigh deeply and add, "And if it makes you feel any better, I've felt miserable all night for what I said. Because it isn't true, Peyton."

I stand there for another minute waiting to see if she appears, and when she doesn't, I turn toward the house. "Nice job, jackass," I say under my breath. Only I would pour my guts out to a garbage can.

On the porch, I go to open the door, but the knob doesn't

give. Stuck again. Dad's been saying he'll get around to fixing it for forever, but that day has yet to come. I jiggle it again, a little harder this time, but nothing. *You've got to be kidding me.*

I look for a stick on the ground, and when I find one approximately the right thickness, I attempt to jimmy the lock, but the stick splinters in my hand.

*Unbelievable.*

I have no choice but to knock gingerly for Dad. He doesn't answer. I knock harder and step back from the door, jogging in place to try to keep warm. My adrenaline starts pumping, anticipating what's to come.

I hear Dad stirring inside, cursing and stumbling his way to the door. "Who the hell is knocking at this hour of the night?" he bellows. He throws open the door, his brow lined with annoyance, prepared to give whomever is on the other side a piece of his mind, but his eyebrows shoot up in confusion when he sees it's me.

"Hank? What the hell are you doing out there? What happened to your clothes and shoes? Somebody messing with you?" He peers past me as if the answer is hiding behind me in the shadows.

"Everything's fine, Dad." I push past him into the house,

leaving muddy footprints on the carpet as I pass, but not caring because it's warm in here.

He closes the door behind him and grunts. "How could everything be fine? You're outside half naked in the middle of the night. Are you telling me that's normal behavior?"

"I heard something outside, so I went to check it out. I got locked out. Sorry to wake you, Dad," I say and start for the stairs. It would be a miracle if he lets me off this easily.

He doesn't.

"What the hell is that in your hand?"

I look down to see that I'm still holding the charbroiled Barbie. "Oh, this was on the porch. I think a stray cat left it. Probably got into someone's trash." I force a smile and tuck the gnarled plastic into my pocket. "'Night, Dad."

I make it up three stairs before he stops me.

"Since when are you a Boy Scout investigating noises?" He chuckles and reaches for his half-empty beer on the coffee table and takes a swig. "You gonna clean up this mud you tracked in? You think I'm your maid or something? Get down here."

"Yes, sir." I slink my way to the kitchen for a rag. I wet it, put a little dishwashing soap and water in a small bowl, and head back to the living room, where he stands over me as I get on all fours and start to scrub at the stains.

After a minute of supervising, Dad plops himself on the couch, throws back the rest of the beer, and then says, "You think I don't know what you're up to? Sneaking around in the middle of the night? Probably up to some trouble, and I won't have it. I got enough crap to deal with without having to mop up your messes." He says the last part with a scowl.

"I wasn't sneaking around, Dad. I told you, I heard a noise." I keep my head down and concentrate on making concentric circles. I know better than to make eye contact with him when he gets like this. It's the liquor talking. I won't let him bait me.

"Don't you mouth off to me. I'll knock you into next Sunday."

I can feel his eyes boring into me, daring me to look up. He's never actually hit me, though he's come close a few times. I've learned to stay out of his way when he's like this.

"We both know you're as chickenshit as they come. Scared of your own goddamn shadow. You expect me to buy that excuse? What were you gonna do, fight off an intruder? You don't even know how to throw a goddamn punch."

I really want to tell him that's because he's never taken the time to show me anything worthwhile, but I opt to keep my mouth shut instead. It's not worth it. Not when he's like this.

"What happens when you graduate this year? *If* you

graduate. What are you gonna do with your life? You want to end up like me? Do ya?"

This is what's known as a trick question, and Dad is loaded with them. If I answer no, then he'll go on a tirade about how I look down on him, how I think I'm better than him. If I say yes, we'll both know it's a lie because his life is shit, a wretched existence shadowed by a series of unfortunate events and bad choices, made tolerable by an abundant supply of cheap beer. I can tell you, whatever I do with my life, it won't be working some crap-ass factory job, getting drunk every night, and talking down to everyone around me to compensate for the fact that I'm a miserable son of a bitch.

I may not be an AP Scholar or the quarterback of the football team, but it wouldn't matter if I were. At the end of the day, I'm the one who's still here and my mother and brother are the ones who are six feet under. And that pisses him off. They were the only bright spots in his life, and he'll never let me forget it. What he doesn't realize is that Mom and Mickey were the only good things I had too. We're in the same damn boat, he and I, and he can't even see it.

Dad pounds the empty beer bottle on the table and it falls over, but he doesn't pick it up. It rolls in a semicircle, then falls to the floor. He stands up, stepping over it, and heads toward the stairs, bumping into me as he passes. "You better watch yourself, kid."

I don't answer. I just keep scrubbing.

It takes another fifteen minutes to get every trace of the mud out of the carpet. I pick up the abandoned beer bottle, throw the empty food containers in the trash, shut off the television, and head back to my room. I can hear him snoring through his closed door, like someone is drilling into the sidewalk. In the morning, he'll act like nothing ever happened.

By the time I get to bed, it's past 1:00 a.m. I close my eyes, but I can't sleep because my brain is going a hundred miles an hour. What happened with Dad is bad enough, but this thing with Peyton is eating away at me like a cancer.

The girl burned a Barbie with my name on it. She only does that when people genuinely hurt her, and I know I did. But someone can only hurt you if they matter to you in the first place. And this weird sense of loss I'm feeling, believing I've caused some irreparable damage to our friendship, makes me realize that in some messed-up way, she's started to matter to me too.

Which is crazy.

The thing is, my gut tells me it's about to get even crazier.

# 9

BY THE END OF THIRD PERIOD, I'VE PRETTY MUCH resigned myself to the fact that Peyton (a) isn't at school, (b) is completely avoiding me like a flesh-eating virus, and/or (c) is off somewhere sticking pins in a voodoo doll that bears an uncanny resemblance to me and I will be stricken with zits the size of bowling balls. The way I see it, I'm simply screwed. The charred Barbie could be the tip of the iceberg.

As if she wasn't pissed enough last night, the turn of events at school this morning probably isn't going to help. Amanda Carlisle's website went live. And *everybody's* talking about it. So many people tried to log on that the site crashed.

So even if Peyton ratted me out, at this point why would anyone believe her? Practically the entire male student population of Kennedy High is lying their asses off, hoping to take Amanda to prom. It's not a matter of truth; it's a matter of winning. It's like the whole school turned into Crazytown overnight and Amanda's the new mayor.

I pass Nick on the way to my locker before lunch, and he jackknifes in front of me, sporting this goofy grin. "Have you checked out Amanda's website yet?"

I try to act nonchalant. "Not yet. The server was down." I don't tell him I've spent half the morning trying to get on, the same as everyone else.

"I heard it was back up again. There're already, like, three hundred and sixty responses logged. She has a counter." He says it with authority, as if he's sharing an insider tip.

"Seriously? That's nuts." The only thing nuttier is how three hundred and sixty guys are trying to take credit for my epic fuckup so they can go out with Amanda.

"I filled out the questionnaire. It's totally anonymous. What the hell, right?" Nick rakes his fingers through his hair and checks out a group of freshman girls walking by.

"So what kind of questions does she ask?"

I throw my books in my locker and we head toward the cafeteria. He says, "I don't remember exactly. Just stuff about that night. I don't know how she's gonna weed out the liars."

"They're *all* liars though. Yourself included." And then to cover my ass, I add, "Unless, of course, you set the fire."

Nick scoffs and says, "I didn't set that fire, man. I'm not *that* stupid."

True, because only one guy is *that* stupid.

I can tell it's Taco Day long before we hit the cafeteria. The smell of greasy ground beef hangs in the air like a radioactive plume, and I suspect it's no less toxic.

"Aw, man," Nick says as we grab our trays. "Last time it was Taco Day I spent half of sixth period doubled over in the friggin' bathroom. I think they're trying to kill us."

My stomach feels queasy as the lunch ladies dole out the tacos, give them each a squirt of sour cream from a bottle, and ladle fluorescent-orange Mexican rice and runny beans onto our plates. Since they make the tacos ahead of time, by the time you sit down to eat them, the bottoms are soggy and they fall apart. I imagine prison food is better than this. So are Monica's attempts at cooking.

On the plus side, the lunch lady gives me an extra vanilla pudding.

We wind our way to our corner table, which is usually empty, but today someone is already sitting there. Before I see her face, I recognize the long, frizzy hair and the fork in her hand, maniacally picking off the tomato bits and olive slices. It's Peyton, and I don't know whether to be relieved or nervous as hell. Nick's face lights up as we draw closer, and he says in a low voice, "Hey, it's your friend. You told her I said hi, right?"

"Definitely."

"What did she say?"

"Not much."

His jaw tenses and he stops for a second. "Whaddya mean, 'not much'? Did she look interested? Happy? Suicidal? What?"

I shrug. "I don't know. Happy, I guess. She definitely knew who you were."

"Yeah?"

"Yeah."

"Excellent." He grins and bobs his head, then runs his hand over his hair, smoothing it down. "I'm in."

"Hold up a second, Romeo. What about Amanda Carlisle?"

"I should have such problems," he jokes as he picks up his pace and I trail behind him.

On the way, I catch sight of none other than Amanda, holding court at the center table, surrounded by her group of girlfriends. She's mid-story, because she's the only one talking, while the others sit there slack-jawed, hanging on her every word as usual. She glances in my direction and we seem to make eye contact so I smile, and I swear she smiles back for a split second before she looks away. It's not as if I expect her to wave, though less than twelve hours ago we were having a conversation in the pouring rain like something out of a movie. Of course, it's entirely possible that she didn't see me just now.

Nick sets his tray down across from Peyton's, leaving me no choice but to sit next to her. She doesn't even look at me. I wonder if Peyton's ever burned a blond Barbie with "Amanda" scrawled across it in black Sharpie—maybe last night, in particular.

"Well, hello there. We meet again," Nick says. His voice is an octave higher than usual. He sounds like a prepubescent middle schooler. Smooth.

"Hey," Peyton says and pushes at a blob of sour cream to make sure she has removed every last bit of unwanted tomato and olive. I'm wondering why she doesn't bring lunch.

"You're not gonna eat those olives?" Nick asks, eyeing them.

"How'd you guess?" She extracts yet another tomato embedded in the sour cream, then licks her fingers.

"I love olives. Can I have at it?" he asks.

She slides her napkin, which is piled with them, toward Nick, and he dumps the contents on top of his taco.

Peyton makes a face. "Olives are disgusting," she says and pokes her fork around in the beans, stabbing them one at a time and eating them. At this rate, she'll be done with lunch by dinner. "Not to mention they're super high in salt. Salt can raise your blood pressure and cause heart attacks and strokes. Plus, they have skin and pits and taste gross. It's so much work to eat them. I don't understand why anyone would bother."

"Most things with skin and pits are a pain in the ass to eat. Look at humans, for example," I joke. I can see her fighting back a smile. The ice has been broken.

"I'm Italian," Nick says. "If I didn't love olives and tomatoes, my relatives would think I was adopted."

"Don't even get me started on tomatoes," she says.

"Don't you eat pizza? Or spaghetti?" I ask.

"Of course." She shoves a bite of rice in her mouth, then crinkles her nose and takes a big swig of her chocolate milk.

"Last I checked, I'm pretty sure those dishes are made with tomatoes," I tell her.

"Yeah, but they're cooked down. No skin or seeds or runny, nasty bits. I gotta say, I don't think anyone has ever taken this much interest in my eating habits except maybe my pediatrician." She lifts her taco gingerly with her fork, and the bottom of the soggy shell sticks to her tray, causing reddish-brown meat to ooze out of the tear like a slow-moving lava flow. "This is foul. I cannot eat this."

"You should come to my house for dinner sometime," Nick says, popping an olive in his mouth like candy. "My mother makes a marinara sauce that will knock your socks off. My great-grandmother's recipe."

"Is that an invitation?" she asks, and Nick's face flushes.

He beams, encouraged, his chest practically puffing out. "Yeah, absolutely. Anytime."

"Can Hank come too?"

Nick instantly deflates, but Peyton doesn't notice because she's turned to look at me. And when she does, I can tell that she heard everything last night.

Every last word I said to those garbage cans.

And when she smiles, even though it's kind of tight-lipped, no teeth showing, I know she's forgiven me.

Nick looks at me, then her, then back to me. He's trying not to seem ruffled by the fact that she invited me along on their date, which is most definitely a buzzkill. "The more the merrier," he says.

"When?" she presses, putting him on the spot.

He raises his eyebrows. "When? Uh…how about Sunday night? My mom makes marinara for dinner every Sunday."

"I'm free Sunday. Are you free Sunday, Hank?" She and Nick both stare at me, waiting for an answer.

"I don't have anything going on," I tell them.

"Do you ever?" Nick cracks himself up, and I give him the

finger. Karma takes over because Nick takes a bite of his taco and the whole thing falls apart all over his frickin' lap.

He jumps up, cussing in Italian. Peyton and I stifle our laughter while Nick dabs at his crotch, but the score is definitely Taco Stains 1, Nick 0. His face is beet red with embarrassment.

"Your jeans are black and your shirt will cover it up, man. No one can even see it. Don't worry about it," I reassure him.

He's stressing though, looking around like people will notice, will laugh. Or maybe he's upset he did that in front of the girl he's trying to impress. I've never seen him like this. Usually stuff rolls right off him. Well, except for the taco.

Peyton must sense his distress too because she does the damnedest thing. She reaches over, grabs her chocolate milk, and knocks it accidentally on purpose into her lap. She watches as the brown stain spreads on her jeans and says, *"Seriously?* I'm such a klutz. Hank, can I borrow your napkin?"

Nick glances up as I hand her my napkin and tell her, "You don't even have to give it back."

"This table is jinxed," he says.

"That seals the deal. I'm sticking to vanilla pudding for lunch." I push aside the remainder of the contents on my tray, peel back the foil on the top of the container, and dunk my spoon.

"I'm gonna grab some more napkins. You need some?" Nick asks Peyton and she nods. As soon as he walks away, an awkward silence sets in.

"Listen, Peyton, about the other day—"

She cuts me off. "So are you gonna do it?"

"Do what?"

"Fill out the questionnaire. On Amanda's website. I mean, you'll know all the answers, right? Nothing to hide anymore." She looks at me but she isn't smiling.

"You heard about that too, huh? It's pretty insane."

"You'd have to live in a cave not to know about it. This has all worked out perfectly for you. You tell your story, you take the girl to prom, and everybody lives happily ever after. That's what you wanted, right? To go out with her?"

"Well...sort of. All these guys are trying to take the blame for the fire, so ironically I have no proof it was me." I pop another spoonful of pudding in my mouth.

"You've got empty sparkler boxes."

"Yeah, but anyone could order those off the Internet. That's how I got them."

"How come you got two puddings?" She balls up her wet napkin, throws it on the table, and steals the extra dessert off my tray.

"I think the lunch lady is into me."

"That must be it." She starts in on the pudding and says, "As I see it, you've got something the others don't."

"Two puddings?"

"A witness."

I freeze. "You'd do that for me?"

"If that's what you wanted."

"I mean, I think it is. I haven't figured out what I'm going to do. The whole thing is weird, right?"

She nods. "Let me know. Happy to help."

"Thanks." I look over at Nick, who's across the cafeteria pulling wads of napkins out of the dispenser. "That was pretty cool, spilling your milk so that Nick wouldn't feel like an asshole."

"No big deal. I felt bad for him."

"I did too, but I didn't take a lunch in the lap for the guy."

She turns her head and looks me straight in the eyes. "Perhaps that's the difference between us. Maybe we have different versions of what it means to be a friend."

I deserve that jab after what I said to Amanda.

"Peyton, I just need to say—" I start but she cuts me off again.

"You want to get out of here?"

I sweep a glance around the cafeteria and then back at her. "Yeah, sure. We can go to the library until the end of the period."

"No, I mean outta here. Like leave school."

"As in ditch class?"

She raises her eyebrows and smirks. "Do you seriously expect me to believe you've never ditched?"

I say casually, "Of course. I do it all the time." Which is total bullshit. I'm not up for the fallout if Dad found out, and quite honestly, there's never been anywhere I wanted to go.

Nick comes back with a wad of napkins and shoves half of them in Peyton's face. She sets them down on the table, seemingly unconcerned with her stained clothes at this point.

"What'd I miss?" Nick asks, looking at each of us.

"We're thinking about bailing. Getting out of here for the rest of the day," she tells him.

"I'm in," he says.

"We've got English next period with Vaughn, Nick. I don't know if that's a great idea," I say, feeling a little nervous about pushing the envelope so soon after what happened last night with Dad. "Plus, I gotta be home by six. My dad knows I'm not working tonight."

"You've got plenty of time. And, dude, Vaughn is totally

cool with people ditching class as long as you bring him back a cheeseburger." Nick laughs.

"We won't be coming back though," I remind him.

"I'm sure he'll take a rain check. But how are we gonna get out of here? There're security guards at the exits, and they only let seniors out during free periods."

"Unless there's a distraction and security is needed elsewhere. Leave it to me," Peyton says. "Meet me in the faculty parking lot during next period."

"How? Just get up and leave?" I ask.

She says, "You won't have to. You'll already be outside." Nick and I look at each other in confusion as she adds, "Bring your backpack to class. By the time they figure out we're gone, school will be over."

"What about my bike?" I ask.

"You'll come back for it later. Trust me. I have a plan." She takes a final bite of pudding, drops the empty container on my tray, stands up, and walks away. Clearly this is not her first rodeo.

Nick watches her leave. "That girl is an enigma, man. I am so completely turned on right now."

"Look, I don't want to get busted, Nick. I'm kind of walking on thin ice at home as it is. Maybe just you should go," I tell him, but he shakes his head furiously.

"Hank, don't be such a pussy. You gotta go. I think she's nervous is all. Like with dinner. She wants you there too, like a chaperone or something. And that's cool. If I can talk her up a little, I can get things going. Then you can take off or whatever. C'mon, you gotta do this for me, man."

He gives me a pleading, desperate look before one eye starts roving toward the window, and between that and the stains on his pants, I can't help but think about Peyton's comment and the kind of friend I want to be. So when the fire alarm goes off during English because, rumor has it, someone set a small fire in one of the classrooms, I can't help smiling because I have a pretty good guess who was behind it.

The administrators are freaking out because this is no drill. It's a bona fide fire, and even though it only burned a bunch of recycled papers in a trash can—and a teacher put it out with an extinguisher—you'd think it had been an inferno. Teachers are flailing their arms and barking directions and hustling us out of the building to the athletic field. Taking in the controlled chaos, it hits me. Peyton set a real goddamn fire. It's serious business pulling an alarm, but setting an actual fire? Is she crazy? What if someone had actually gotten hurt?

The fire engines arrive on the scene, their sirens wailing and lights blazing. It will easily take the whole period to line everyone up and wait for the fire department to give the all clear, and by the time they let us inside, last period will be underway, so there won't even be enough time to take attendance. It's perfect. Nick and I find each other and slowly maneuver our way to the back of the pack, slipping out the side gate with ease while everyone is distracted, just as Peyton had said.

We make a beeline for the faculty parking lot, shooting glances over our shoulders like we've just pulled off a jewelry heist. And there's Peyton, casually sitting on the hood of Principal Drucker's car, lighting a stack of flyers about an upcoming pep rally one by one and casually reducing each to a pile of ash on the ground beside the front tire. There's a look in her eyes that rattles me a little, as if she gets some sort of a release from this, like scratching an itch.

She sees us and a smile spreads across her face. She abandons the remaining flyers and jumps down, leaving a slight groove in the hood where she's been sitting.

Nick keeps on moving, all arms and legs, anxious to get out of the parking lot undetected, and he motions to us to hurry and follow him.

"C'mon," I urge her because she's moving in slow motion and I'm starting to panic that someone will see us too.

She shoves something in my hand as I pass her. I look into

my palm. It's a red matchbook with "Lombardi's Liquors" scrawled across the front. I flip it open and it's empty. All of the matches have been used. I shove it in my front pocket. She smiles at me and says, "I guess it's true what they say. Children really shouldn't play with matches."

And then she's running ahead of me and I'm running after her, and my heart is pounding with adrenaline. Even if it's only for a couple of hours, we don't have to answer to anyone except ourselves. For the first time in a long time I feel free. I have no idea where we're going, but it really doesn't matter. Maybe Peyton's dangerous, maybe she's crazy, but whatever she is, I want to follow her and find out.

# 10

EVEN THOUGH DITCHING SCHOOL TWO PERIODS early is hardly jacking a car or robbing a bank, I feel kind of badass about getting away with something I shouldn't have. If the last two weeks are any indicator, I'm becoming somewhat of a pro in this department.

The only problem is that between the three of us we have no car, a stick of gum, and about three dollars in change, so our options are limited. We end up at Ziggy's sharing an order of chili cheese fries. Peyton has never been there before, and she points to the giant bell hanging from the wall by the cash register.

"What's that for?" she asks.

We tell her about the How High burger, how every time someone orders one, they ring the bell as they bring it out, and how someday Nick and I are each going to order one, finish it, and get our pictures on the wall.

"You seem pretty serious about this," she says.

"There is nothing *not* serious about a How High burger," Nick says as he stuffs his mouth full of fries. A lone strand of cheese dangles precariously from his chin, but neither of us has the heart to tell him it's there. It's far too amusing.

"The name alone. It's like a dare." I drain my water, then shake the ice in my cup, hoping it will inspire the waitress to stop reading her *National Enquirer* and actually bring us refills.

"It sounds disgusting," Peyton says.

"Don't knock it 'til you've tried it. Your face could be up there too. Hank and I are going to be legendary. Just sayin'. Before we leave this town, our pictures are going to be up on that wall." Nick says "we" but I don't correct him. Not here in front of her, but the fact is he's the only one of us who has any hope of getting out of this town anytime soon.

The three of us leave our money on the table and head outside. We're still good on time but have zero funds left, so we start walking and talking about random crap.

"What's the grossest thing you've ever seen?" Nick asks as he picks a leaf from a low-lying branch in our path.

No-brainer. "That would definitely be Joey Tuscaluso picking his nose in seventh grade and sticking the boogers under his desk. By the end of the year, there must have been two hundred of them under there," I say as Nick howls like a frickin' hyena.

"I remember that guy. What ever happened to him?"

"Who knows? Probably got a job at the Kleenex factory."

"The grossest thing I ever saw was my mother having sex with this guy who came to fix our TV," Peyton says flatly, and both Nick and I abruptly stop laughing.

"You had to watch your mom have sex? That's messed up," Nick says.

"Our TV broke so this repairman arrived. Long, greasy brown hair, goatee, tats up and down his arms. Mom must not have had the money, but clearly they worked out a payment plan, because I come out of my room to get a drink of water, and there they are, going at it on the couch. They were both totally into it."

Nick and I groan. "Nasty. Did she see you? What did your mom do?" I ask.

Peyton has our full attention, and she seems to be enjoying it. She blows her bangs out of her eyes and smiles. "Nothing. She looked right at me and put a finger to her lips, like I should be quiet. You'd have to know my mom, but this might be one of the least shocking stories I could tell you about her. In my opinion, that definitely trumps a desk full of boogers."

"She's got you there, Hank," Nick agrees. "Holy shit."

"What's the grossest thing you've ever seen, Nick?" she

asks. I can practically see him push his shoulders back because she's called him out. He grins goofily as he lets the bomb drop.

"I once saw this guy with his brains blown out the back of his head. Gray matter everywhere, and tons of blood. And this…crater missing from his head."

He creeps me out with how he says this with a smile on his face.

"Oh man, that's sick." I wave my hands as if that will make the image disappear.

"Did your dad kill him?" Peyton asks without batting an eye.

Nick snorts. "What?"

"Your dad. Did he kill him?"

I start to feel nervous. No one says that kind of stuff to Nick. At least not to his face. I can't believe she just asked him that point-blank.

"Why would you think my dad killed him?" Nick's tone is dead serious.

Peyton licks her lips and narrows her eyes, then says, "People talk at school. They say your dad is…a hit man or something."

"My dad is in waste management," Nick replies and swallows. His Adam's apple bobs up and down like a fishing lure in his throat.

"As in a garbageman?" I ask, hoping to clarify.

Nick's mouth hangs open as Peyton shrugs and says, "Whatever you want to call it. It makes perfect sense, actually. Such an easy way to get rid of the evidence. It's cool if he is, you know. I honestly don't care. I was just curious. My mom once dated this guy who worked at a funeral home and sidelined at a real estate agency. Folks would kick the bucket, and then while the family was grieving and vulnerable, he'd get the listing for their rent-controlled apartment. People do all sorts of messed-up shit, and they all have their reasons why. Who am I to judge?"

Nobody says anything for a few minutes. I mean, what can you say in those circumstances? A comment like that is sort of a conversation stopper. Instead we watch cars driving by, the cracks in the sidewalk, the street sweeper blowing up a mini dust storm.

Nick kicks at a rock on the sidewalk, and it goes skittering into the road. "My dad's a great guy. He's honorable. He stands up for what he believes in. He loves his family, his friends, and his community. He goes to church."

*So did the Sopranos.*

"Hey, like I said, I don't care if he takes out the garbage or he 'takes out the garbage.'" Peyton uses air quotes to drive her point home. "I'm just saying that who our parents are doesn't have to define who we are. At least not to me."

"So what's the deal with the guy with his brains blown out?" I ask as we walk toward Main Street. Nick looks visibly relieved by the change in topic.

"It's some video I saw once on YouTube," he says. "You can see all sorts of weird shit like that on the Internet. Mutilated bodies, people having sex with animals: you name it."

We end up at Metropolis Comics. Victor doesn't even bat an eye that I'm showing up before the end of a school day. He greets me by name as if I'm a regular at the local bar. He grabs his cane and gets to his feet.

Victor has one wooden leg. His real one got shot off in the war a long time ago. Sometimes he says he can still feel it, like it's still there. They call it phantom pain. I get that sometimes too. Stuff will happen and I'll want to tell Mom or Mickey. And then I remember they're not here anymore either.

"This must be Nerdvana for you," Peyton says, taking in all the posters on the walls and the display cases of back issues and collectible figurines.

"I like to come here. Victor doesn't mind if I sit and read in the back. He's awesome," I tell her as Nick pushes past us to look at a Spider-Man anthology that's grabbed his attention.

"Hey, Hank. I got something that I think you're gonna want to see," Victor tells me with a knowing smile. He tilts his head, summoning me to the counter.

"New Avengers?" I ask him. Sometimes if he gets in an issue early, he'll let me check it out even though he's not supposed to put it on display yet. He used to do the same thing for Mickey when he was alive. Victor has always looked out for us. I think it's because he once had a kid too, but his kid died. Drowned in a pool or something messed up like that.

"Better." His New England accent is so thick that the word comes out sounding like *bett-uh*. He wiggles his eyebrows as I make my way over.

"What's better than a new Avengers?" I ask.

"What's the one thing you've been asking me about for years? *Nev-uh* come through here before, *nev-uh* even *seen* one, and then yesterday it shows up. Some old guy bit the dust, and his nephew comes in and sells everything. I didn't put it out because I wanted you to be the first to see it."

"You're killing me with the suspense, Victor," I say.

He reaches into a drawer behind the counter, and my eyes bug out of my head when he pulls out a beat-to-hell copy of Marvel's *Fantastic Four #48:* "The Coming of Galactus!" and lays it down in front of me. Nick and Peyton lean over my shoulder as I run my finger over the battered cover and then carefully hold it in my hands. I can't find the words.

"What's the big deal? It's just some old comic," Peyton says, and Victor chuckles.

"This is not just any old comic," I tell her. "This is the March 1, 1966, issue of *Fantastic Four* where the Silver Surfer character is introduced for the very first time. He comes to Earth as a scout for Galactus, and they battle with the Fantastic Four and the Watcher." I can't believe I'm actually holding a copy of it in my hands.

"Unfortunately, this one is in wicked poor shape," Victor explains. "The spine is split, especially between the staples, and there's a lot of edge wear and small tears in the pages. And half the back cover is missing. But you don't turn one of these down when it comes through, even if it's low grade."

The condition doesn't matter to me. It's not like I'd turn around and sell it, not when I've wanted it for so long.

"How much is it?" I ask. I'm willing to bet I don't have near enough to buy it.

"In this condition? Around $275."

It's like I found a winning lottery ticket, only to have it swept out of my hands by a gust of wind and blown into the gutter. Not that I know what that actually feels like. I'm just guessing it feels a lot like this. Here one minute, gone the next. Never really mine to begin with.

Nick whistles and leans in for a closer look as I carefully open the cover, taking in each glorious yellowed page. Peyton shakes her head in disbelief. "For a ripped-up comic book? Who would pay that?"

Victor says, "People will pay upward of seven or eight grand if it's in mint condition. This one's very popular. People are always looking for it."

"That's like…a car," she rationalizes.

"A shitty car," Nick says. "With no air-conditioning and bald tires."

"I put it aside just for you, Hank. Thought I'd offer you the first shot at it," Victor says with a grin.

I sigh. "Man, I wish I could. I don't have that kind of money."

I thumb through the pages, wishing I were here alone so I could sit in the corner and read the whole thing. When I reach the end, I gingerly close the cover, running my fingers over it again before reluctantly handing it back to Victor. God knows how many times Mickey and I talked about wanting to find this issue. He'd be beside himself right now. Giving it back is killing me.

Victor carefully slides the comic back into its plastic sleeve

and locks it in the drawer behind the counter. "Well, I'll wait a
while before putting it out. How's that? Maybe you'll be able to
scrape it together, huh?"

I smile, knowing that unless I rob a bank or discover I am
the sole heir of an unknown rich uncle I have zero chance of
ever owning that comic. "Yeah, maybe."

Victor turns to Nick and Peyton and beams with pride as he
says, "Your friend Hank is quite the artist himself. One day I'll
be selling his comics for top dollar. You can bet on that. They'll
be lining up outside to wait for the latest issue."

"I wouldn't hold your breath, Victor," I say and he pats me
on the back good-naturedly.

I can tell Victor feels sorry for me because he tells us all
to go ahead and pick out a comic from the Last Chance
Clearance bin, on the house. Most of the time, I hate when
people feel sorry for me. When people find out my mother
and brother are dead, or that I have no money, or that my dad
spends more time with the drunks at the local bar than with
his one non-dead kid, they treat me differently. Their eyes get
this pitying look, and they go out of their way more than they
would for other people.

When people feel sorry for me, it's because they see me as
broken, and sometimes I wonder if there's truth in that. But it's

weird; I don't. I know my life is pretty messed up, but I gotta believe there's more to life than this. Otherwise I'm no better off than my mother and brother, pushing up daisies from six feet under in the cemetery up the road.

I'm like the Silver Surfer. Despite the considerable evidence that the world is pretty screwed up with people who do bad things, the Silver Surfer believes there is still good in the world. And as I look at Nick and Peyton digging through the bins, and Victor smiling as he watches the three of us, I think I'm standing in the middle of it.

✳

I finally make it home about twilight after going back to school to get my bike. I walk in and am greeted by a view of Monica bending over in front of the oven, her leopard-print thong showing over the top of her denim cutoffs.

"Oh, hey, Hank! I thought I'd make you guys some dinner before I head out." Monica removes some cremated thing in a Pyrex dish from the oven, fanning her oven mitt over it furiously. Literally, the top is charred and I have no idea what it is, but at this point I'm starving and there's a short list of other options.

She places a huge slice of whatever it is on a plate and hands it to me.

"Lucky me." I thank her and smile. I try to cut off a piece with my fork and knife, but the mass won't separate. I try to approach it from another angle, but still no luck, so I pick it up with my bare hands and tentatively take a bite. It pretty much tastes as good as it looks, but Monica's staring at me expectantly, so I force myself to chew and swallow it as quickly as possible.

"Whaddya think? It's spinach-stuffed meat loaf with black-ened mashed potatoes on top. I saw it in a magazine. It's like everything is all in one place. No side dish necessary. You like it?"

"Oh yeah, it's great." I've never wished we had a dog as much as I do at this moment. But I'm guessing a few bites of this meat loaf would quite possibly kill it or, at the minimum, give it the shits all over the living room floor.

She beams as the front door slams and my dad stumbles into the kitchen, raking his hands through his hair and sighing deeply. He doesn't say hello to either of us—just looks at the contents of that Pyrex dish and curls his lip. "What the hell is that supposed to be?"

"It's meat loaf stuffed with spinach and topped with black-ened mashed potatoes," I tell him and take another tiny bite.

Dad reaches over and pokes at the leathery potato topping,

then walks to the fridge and grabs the first of who knows how many beers he'll drink to make this edible. I almost want to ask for one myself.

"Hank likes it. It's good, right?" She looks at me and I nod, still chewing.

Dad turns, downing half the beer in one swill, and pulls Monica to him, then tells her with a laugh, "Honey, I'm starting to wonder if you shouldn't stick to dancing."

She sticks out her bottom lip in a mock pouty face and says, "You're so mean." He chuckles, leaning to give her a kiss, and I can tell by the way they look at each other that despite all the good-natured ribbing, they're genuinely crazy about each other. I definitely don't need to see where this is heading.

That's my cue to grab my plate. "I'm gonna take this upstairs. Got a lot of homework."

They don't even notice.

In my room, the first thing I do is chuck the spinach, meat loaf, and potato missile out the window. It gets good distance and lands with a *thwack!* against something in the neighbor's yard. A cat lets out a yowl, so I'm guessing it may have hit the cat. That meat loaf is just spreading misery wherever it goes.

I throw on some sweats and turn on my piece-of-shit computer so I can start my homework. The computer is old and there's a white line across the screen where the pixels dropped out, but it gets the job done. As long as it runs, it falls into Dad's category of "If it ain't broke, don't fix it, and even then, don't fix it." I pull my well-worn copy of Charles Dickens's *Great Expectations* out of my backpack and try to figure out how I'm going to write a ten-page essay about it by the end of the week. The book is basically about this guy who falls in love with this wealthy girl who's totally out of his league and spends his life trying to impress her. It makes me think about Amanda.

I know I should focus on my essay, but I have to see what everyone is talking about. I have to look at her website. The whole thing is so frickin' insane, and judging by earlier, I probably won't get on anyway. But either everyone's busy having dinner or people have started to come to their senses, because just like that, the site loads and I'm in.

And then I do something that may change the course of history.

Or at least my history.

# 11

THERE SHE IS. AMANDA CARLISLE IN HER SENIOR portrait. Next to her photo is a blue box with a big, white question mark. Underneath, it says in a pink swirly font:

> Are you my Prince Charming? Answer the following questions about the night of the fire, and my true prince will take me to ball.

I snort at her typo, because you know that's what every guy is hoping will happen by the end of the night. It's not like any of us honestly give a crap about going to some dance, myself included. But the truth is I'm not exactly sure what I want anymore.

Asking Amanda to prom was a moment of temporary insanity. I knew it was a long shot, and her lawn catching fire probably saved me from a very awkward and humiliating rejection. If I were a smarter guy, I'd leave well enough alone and let some other poor bastard reap the rewards.

But then I think to myself, can I live with some other guy enjoying a night that might have been—that *should* have been—mine?

I scroll to the first question. It says:

No one has come forward about setting or seeing the fire that night. But I know I saw someone in the yard. The fire chief said he may have been trying to warn me of the danger or convey another message. Which is it? If you were trying to warn me, why didn't you stick around? And if you had a message, what was it?

My eyes linger on "No one has come forward" because that means Peyton hasn't told anyone what she knows, despite all that's happened between us. Turns out she's pretty cool. Technically, she's the reason all this is happening. If not for her, I'd probably be in the juvenile detention center making friends with kids named T-Bone and Doomsday.

I stare at the blinking cursor for a few minutes. *Keep it short. Keep it simple*, I tell myself. And then I start typing.

I spelled out "prom." I was trying to be original to get your attention. I see it worked. (Sorry about the tree.) I couldn't stick around for your answer because I had a dentist appointment, and those people charge you big bucks if you don't cancel at least twenty-four hours in advance. Good oral hygiene is a priority in my life.

Question number two:

*If the answer was that it was a message, what did you use to write the message?*

I write:

Sparklers. I thought they'd be more festive…and less dangerous than lighting a bunch of candles because sparklers just burn themselves out. Apparently, this was not the case.

Question number three:

*It was dark, but I caught a glimpse of your outfit. What were you wearing—and what was that logo on your chest?*

I write:

Since my superhero costume was at the cleaners, I wore a
Batman hoodie and a pair of jeans. And Captain America
boxers. I was mixing it up with the Marvel/DC franchises
because that's how I roll. I'm a rebel.

I chuckle out loud for a minute at what a witty bastard I am.
Question number four:

Do I know you?

Yes. And no. Kind of. I wouldn't say we're friends, but we're
not *not* friends. But I guess we're closer to not friends than
friends. But not in a bad way. I'm certainly hoping that we
can move past this whole crazy incident and get to know
each other better.

Question number five:

Tell me something about that night only you and
I would know.

This is a tricky one. I wrestle with how to answer it. Should I tell her how pretty she looked that night? Or what the weather was? Or how fast the fire department responded? How will what I say stand out from all the other entries? I go for humor.

If you want to ask someone out, lighting sparklers in a pile of mulch is a surefire way to get their attention. We can honestly say our friendship started with a spark.

Question number five:

Describe our perfect prom night.

Technically, this is not a question, it's a short-answer essay, and I'm not much for essays. I opt for the truth since, ironically, I'm likely out of the game anyway.

You have an adventurous spirit, right? Well, if I take you to prom, I'd roll up on my bike and prop you on the handlebars. I promise to try like hell to avoid potholes. (My dad has a car, but the odds of me coming down with Legionnaires' disease are higher than him handing over the keys.) I'd probably pick you up early so we could grab a bite to eat first. I guess it's safe to say that if I pick you up on a bike, it's pretty much a given I can't take you somewhere with fancy napkins and candles. But Ziggy's makes a great burger. Unless you're a vegetarian. It's totally cool if you are. I'm pretty sure they have salads there too.

We'd eventually go to the dance and might stay for a while, if that's your thing. But I'm guessing as soon as you see my mad dance moves you'll be much happier with Plan B, which is to catch a movie at the dollar theater on the other side of town. After that we'd head over to the park with a fresh bag of chips (your choice of flavor, of course) and two Cokes (Unless you prefer Pepsi. I can be down with that too.) and lie back to watch the stars and talk about the mysteries of the universe. Once we've answered life's greatest questions, we'd hop back on my bike and pick up some ice cream before I take you home. So, in closing, if you choose me, it would be cool if you remember to bring a helmet.

And last but not least, question number 7:

Do you have any proof that it was you?

My fingers hover over the keyboard. I think about what

Peyton said to me in the cafeteria. This is the one question that could swing my entry from a maybe to a yes. What do I have to lose? I smile and type:

**I have a witness.**

I hit Submit, and the following screen notifies me that I am entry number 456 and to remember my entry number. Unbelievable. Four hundred and fifty-five people are willing to risk a brush with the law for a chance to take Amanda to prom. This is so out of hand. A new screen pops up asking if I want to edit my current entry or finish and return to the main screen. I hesitate for a moment; then I press the Finish button. A spinning rainbow cursor appears, indicating the website is processing my entry.

After the fourth revolution, I close my eyes and try to imagine Amanda reading my answers and contacting me, letting me know she wants to meet to me in person.

I start to feel queasy, but not because I ate the leftover chicken wings and washed them down with three-days-past-expiration milk straight from the carton. No, it's the queasiness that comes with leaving your comfort zone, then wishing you could go back because you're not ready for this kind of change. It's the intestinal twisting that follows stepping into the spotlight when you are much happier being backstage—if not under the stage, let alone anywhere near the frickin' stage. The light-headed, contents-of-your-dinner-rising-in-your-throat, pukish sensation of being given a second chance to make an important decision and screwing that up too.

Sometimes, the best course of action is inaction. Even though answering seven stupid questions may alter the entire course of my crappy teenage existence, it could be argued that not answering them does too. At least I know what to expect.

So I decide to delete my entry.

Every last word.

I frantically hit the Back button, trying to return to the previous screen, but nothing happens. The rainbow cursor keeps spinning. I slam at all the keys, but the screen is completely frozen, leaving me no choice but to reboot the computer. By the time I get it up and running and log back onto Amanda's website, the count is now up to four hundred and seventy three, and I have absolutely no way of knowing if my entry is one of them.

Well, isn't that perfect.

# 12

THE LAST TIME I ATE AT SOMEONE ELSE'S HOUSE was after my mom and Mickey died. Some lady from church invited Dad and me over for dinner. He made me wear a stiff, uncomfortable collared shirt and lectured me that I'd better eat every single thing that was put in front of me or it would be disrespectful to this kind lady's hospitality.

I had no appetite whatsoever, but I was too scared to protest so I ended up sitting alone in the kitchen and eating six times my weight in turkey tetrazzini casserole, while the woman from church "comforted" my dad. I got the feeling she'd been "comforting" him for some time, even before my mother died. I'm not sure if it was that epiphany or the turkey tetrazzini, but I spent the entire night doubled over the toilet puking my guts out.

My mother would have massaged my back or brought me a cool washcloth. Hell, even Mickey would have climbed out of bed and said, "Hey, buddy, can I get you anything? Glass of cold water?" But my dad never even checked on me. He just sat in a chair downstairs, staring into space until the sun came up.

Thumbing through my closet, I see the shirt still hanging there toward the back. It's tiny because it is meant for a twelve-year-old, and if my mother were still here, it would have long since been donated. All I have at this point is a bunch of well-worn T-shirts, sweatshirts, and one faded-looking navy button-down flannel, but at least it has a collar, so I decide it will be decent enough to wear to Nick's.

Nick lives in the nicer part of town, where the houses are bigger and not sagging at the corners, and the cars in the drive-ways are actually from this decade and not on blocks. I am a little intimidated when I first see his house. It's a two-story brick monster with tall, white columns and black shutters on either side of the windows. It is set back from the street and surrounded by a wrought iron gate with a little camera turned on the entrance to the driveway.

As soon as I roll up on my bike, it's like they can see me because the gates creak open, then close after me as I pedal in. People in "waste management" make a hell of a lot more money than I expected.

I park my bike behind a sweet-looking older model Mercedes with tinted windows. I can't help it; I imagine a body, gagged and bound, stuffed in the trunk. I swallow hard and resolve to be extra polite so that's not me at the end of the night.

Nick opens the door and greets me with a big smile, ushering me into the foyer. He's all suited up for the occasion, and I feel underdressed but grateful I'm wearing a shirt with buttons.

"Fancy," I say.

"Peyton just got here," he tells me and wiggles his eyebrows. "So far, so good. She dug the suit. Chicks are into suits. I hope you're hungry because my mother made enough food for an army."

"I'm starved," I tell him, and it isn't even a lie. My stomach has been rumbling with anticipation for hours. Not to mention that this could be the last decent meal I get for a while, so I need to store it up like a camel.

"Now remember, we eat, and after dinner, once Peyton loosens up, I'll give you the signal and you can go. Say you have to pick up something for your dad or whatever."

"Pick up something. Got it." I flash him a thumbs-up.

"Thanks for doing this, buddy. I owe you one." He gives me a smack on the back. "C'mon, everyone's in the kitchen." I follow him down a hallway filled with dark wood and marble with gold accents. I've never been in such a nice house. Everything is polished and in its place. And there's the most amazing aroma of garlic and herbs, unlike at my house, which always smells musty, like spilled beer and wet dog—and we don't even have a dog. Pack me a bag. I'm ready to move in with Nick's family.

Nick leads me into the kitchen, and when Peyton sees me, she smiles, visibly relaxing. He introduces me to his mother, Angela, who has a nest of curly black hair, bright-red lipstick, and a round body crammed into clothes meant for someone half her age. She comes at me with her arms stretched wide like I'm some long-lost relative and pulls me into a hug that crushes me to her gigantic breasts. They're soft and doughy against my chest, like I'm lying on a pillow.

"So nice to meet Nicky's friends," she gushes. "He never wants to bring anyone by. It's like he's ashamed of us."

"Ma, I'm not ashamed," Nick protests.

"So why haven't you ever had your friends over before?"

"They're here now, aren't they?" Nick's father interrupts and extends his thick, meaty hand to give mine a strong shake. "Dominic Giuliani. Welcome."

He's tall like Nick, and it's clear who Nick inherited his unibrow from. But that's where the resemblance ends because Dominic Giuliani has enough paunch around his middle to show that he's a fan of his wife's cooking. When he smiles, there is a gap between his two front teeth, and when he says the letter *S*, he makes a slight whistling sound. His voice is deep and rich, and when he laughs, his whole body shakes. In fact, he's so pleasant and welcoming that I forget he may be a hit man until the doorbell rings. His expression turns gravely serious. He frowns at Nick. "Who's that? You said you invited two friends."

Mr. Giuliani crosses the kitchen to look at a small TV monitor. As he passes me, I shoot a glance at Peyton. She looks different tonight. Her hair is actually pulled back from her face, which makes her eyes really stand out. Tonight they look especially blue. Like she might be wearing makeup. And instead of one of her oversize rock band T-shirts, she's wearing a plain black sweater and a flowy red skirt. Cleaned up like that, she looks nice. Pretty, even. Nick must think so too because he can't stop staring at her.

Mr. Giuliani lets out an exasperated grunt and presses a button. I watch the iron gates swinging open on the monitor as he tells Mrs. Giuliani, "It's Giovanna. She must have misplaced her remote again. I swear, if that girl's head wasn't attached to her shoulders, she'd lose that too."

Mrs. Giuliani waves her hand at her husband dismissively and says, "Go easy on her, Dominic. You know she's having a tough time."

Nick leans in and says, "She broke up with her boyfriend."

"Her *fiancé* broke up with her. Two months before the wedding. Can you believe it?" Mrs. Giuliani says, and I can see a vein bulge in Mr. Giuliani's forehead.

"We don't talk about it," Nick says.

"No problem," I assure him.

"I could wring that bastard's neck," Mr. Giuliani says as he goes to the front door to let in Nick's sister. Peyton and I exchange a glance, and she raises her eyebrows, as if telling me, "I told you so." Admittedly, I'm glad I'm not Giovanna's ex-fiancé.

"He got cold feet. Ended things via a friggin' text message. My father is ready to have an aneurysm," Nick explains.

Not gonna lie: Nick's sister is totally hot. Her stick-straight black hair shines like a shampoo commercial. She has a mole right above her lip that draws my attention to her mouth, which is painted deep purple, like she sucked all the color out of a grape. She's so skinny she looks like she could break if you hugged her hard enough, but the plunging vee of her sweater reveals that she takes after her mother in that area. Giovanna seems to be around Monica's age, but she looks far more exotic. She plops her oversize, studded purse on the kitchen island and inspects Peyton and me as if we've both sprouted two heads.

"Who is this?" she asks.

"What kind of way is that to greet company?" Mrs. Giuliani asks. "These are Nicky's friends, Peyton and Hank."

Giovanna plasters on a smile. She arches an eyebrow. *Very sexy.*

"Nicky has friends?" she asks innocently.

"Shut up," Nick says as she cackles. I think she might be more intimidating than Mr. Giuliani.

"I'm teasing. Nice to meet you, Nicky's friends," she says and shakes our hands. As we sit around the kitchen table to eat, Peyton slides into a chair between Nick and me. She catches Nick staring at her and smiles nervously.

"What's wrong? Why do you keep looking at me like that?" she asks.

"Like what?"

"Like *that*. You keep giving me these weird looks. Is my hair messed up or something?"

She reaches up to smooth it. I want to crack up, because in the brief time I've known her, I never thought she owned a hairbrush, let alone worried about her appearance.

"No, you look fine," he assures her. His cheeks start to turn red. "In fact, you look better than fine. You look really nice."

Her mouth turns up at the corners as she puts her napkin in her lap. "Thanks."

Nick is right; his mother makes the most kick-ass marinara sauce I've ever eaten. I devour three servings of it over the most perfectly cooked rigatoni I've ever had, along with garlic bread, antipasti salad, minestrone soup, and for dessert, homemade cheesecake with strawberries and dollops of freshly whipped cream.

Nick is cracking jokes, telling stories, and trading barbs with his dad. Nick is trying so hard, and apparently whatever he's doing appears to be working, because I've never seen Peyton smile so much.

I distract myself by watching Giovanna lick the whipped cream off her strawberry and try to figure out how someone this smoking hot came from the same gene pool as Nick. Mr. Giuliani is telling a long-winded joke that has almost built to its punch line when Giovanna's phone buzzes loudly. Mr. Giuliani's cheeks flush and his jaw tenses.

Giovanna sees the expression on her father's face and says, "What? I'm expecting a call."

"Who is more important than Sunday night dinner with your family and guests?" he asks as his face begins to redden.

"It's Bobby," she says quietly.

The way his face is turning red, Mr. Giuliani looks like he just ate a chili pepper.

"Bobby," he says calmly. "Is this the same son-of-a-bitch Bobby that decided to dump you two months before the wedding I paid for? That didn't have the nerve to say it to your face?" Now he's not quite so calm. He looks like his head is going to pop off.

"Daddy, relax. He just wants to talk."

"Do you have no self-respect? This *stronzo* has no further business with you."

Giovanna pouts. "Daddy, I'd thought you'd be happy for me. Bobby wants to work things out. He knows he made a mistake."

"His mistake was calling before Dad could finish his joke," Nick says, trying to lighten the mood. He catches sight of the uncomfortable look on Peyton's face and reassures her, "Don't worry. They're not really fighting. This is just how my family talks."

Mrs. Giuliani pats Giovanna's hand and says, "Go talk to Bobby. Relax, Dominic. Every girl should be so lucky to have a father who loves her so much."

Giovanna gives her father a kiss on the head as she bolts from the room. There is an awkward silence as we all eat our cheesecake, and I try to imagine what it would be like to have my dad care about me that much. I glance at Peyton, and I can tell from the way she's looking at Mr. Giuliani that she's probably thinking the same thing. Then she pipes up and asks, "So how did the joke end? What happened to the nun and the fifty-pound canary?" And just like that, she reels Mr. Giuliani back in.

All I can think is how much I wish I had someplace I belonged with people who care about me the way Nick's family cares about each other. I used to, but that was a long time ago. I wonder if Peyton has ever known what that feels like. Honestly, I'm not sure which is worse: to have it and to lose it, or to never know it at all.

Nick turns to me. "Hey, Hank, don't you have to leave soon? You know, to pick up that thing for your dad before the store *closes*?" He puts emphasis on the last word and raises his eyebrows as if I may have forgotten the cue.

"Oh, right. That thing for my dad. Yeah, I better get going. Thank you so much for dinner, Mr. and Mrs. Giuliani. It was delicious."

I start to push back my chair when Peyton asks me, "What do you have to pick up at this hour?"

I think fast. "Um, I have to get to the pharmacy before it closes. I gotta pick up some cream. My dad's got this rash... It's pretty nasty actually. On his feet. Been going on for a while now and I keep telling him he's gotta get it checked, because he's…um…always scratching and it's spreading."

Everybody seems thoroughly repulsed, so that's my exit. Mr. and Mrs. Giuliani shake my hand, and Peyton and Nick walk me to the door. Nick is all smiles.

All the way home, I imagine the two of them together. I wonder if he'll make out with her. If she'll sneak him into her room, maybe take a picture of him standing there gazing up at those forty-fives. Her hanging a photo of *him* on her wall.

What if she tells him things she doesn't tell me? That's cool, I guess. She's entitled. It's not like I'm her shrink. Hell, it's not like I asked to hear half the stuff I know about her.

I'm not jealous or interested in her. I just like it when all three of us are equally miserable. And for some reason, the two of them being happy together without me pisses me off.

At home, I intend to unwind and work on *Freeze Frame*, but I'm too distracted. I can't stop thinking about Peyton.

Peyton, with her hair pulled back like it was tonight, her skin so white it's practically glowing, lying back on her bed, her lips slightly parted.

Peyton, who for all I know is making out with Nick Giuliani right now.

Peyton, who probably thinks Nick is all that because his dad drives a Mercedes and doesn't come stumbling home drunk, calling him names. He lives in a fancy house and doesn't have to worry if there's anything in the refrigerator that doesn't have an alcoholic content of at least five percent.

Meanwhile, a year from now—ten years from now—I'll still be here, bagging groceries at the Shop 'n Save. If I'm lucky, I'll have moved up to produce manager. Then I'll get to wear one of those green aprons instead of my black one. Something to aspire to.

I pull out my sketchbook and try to push it all aside. For the next few hours, I lose myself drawing my superhero Freeze Frame as he frantically searches for his love interest, Rowena. She's been kidnapped and the Dark Overlord has hidden her somewhere in the bowels of the city. She dropped her timekeeper talisman so he can't track her, but based on where he's picked up the signal, he believes she's left him a clue.

When I'm done with the final panel, it's two forty-five in the morning. I look over the pages. They're good. Really good. Maybe some of the best stuff I've done. I wish I could show the comic to someone.

The truth is, I want to show it to Peyton. Other than Victor, she's the only person who knows about *Freeze Frame*. She gets how personal my art is to me, how when I'm drawing *Freeze*

*Frame*, I feel most like myself. It's weird, but I don't mind being vulnerable with her. I trust her. And now I just hope that won't get awkward with things taking a romantic turn between her and Nick. I can't let it.

I steal another look at the clock. I can't wait until tomorrow.

I pull on my jeans and grab my Batman hoodie and my sketches, because I don't give a flaming fuck what time it is. I crack my door. Dad's snores carve through the silence, loud and guttural, like he's under deep and won't be getting up for a long while. He's in his room this time thankfully, so I sneak downstairs, hop on my bike, and ride in the direction of Peyton's neighborhood.

Her house is dark and quiet. Her window is open.

I make out her silhouette lying in her bed, the covers curled around her. There's no sign of Nick, for which I am relieved. I open my mouth to wake her up but stop. I don't want her to get scared and scream. Pete's frightening enough during the day. No need to incur his wrath in the middle of the night. Instead, I lean in and stretch my arm to gently lay the sketches next to her.

Seeing Peyton now almost feels more normal than seeing her during the day. I swear, since I met Peyton, I haven't had a full night's sleep, and yet I'm not tired. In fact, I've never been more wide-awake.

# 13

"DID YOU MAKE THE FINALS?" NICK ASKS ME AS we're walking toward our lockers at the beginning of nutrition break on Monday.

I worry that maybe I forgot about some test or competition in gym class. "Finals? What are you talking about?"

He raises his eyebrows and shakes his head. "Dude, it's like you live in a cave sometimes. Amanda posted who's moving on to the next round. If your number is listed on her website you have to answer more questions."

With everything that has been going on, I'd nearly forgotten about Amanda's site and whether or not my answers had actually gone through. "I haven't checked. How about you? Did you make the cut?"

He grins and rubs at his bad eye, almost as if he's trying to guide its gaze back into place. "I did. I had some pretty smooth answers, so I'm not surprised. I'm not sure what to do though, because I got this thing developing with Peyton, right? I wouldn't want to have to break Amanda's heart if I'm dating someone else. It wouldn't be fair."

I bite the inside of my cheek to keep from laughing. "Definitely. So what's the deal with you and Peyton? Are you guys, like, going out now or what?"

"She's definitely into me. I can tell. Who could resist the Giuliani charm? Dinner went really well, except for the part when you and my parents were hanging around messing up my mojo." He gives me a mock punch in the arm. "What was up with that foot rash story, man? That was disgusting."

"Well, you drove her home, right? You were alone then. Did you put the moves on her or what?" I'm razzing him, but I'm more interested in the answer than I'd care to admit.

Nick shoots a glance over his shoulder and rakes his fingers through his hair. "Nah. I just drove her home, you know? I didn't want to push my luck. Had to be a gentleman. Of course, if she'd invited me in, I might have been willing to bend the rules."

"Of course." I smile and say, "So did your sister get back together with her boyfriend?"

He snorts. "Not yet. My father is ready to have a friggin' coronary because he never liked Bobby in the first place, but he also doesn't like to waste money. My sister dropped

some serious cash on a dress, and there was a nonrefund-
able deposit for the caterer. I know they'll get back together,
but Giovanna is drawing it out and making Bobby beg for
her forgiveness. Can you imagine if my father knew she was
knocked up?"

"She's *pregnant*?"

"Let's just say you don't need to be Sherlock to notice she's
in the bathroom throwing up most mornings. When my father
finds out, it won't be pretty."

"Wow."

"Family. It's the original *f*-word, am I right?" He cracks
himself up, then tries to act all casual as he asks, "So have you
seen Peyton around today?"

"I haven't." What I don't add is that not seeing her has been
driving me nuts. She hasn't said a frickin' word since I left that
comic on her pillow. I don't know what the hell I was thinking,
showing her my stuff like that anyway. I'm not used to letting
anyone else into my head. It's a bit like standing naked onstage
during a school assembly.

We separate, heading to our respective lockers. I still have
seven minutes before nutrition is over, so I dart around the
corner to the school computer lab and log on to Amanda's
site. I scroll down the list of twenty-five or so numbers that've

moved on to the next round for further questioning, and there it is: entry number 456. Holy shit. It took.

This is really happening.

I don't have time to read through the new questions since I have to get to my next class, but the odd euphoria of feeling one up on those who didn't get chosen makes me smile. Part of me wants to show everyone I'm not the loser they think I am, but another part of me doesn't care because the whole thing is so inane to begin with. It's like what Monica said: life and people never live up to expectations. I'm supposing Amanda would be no different, but I'd love a chance to prove that theory wrong. Although we've only talked once since the incident, I feel like our conversation gave me a better sense of who she is as a person, and I'd be lying if I didn't say she still seems pretty fantastic.

I'm sitting in the back of bio, doodling in the margins of my notes and stealing glances at Amanda, calculating my chances for being her escort to prom, when the fire alarm goes off. There is a mix of cheers and grumbles as our teacher jumps into emergency response mode and hustles us single file out the door.

The faculty shepherd us through the halls, while a group of freshmen whisper back and forth about two fire alarms in two weeks. I smile, sensing this is most definitely not a coincidence.

I shove my hands in my pockets, and on a hunch, I casually make my way toward the faculty parking lot. Lying right in front of the gate is a matchbook, the cover folded neatly back and tucked in on itself, a single unlit match sticking up like a middle finger. I pick up the matchbook, closing the cover. This one is from Purple Haze Hookah Lounge. I laugh and shove it in my pocket, then slip through the gate into the parking lot.

I find Peyton sitting cross-legged on the asphalt next to Vice Principal Jergensen's Volvo wagon, which has the bumper sticker "Are you following Jesus this close?" As I get closer, I see that she is reading the *Freeze Frame* pages that I left on her pillow. She has not set them on fire, so I'm hoping that means she thinks they're decent.

When she hears me approaching, she looks up and actually has tears in her eyes.

"Hank, this is amazing," she says, shaking her head and thumbing her way to the next page.

Admittedly, it's what I've been waiting to hear, and it fills me up. "I'm glad you liked it. I wanted to show it to you because I'm pretty proud of it actually, and I'm excited to hear what you think. But…we could have met up after school or something. You didn't need to pull the fire alarm."

She laughs. "No worries, I only burned a few paper towels

in the girls' restroom. It's all tile and toilets. I'm sure it was out before the fire engines got here. Though all that hair spray residue does up the flammability factor. Hmmm."

As much as I want nothing more than to get her feedback, and I'm flattered that she couldn't even wait until lunch to talk, I'm also unsettled by how flippant she is about what she's done. She throws caution to the wind. Like she doesn't care if she hurts anyone because she's got nothing to lose.

"Seriously, what if someone got hurt? Or the fire got out of control? You should stop. What if someone catches you? You'd get kicked out." I glance nervously toward the school, afraid that at any minute one of the teachers will sweep the parking lot for stray students and find us.

"Can we please talk about this instead?" She grabs my wrist and pulls me down next to her. "Hank, you are very talented. I'm not kidding. You have to do something with this."

"Do what with it?"

"I don't know. You need to show this to someone. I imagine all the art schools in the country would beg you to come if they saw your work. Or you could send it to a publisher. There have to be special publishers for this kind of stuff, right? We could write to them, and maybe they would take a look at it."

She seems genuinely excited. Having Peyton look at my

pages and judge them was hard enough; I'm not sure I could handle a college or publisher telling me my work is no good.

I bite my lip for a moment. "That would be pretty amazing. But the reality is that colleges have already closed applications for the fall. I have greater odds of being hit by lightning than getting in, not to mention being able to afford tuition. And I don't know squat about how to find a publisher."

Peyton rolls her eyes. "There's this amazing thing called the Internet, Hank. It's like a genie. You ask it questions, and it gives you answers. Also, there's this awesome school called the School of the Museum of Fine Arts in Boston. They have rolling admissions, so you can still apply. It's not too late. Their admissions people look at your stuff and let you know their decision in a month or so."

"How do you know so much about their admissions policy?"

"Again, Hank, the Internet. Are you listening to me? You owe it to yourself. I'll help you figure out the details. It's just... This is too good. The world should know who Hank Kirby is. You have so much talent, and you're a good person. You *deserve* good things. So many people don't. But you do." She squeezes my arm as if that will drive the point home, then swallows hard, tucks a loose strand of hair behind her ear, and adds, "And most of all because I know it took a lot of courage for you to show me this. I've never had anyone trust me that much."

"Well, I have more pages. I mean, I'd love to show you more of them if you're interested." I'm hoping she is.

"Of course I'm interested." She beams and hugs the papers to her chest. "Can I keep these for a while?"

"Sure. Whatever blows your hair back."

She reaches into her back pocket and pulls out a pack of bubble gum, offering me a piece.

"Wow, matches and gum at school. You're a rebel."

"I've never been much for following rules I didn't agree with. That's probably the reason I'm not Student of the Month," she says and blows a ginormous bubble. "So did you know that the guy who invented Captain America and the Fantastic Four and a bunch of other famous superheroes was named Jack Kirby? Maybe he's, like, your long-lost uncle six times removed."

"Where'd you learn that? I mean, *I* knew that, but…I'm impressed that *you* do."

She leans into me and says, "If I'm going to be friends with the next big comic book artist and writer, it's in my best interest to be up on my superheroes. You can't ever be too informed."

I smile and give her a playful nudge, intended to convey how much it means to me that she looked up this stuff because she knew it was important to me. That's pretty cool. "It's true. You never know when you could be in a life or death match of Trivial Pursuit."

"I will have you know that I kick ass at that game. I used to play all the time when I was in the hospital."

It slides out of her mouth and from the look in her eyes, she wishes she could reel the words back in. But before I can ask her what she's talking about, we are interrupted by the sound of footsteps. Then our English teacher, Mr. Vaughn, skitters past, his head down, covertly sneaking a puff off a joint. He spies us mid-inhale and freezes as if deciding his best course of action, looking every bit as surprised to see us as we are to see him.

Mr. Vaughn is pretty chill as teachers go, and he exhales loudly as he brushes back the hundred or so hairs—each of them shoulder length and gray—that remain on his head. He's the kind of guy who must have been to a million Grateful Dead concerts. I wouldn't be surprised if he stays at just the right level of stoned to make it through us kids massacring the English language every day in his class.

"What are you two doing back here?" he asks, trying to be all official, which is hard when you're cupping a joint in one hand.

"We're taking a break," Peyton tells him. "What are *you* doing, Mr. Vaughn?"

He studies the ground for a minute, as if the proper answer will manifest itself there, and then looks at us and grins. "I guess I'm taking a break too."

Peyton nods. "I think it's good to take a break now and then."

She may be up for casual conversation, but I'm practically pissing myself at the thought of Mr. Vaughn turning us in. But I suppose catching a teacher smoking a jay cancels out two teenagers reading and talking about superheroes during a fire drill, even if one of them was responsible for the fire that caused the drill.

Mr. Vaughn notices the stack of papers in Peyton's lap. "Whatcha got there?"

Peyton hands my comic to him, and I feel my cheeks burn with embarrassment. I reach out to grab the pages back but Peyton swats my hand away.

"It's a comic Hank writes and illustrates. He's going to be famous," she says with authority.

Mr. Vaughn flips through the pages and starts smiling, then laughing, but in a good way. He takes another puff of his joint. He exhales and says, "This is really good, man. You going to art college next year?"

I can practically hear Peyton say, "See? I told you so!"

"That's not the current plan. Possibly junior college in the next year or two, if I can swing it. I'll be working so it might be tough. My schedule changes every week," I tell him. I don't want to share that I also probably can't afford it. I've heard all the scholarship talks from the counselors, but I know my dad is counting on the extra money I will bring in once I can bump up to full time.

Mr. Vaughn's face falls. He sees through my bullshit. "You show a lot of promise, Hank. You should stick with your studies."

Nobody has ever told me that before.

He gives Peyton the stack of papers and sighs deeply. "All right. Back to the unruly masses. We're bound to be missed. Me especially." We all laugh at that. "Hey, you by chance have an extra stick of that gum?"

Peyton roots out the pack and hands him one. He pops it in his mouth, salutes, and says, "Thanks. I'll let you two lovebirds finish your moment. Sorry to interrupt."

My jaw involuntarily drops and I want to insist that it's not like that—we're not making out or even *thinking* about exchanging bodily fluids of any sort—but his back is already to us.

"I guess we looked like a couple," she says.

"Yeah, well, he was high. Now we know why he's always asking kids to bring him cheeseburgers if they ditch, right?"

We stand up, and she kicks at the rear tire of Jergensen's car with the graffitied toe of her Converse high-tops and says, "Would that have been such a crazy thing?"

"What?"

"If we were a couple."

"I didn't say that."

She straightens and digs her hands in her pockets. "You basically did. I mean, you said he thought we looked like a couple because he was high, as if the idea was completely ridiculous."

It is, but because I can't imagine what she would want with a guy like me. She should be with someone who can take her to nice places, make her laugh, and give her gifts to show her she's special. I can't offer her a damn thing.

"It's not that. It's just…now there's this thing going on between you and Nick. He's my friend." My hands start to get clammy. It's weird to be talking about this kind of stuff with her.

She casts her gaze toward the doors where everyone is filing back into the school. "You're right."

"So…it's working out between you guys then?"

She shrugs. "I guess."

"He's a decent guy. You can't really do much better than him."

She raises her eyebrows and cocks her jaw. "What's that supposed to mean?"

I realize how that sounds. "I didn't mean you *couldn't* do any better. I merely meant he's a stand-up guy. You two are good together is all."

She hugs my comic to her chest and stares at me. "You think?" I can't read her expression. She deserves someone who has his shit together, someone with options in his life who can make her happy. Someone like Nick.

The way she keeps looking at me makes me start to feel dizzy. It's probably the secondhand smoke, but for a moment, I can see past her frizzy hair and baggy clothes straight to her soul, and I swear she's so beautiful. Here we are, only a few inches separating us, and all I want to do is lean over and kiss her. I wonder if she'd push me away. I don't even know why I'm thinking crazy like that.

It's as if she can read my mind because she takes a step closer to me. It would be so easy to kiss her, but Nick likes her, and that would be a shitty thing to do. So I clear my throat and step back, saying, "So, um, earlier. What did you mean when you said you were in the hospital?"

She faces away and doesn't answer me.

"Were you sick or something? Was it serious?"

"Forget I said that. It was nothing."

"How can it be nothing if you were in a hospital?"

She pulls at a loose thread on her shirt. "I did something stupid, and I had to stay there for a little while until I got better. It's not that big a deal. I don't really want to talk about it, okay?"

"Okay." I've definitely hit a nerve. I can tell that pressing her is only going to upset her. I shift topics despite having a million questions. "Oh, guess what? I made the cut on that Amanda thing. Turns out I had the right answers. Who knew?"

Our moment, whatever it was, is over. Just like that.

She cracks a half smile. "That's good, right? That's what you wanted."

I shrug as we walk back toward the gate. "I guess. Let's be serious. It's not like she won't be disappointed if she finds out it's me and not Clay Kimball or one of those other jockstraps. Everybody wants Cinderella to end up with the handsome prince, not the stable hand."

"Clay Kimball? Please. You're so much better looking than he is."

"You're right. Girls are so busy looking at me that they hardly notice him these days."

"Are you kidding? Plenty of girls look at you."

"Uh-huh."

"You're so completely oblivious. It would be charming if it

wasn't kind of annoying." She shakes her head and lets out a loud sigh. "Besides, Clay Kimball is a walking steroid. Not to mention he has a thing for Miles Pederson."

I start cracking up. "What? Where the hell did you hear that?"

"I know things. I saw them once."

"What? When?"

"I was at the park over on Crescent. I'd had a crappy day but had found this pack of matches on the ground so I decided to go burn some old leaves. Nothing that I couldn't stamp out or anything. I was just worked up and needed a release. When I turned the corner, there they were."

"You really should consider yoga instead. Far less potential for jail time."

She elbows me and says, "Do you want to hear my utterly scandalous story or not?"

"Definitely." Although I'm not much for gossip, I admit that having top-secret insider dirt on one of the most popular guys in school is pretty amusing. My interest is piqued.

"Okay then. So Clay had Miles pinned against a tree, and they were playing serious tonsil hockey. I hid and watched them for a while. It got pretty intense. They seemed really into each other. There's more to everyone if you get below the surface. Even Clay Kimball. Or you."

I love how Peyton tells shit like it is. No judgment or beating around the bush. She gets right to the heart of it. I've never talked to a girl like her before.

We slip back through the gates onto the school grounds as Nick is making his way toward us. Seeing us together seems to catch him off guard. His eyes dart back and forth between us, assessing the situation. He stiffens, keeping his gaze on me and trying to ascertain if I've made the moves on the girl he likes, but Peyton answers that by stepping between us and saying, "Hey, Nick. We should hang out again soon. Maybe this weekend or something?"

He relaxes. "Yeah, sure," he replies, rubbing at the stubble on his chin, trying to be cool. "What do you guys want to do?"

"Oh, I meant just you and me."

Nick looks at me and I say, "Yeah, I have some stuff I gotta do. You guys hang without me."

He nods his head, trying to mask his delight that I will not be joining them. "Sweet. I mean…some other time, Hank."

"Excellent. I'm *really* looking forward to it." Peyton stares at me when she says it though.

I smile to look happy for them. I mean, I *am* happy for them. I have no reason not to be. *They* seem happy, so it's all good. Not to mention that I'm closer than I've ever been to having a date with Amanda, and two people saw *Freeze Frame* and actually thought it was decent. As far as days go, this one is borderline epic. In fact, life is all rainbows and smiley faces.

There's only one thing that can kill this buzz, and it's waiting for me when I get home.

# 14

I CAN PRACTICALLY SMELL THE BOOZE FROM THE street, and the TV is cranked up much too loud. Dad's yelling in a booming voice, though I can't make out the specific words. He's on a bender. My body immediately tenses. There's only one reason my dad would be home, plastered, in the middle of a Monday afternoon, and it isn't to make me an after-school snack. This can't be good.

"Hank!" he says, trying to focus on me as I pull the front door closed behind me. "Have a seat." He pats the sofa cushion next to him and nearly falls over in the process.

"Dad, what are you doing home?"

Monica comes out of the kitchen, dressed for work in a skimpy tube top and cutoff shorts. She is visibly stressed, and mascara trails down her cheeks. *Why has she been crying?*

She jiggles her keys in her hand and says, "I'm glad you're home, Hank. Your dad got laid off today, and I didn't want to leave him here alone. Not like this. But I gotta go."

"He what?" This is so very not good.

"I don't need you to babysit me," my dad slurs at Monica. "Don't you have a pole to twirl around? Stick to what you're good at."

She glares at him tight-lipped. "When your father gets drunk, he says a lot of shit he doesn't mean."

"Shit I don't mean?" Dad's eyes narrow. "Honey, wake up. You wrapping yourself around that pole is what made me notice you in the first place."

"Dad—" I start to defend Monica even though I know it's going to piss him off more. Mickey and I were never brave enough to say anything when he talked to our mother that way. I'm not going to make that mistake twice.

My dad does not like being confronted. Especially in front of other people. Even when he knows he's wrong. He has too much pride to back down. But he has to realize that if he stops giving a shit about everybody else, eventually people will stop giving a shit about him too. I have a feeling this is about to be one of those times.

Dad cranks the TV volume from loud to ear-splitting, ignoring us both. Monica shakes her head. Her mind is already made up.

"Look," she says to me in a low voice, "I made a tuna

casserole. It's on top of the stove. All you need to do is reheat it in the oven. Just get some food in him to soak up some of that liquor." She bites back tears. "You take care of yourself, Hank. You're a good guy. Maybe I'll see you around sometime."

She leans in and gives me a hug. That's when I notice the suitcase by the door.

Her suitcase.

The green one with rainbow-colored ribbons tied around the handle that's been sitting in the hall closet for nearly a year, ever since she unofficially moved in.

And it becomes clear that today she is officially moving out.

"What?" I'm seriously hoping I've misheard her. "No, Monica, wait. You can't go!"

I grab her hand as she heads toward the door. I'm frantic at the thought of her leaving. She's about the only thing keeping Dad sane. Without her, I don't know what's going to happen.

"I really care about your dad, but I can't do this anymore. I can't take how he gets when he drinks. I told him he needs to stop, but lately he doesn't seem to care about anything or anyone else. And now this. I told him if he wants to be with me, he needs to get his shit together. If he does, he knows where to find me." Tears run down her cheeks. She angrily brushes them away. "I'm sorry."

"Look, he doesn't mean it, Monica. When he sobers up, he'll be his usual self again. You know that. Please. Stay." I plead with her, but she's already got her hand on the doorknob.

"It'll be okay, Hank."

And just like that, she's gone, and I'm standing there, jaw half open, staring at the back side of the door. I contemplate running down the driveway, throwing myself in front of her car, begging her to stay. Part of me wants to get in the car with her and never look back. But I can't.

I slowly turn to look at my dad and see he's lost in the television, his eyes at half-mast. If he notices that Monica has left, he doesn't show it. From the lineup of empties in front of him he's at least halfway through a six-pack and not showing signs of stopping anytime soon.

Dad belches and brings his beer to his lips for another swig; then he wipes at his mouth with the back of his fist. He grabs the remote and turns the TV down to a semi-normal volume. "Don't you dare heat that crap. Smells like cat food! I ain't touching it."

"What's going on, Dad?" I ask quietly.

"You heard her. I got fired."

He starts flipping through channels. Suddenly, the house is filled with the proclamations of someone hawking a blender that does it all: slices, dices, and practically folds your laundry. Dad is riveted.

"Why?" I'm scared to hear his response.

He turns to me with narrowed eyes. "Because the sons of bitches at work set me up is why. And I caught them at their own game. I have a good mind to take them to court for violating my personal privacy." He spits as he says the letter *p*.

This sounds serious. "What happened?"

"They set up these little cameras all over, see? Like government spies. My supervisor claimed he saw me sneaking a drink by my locker. I called him a liar. Then he shows me the goddamned video, so I called him a pervert with nothing better to do than sit around jerking off and watching his employees all day. Then he pulled out *my* flask that he stole from *my* locker without *my* permission, and he tells me I'm gonna have to leave. Twenty-one years of service and they let me go without blinking an eye."

I can feel the blood drain from my face. Folks won't exactly be lining up to hire Dad. I'm guessing there's not a huge demand for alcoholic factory workers in their midforties with a high school degree.

"You should go talk to him," I suggest. "Ask him to give you a second chance. Like you said, you've been there a long time. Maybe he'll reconsider."

He laughs, and he doesn't let up, so finally I join in because I'm not sure what else to do. "You think life is like one of those comic books of yours, don't you? Where justice prevails. Where the good guy friggin' wins." He erupts with laughter again, and then he starts coughing so hard that he drops his beer. As he reaches for it, he clips his temple on the edge of the coffee table and it draws blood. Now he's cussing and throws the beer can across the room. Then he starts crying.

Like, really bawling.

It all happens so fast that I still have to wipe the smile off my face and shift gears. I run to the kitchen, throw some ice in a plastic grocery bag I find under the sink, and wrap it in a dish towel. I give it to him to put on his head and then grab another dish towel to clean up his mess. I know better than to talk to him, so I just keep working, keep trying to make it all be okay.

I sneak a glance at him. He looks like hell, his face all red with a smudged line of blood down the side and snot bubbling out his nose. The last time I saw my dad cry was when Mom and Mickey died. He did it mostly in private, not wanting to share his grief with me. Even now, I'll hear him late at night when Monica's working and he thinks I am sleeping. He'll go into Mickey's room and sit there in the dark and talk to my dead mother and brother. He tells them all the things he should have told them when they were alive and what's going on now. Ironically, I am in the next room but he won't say a word of it to me.

"Just leave it," he says.

The knees of my jeans are now wet and beer-stained. I keep dabbing at the soaked carpet, but the dish towel is already saturated.

"I said, 'Leave it!'" he booms, and I stand up, still trying to avoid looking him in the eye.

"Okay."

He examines the bloody dish towel in his hand and then shifts his focus to the TV, flipping through the channels again like nothing's happened. "You're blocking the TV."

I move aside as he settles his focus on some game show. I leave him be, picking up the beer can he threw and setting it on the hallway table. As I do, I catch sight of the stack of mail sitting there. I thumb through to see if there's anything for me, not that I get much mail, but it's envelope after envelope of unopened bills, some of them with ominous red stamps that say "Final Notice" in big caps.

It's amazing, really, what with Dad's anti-sobriety stance and his hair-trigger temper, that he's been able to keep this ship afloat until now. I'm wondering how long Dad's unemployment and my part-time, minimum-wage job bagging groceries are going to carry us. I try to tamp down the panic rising from my gut. I have a vision of living under an overpass, pushing a shopping cart of our belongings, holding signs at highway off-ramps, and talking to people who aren't there. I can't let that happen to us.

I can probably convince Mr. O'Callaghan to let me pick up a few extra shifts on the weekends, at least until Dad lands on his feet. That should scrape together enough to keep the lights on, even if we have to eat a fuck-load of ramen to get by. A kid at my school, Walter Zhou, brings ramen to school for lunch every single frickin' day. He always has a smile on his face, so it can't be all bad, right?

*This is only temporary*, I tell myself like a mantra. *Everything* is temporary. If I've learned anything since Mom's and Mickey's deaths it's that the only thing you can count on in life is change. Except, of course, from a vending machine.

I look over at Dad one more time before I head upstairs. His eyes are closed. He's fallen asleep. That's probably good. Far be it from me to disrupt the peace.

I head upstairs and collapse into my desk chair, puffing out my cheeks as I exhale loudly. I'm not much of a pot smoker, but I'm half wishing I'd hit Vaughn up for a joint this afternoon, because I could sure use a little escape right now. I log on to my computer instead.

It seems so trivial in the face of everything that's happened this afternoon, but I find myself on Amanda's page. There's my number listed as a finalist: 456. This whole thing is so damn superficial, yet making it to the next round feels like an achievement, and I am oddly compelled to see it through. I look over the next round of questions, and they don't have anything to do with the incident. They're more like questions you'd find on a dating website:

If you and I had twenty-four hours to do anything, what would we do? Would it be a wild and crazy adventure or a lazy, romantic day?

If you could describe yourself using only five words, what would they be? And how would you describe me?

Why do you think we'd make an awesome couple?

What is something you really believe in? How far would you go for a cause that is important to you?

There are, like, six more questions, but I stop reading. It's as if I'm interviewing for a job that I'm qualified for, but I still need to have the right hobbies to get hired. If she's really looking for the guy that set her lawn on fire, I'm it. But Amanda seems to be looking for her soul mate. And how I answer these questions determines my fate, her fate, the fate of our unborn children and grandchildren, maybe the course of the entire universe.

But the fact is, you can't get the job if you never apply. And since you can't lose what you never had in the first place, I throw all caution to the wind and answer each of her ridiculous questions with witty, charming responses that are guaranteed to make her laugh. At the minimum, it is an entertaining distraction from thinking about what happened downstairs.

This time when I hit Submit, I'm not even mildly nauseated. Maybe the universe will let this one tiny thing go my way. Maybe it will be a sign of better times to come. And if Amanda doesn't choose me, it'll make an outstanding story when I'm old enough to go to cocktail parties.

There are so many things in life that you simply can't control. You just have to accept them, even if they don't make sense. This is one of them.

None of it matters, and all of it matters too much.

# 15

FOR THE LAST FEW WEEKS, MY DAD HAS BEEN sitting on the couch in various states of intoxication and watching television, only getting up to pee or forage for food. I suspect this is what rock bottom looks like. It isn't pretty. I try to avoid talking to him as much as humanly possible, heading straight to work from school and then right to my room when I get home. Working on the next installment of *Freeze Frame* has been a welcome distraction.

I've been thinking about what Peyton said about looking for a publisher for my comic. She'd loved it so much that she'd set a fire to get me out of class to tell me so. Mr. Vaughn seemed to like it too, even if he was stoned. Drawing is the only thing I know I'm good at, other than stacking cans of Campbell's soup. Only one of those talents is delivering a paycheck right now, but for the first time, I'm hopeful that *Freeze Frame* could be my ticket out of here.

O'Callaghan gives me some extra shifts. I'm trying to work as much as I can, not just to make extra money, but also to keep busy so my brain doesn't explode. Amanda still hasn't posted her decision. The word around school is that she's going to in a few days. She pretty much has to, because everyone's making plans for prom, which is coming up soon.

I wonder if Nick is going to ask Peyton. Would she even go? She doesn't seem like the type who would give a crap about a dance, even if it is some major "rite of passage." I wouldn't know because I haven't seen them much. They're probably too busy playing tonsil hockey to miss me. Far be it from me to get in the middle of their love fest.

Bottom line: the less I have to think about my life right now, the better.

Just when I am convinced Dad is going to permanently become one with the couch and never get out of his lucky Red Sox tee and boxer shorts again, a miracle happens. I'm heading out the door to work, and there he is, showered and shaved, with his hair combed and slicked back. He's even wearing a tie.

"Got a job interview today," he tells me. "Haven't had one of those since before you were born."

He paces back and forth in the living room, and there are faint rings of sweat under his armpits.

"Good luck! I'm sure you'll knock it out of the park, Dad."

Truthfully, I'm a little nervous about what might happen if he doesn't.

Maybe this is the week things will be looking up for the Kirbys.

Or maybe only for Dad, because when I arrive at the Shop 'n Save, O'Callaghan hands me a mop and a bucket and sends me off to do a cleanup in aisle five. Apparently, some dickhead decided it would be fun to punch holes in a bunch of V8 cans. The place looks like a crime scene, with sticky pools of red liquid everywhere. O'Callaghan normally doesn't put me out on the floor like this, but he's shorthanded. In a way, it's a promotion, which is sort of exciting and pathetic at the same time.

I'm dunking the mop into the bucket to give the floor a final swab when a voice behind me says, "*There* you are."

I turn and it's Peyton in the Pink Floyd tee she was wearing the night I met her, along with a pair of cutoffs and high-top Converse. She's holding something behind her back. She's drawn happy faces on both her kneecaps again. Her hair is in two long, sloppy braids that make her look about twelve, but it's cute, and the sight of her makes me smile.

"Hey," I say and shake my bangs out of my eyes. "Where's Nick?"

"I don't know. Why?"

"I thought you guys would be hanging out."

I put the mop back in the bucket and glance over my shoulder to see if O'Callaghan is watching. He hates it when I talk to customers. He says time is money, and by talking, I'm wasting his. He's caught up at one of the registers with some old lady who looks to be paying for her groceries in dimes and pennies. I pull out the mop again so he doesn't call me over to help.

"We're not conjoined twins," she says.

"Trouble in paradise already? Or is it his breath? I always tell Nick he should use mints. Chronic halitosis doesn't have to be an issue nowadays."

She laughs. "His breath is fine."

"Yeah? So that's going well then?" I swish the mop around, trying to play it cool, like I don't really care about the details, but part of me hopes she'll say it's boring as hell without me there.

"I guess. We went to see a movie and grabbed a slice of pizza."

"I bet that's not all he wanted to grab," I say, and she scrunches up her nose.

"Well, he didn't get very far, but not for lack of trying. Nick is definitely a touchy-feely kind of guy, emphasis on 'touch with the goal to feel,'" she tells me. I imagine Nick running his hands over her, and the thought makes me feel weird. "Do we have to talk about this? I didn't come here to talk about Nick."

"Then let's talk about something else."

"I came here to give you something. Ta-da!" She smiles and hands me a medium-size purple gift bag, the handles of which are tied together in a sloppy bow with a piece of red yarn. Instead of tissue paper inside, there is a folded sheet of this week's Shop 'n Save circular. "Sorry, I was out of wrapping paper. I had to improvise."

"What's this?"

"It's just a little something I wanted you to have. I hope you'll like it." She has a huge grin and is bouncing on her heels excitedly.

I've never had a girl give me a present before, and it takes me by surprise. It feels really personal, like she was actually thinking about me. I gesture toward O'Callaghan and say, "Thanks. I wish I could open it right now, but my boss is totally on the warpath with me. I think his Lucky Charms weren't magically delicious this morning." I dunk the mop and slosh it over a spot I missed underneath the lip of the shelves.

She bites at her lip, visibly disappointed, and then shrugs it off. "That's okay. You can open it later." She digs her hands in her pockets, rocking back and forth on her heels. "Can I ask you something?"

"Shoot."

"Have you been avoiding me, Hank?"

I stop mopping. "Why would you say that? I'm standing here talking to you, aren't I?" I glance at O'Callaghan again. He's checking me out, so I say in a very loud voice, "Tampons are in aisle twelve, miss. I believe the store brand is on sale."

Her forehead creases with confusion, so I add under my breath, "My boss. Work with me."

She gives me a wink and responds in an equally loud voice, "Thank you. I'm having an especially heavy flow this month. Do you carry the super overnight pads with wings? I need extra protection." And then in a lower voice, she says to me, "Obviously not right this minute. I mean in general. I haven't seen you all week."

I say loudly, "Yes, we have many varieties of pads in all shapes and sizes," then lower my voice and tell her, "No, I've just been working a lot. My dad lost his job last week, and his girlfriend bailed, so it's been kinda crazy…"

Her face crinkles with concern. "That sucks. I'm sorry. When I didn't see you, I thought maybe you felt weird around me after what happened last Friday. You know, during the fire alarm."

I wasn't sure which part she meant: when she admitted to crying over *Freeze Frame*, when she mentioned she'd been in the hospital, or when we almost kissed. Of course, that last one could have been my imagination.

I don't get the chance to ask because Mr. O'Callaghan appears beside me, his bushy brow furrowed, his hands on his hips, saying, "Can I help you with something, miss?"

"I was just directing this customer to the feminine products," I explain, and Peyton nods in agreement.

"Aisle twelve," he tells her, then glares at me. "Hank, get back on a register. I'll finish here. Those groceries aren't going to scan and bag themselves."

I hand him the mop, and it dribbles dirty water onto his shoes. He jumps out of the way and narrows his eyes at me. I just give him my best "at your service" smile and head back to the front of the store. As I walk away, Peyton asks, "Do you also carry douches in assorted scents? A girl has to feel fresh." I suppress a laugh as I try to imagine O'Callaghan's face.

At the registers, there is not a single customer waiting to be rung up. What a tool. I'm dying to look inside the bag, but I stash it under the counter to savor later.

Five minutes later, Peyton is at my register with a big box of tampons, maxi pads, and a bottle of lavender-scented feminine wash. She puts them down at the end of the conveyor belt. I smile cheerfully as I ring her up. "That's gonna be nineteen dollars and seventy-three cents," I tell her.

She digs in her front pocket and pulls out eighty-six cents. She frowns. "I'm a little short."

"Appears so."

"Hmmm. I guess I'll have to get these another time. I'll buy this instead," she says and grabs a plastic disposable lighter, placing it on the counter next to the credit card machine.

I remove the other items from the conveyor belt, place them in the returns basket, and ring her up. "Should I be selling you this?"

"That's a burning question, isn't it?" she replies with a straight face as she shoves her change toward me.

O'Callaghan will be back to check on me any second, but I don't want her to leave yet. Judging by the past week or so, I don't know when I'll get to see her again without Nick. It feels good to talk to her. "I heard a really messed-up joke the other day you might appreciate."

"Hit me."

"What kind of car does a pyromaniac drive?"

She pockets the lighter and a pack of watermelon gum that she did not pay for. "No clue."

"A Blazer."

Peyton laughs as another customer starts unloading her groceries onto the conveyor belt behind her.

"Thanks for the present."

"You're welcome. What time are you done here tonight?"

"Ten thirty."

She smirks. "Well, can I meet you after work, then? I want to watch your face when you open it."

"Yeah, sure," I say and smile, already looking forward to seeing her again.

"See you later," she says as I greet the next customer and start to scan her groceries. I turn back toward the exit to wave at Peyton, but she's already gone.

The next three hours pass excruciatingly slowly, and at the strike of ten thirty, I'm outta there like a shot. Peyton's waiting by my bike with a huge smile on her face.

I tear away the newspaper wrapping, and there in my hands, wrapped in a protective plastic sleeve, is Marvel issue #48 of the *Fantastic Four*: "The Coming of Galactus!" *What the…?*

"Holy shit…" I carefully remove the comic and flip through the pages. When I can pick my jaw off the asphalt, I tell her, "Thank you. This is amazing. Where did you get this?"

"At that comic book store you took me to," she says. "You like?"

"I can't believe you bought this for me."

The question is: *How* did she buy this for me? Where the hell did she get that kind of money?

I know I can't accept such a generous gift from her, no matter how badly I want to. It wouldn't be right.

Would it?

"Well, believe it. It's yours now. It showed up in that store for a reason," she says. She's so genuinely happy that she's practically glowing.

"Does Nick know about this?" I'm annoyed that Peyton's given me this amazing present and that I have to worry about how Nick will react. She and I were friends before she met him. Maybe I'm a prick for feeling that way, but it's the truth. Peyton is the first person who's actually made me feel good about myself in a long time. She's probably the best friend I've ever had, and I'm not willing to give that up just because Nick decides he wants to put sour cream on her burrito.

Her smile cools as she says, "What does Nick have to do with this?"

"You guys are dating, right? I mean, isn't it weird to give some other guy a present? Not that I'm complaining. This is possibly the coolest thing anyone has ever done for me in my entire life."

The glow returns. "Friends give each other presents all the time and it's no big deal. This has nothing to do with Nick. This is between you and me."

I am overwhelmed. "I can't let you spend that kind of money on me, Peyton. Let me pay you back. I can't get it to you all at once, but I can pay you in installments or something."

"It's fine, Hank. Seriously. The look on your face when Victor showed you the comic? I knew I had to get it for you." She smiles. "I'd never seen you so excited. I just wanted to see you that happy again."

"Yeah, well, like I said, nobody's ever done anything like that for me before. So…thanks."

"You're welcome." She leans in and hugs me. She smells good, like laundry detergent. I probably smell like sweat and V8. Not a great combo.

"I wish I could show this to my brother. Jesus, Mickey would flip out that I saw, let alone got, a copy of that issue."

"I wish I could have met him," she says.

"He was a cool guy."

We start to walk in the general direction of Peyton's house—me pushing my bike and her carrying my backpack draped over one shoulder.

"You said he and your mom died in a car accident, right?"

"Yeah, when I was twelve."

"Wow, that must have been rough, especially since you two were close. It's lucky you weren't in the car with them."

"Actually, I was." I can feel my hands start to shake. I've never talked about what happened that day. It's just too personal and painful and confusing. I worry that she might think less of me, but it's a risk I'm willing to take. I've never felt a connection to someone like I do with her. I feel like I could tell her anything.

I want her to know the truth. My truth.

"My mom had dragged Mickey and me on errands. We'd argued over who'd get shotgun so she'd made us flip a coin. He won, and I spent the whole ride pouting like a damn toddler. It started getting dark, and Mom had some extra money in her purse so she took us to McDonald's as a treat for dinner. We each got to order a large fry and shake. When I had my fill, I thought it would be amusing to start throwing fries at Mickey, just to annoy him. It worked." I feel the tears coming, but I fight them back. I puff out my cheeks, exhaling loudly. "I'm sorry. I've never told anyone this before."

When I hesitate, she reaches for my hand and squeezes it lightly, then lets go. "It's okay. You don't have to tell me if you don't want to."

"Actually, the weird thing is, I do."

She smiles and gently asks, "So what happened?"

"It started to piss him off, which only egged me on. Finally, Mickey whirls around, unbuckles his seat belt, and tries to grab my shake out of my hand. Mom turns her head to tell me to stop, so she doesn't see the car in front of us slow down. She swerves and jumps the median into the path of a charter bus full of blue-haired old ladies on their way to the casino to play nickel slots. And then everything started moving in slow motion. I knew what was about to happen but was totally helpless to stop it. Two seconds later, they were gone."

The tears sear my eyes, but I don't want to blubber in front of her like a guest on *The Jerry Springer Show*. I take another deep breath and sigh.

Peyton puts her hand on my arm and stops. She faces me so that she's looking right in my eyes. "It's not your fault. You have to know that."

I swipe my fist at the corner of my eye. "They said the only reason I survived is because Mickey's seat broke my impact. It should have been me, not him. He had everything going for him. And my mom... God, she was an amazing person. She put up with so much, and yet she was always positive. Like a ray of sunshine and you just wanted to bask in her light."

"Hank...it's *not* your fault."

I shake my head, the weight of their loss creeping around me like fog. "I killed them. If I hadn't been such a stupid, obnoxious little kid, they'd both be here today. And my life wouldn't be such a total piece of shit. Everything would be different."

"You don't know that," she says quietly.

"*I'd* be different," I tell her. "And maybe my father wouldn't be the way he is. Mickey was always his favorite. They were into all the same stuff. They even looked alike: same chin, same grayish-green eyes. Mickey made you feel good just by being around him. He used to brainstorm ideas for comics with me. That's how we came up with *Freeze Frame*. We'd work on it when we needed to block out the sound of Dad yelling at Mom. Mickey would write the story, and I'd draw the images.

"When he died, we were about to start a new issue. We'd left the story line on a real cliff-hanger. Then suddenly it was all up to me to figure out what happened next, without him. Now it keeps me going. Whenever I work on *Freeze Frame*, it's like Mickey's there, telling me not to give up, to trust my own voice. My mother and brother were the glue that kept our family together. And ever since they died, everything has pretty much fallen apart."

Peyton says, "You can't blame yourself. It was an accident. *You* didn't kill them, Hank."

I shake my head. "I don't know. I want to believe that. I really do."

"Sometimes, to help make sense of things, we tell ourselves stories and we convince ourselves that they're true, but that doesn't mean they really are."

We walk the rest of the way to her house in silence. When we get to her driveway, we can hear the TV blasting from the street. Pete's car is there. No sign of her mom's. Peyton hangs back slightly, as if she's hesitant to go inside.

"Hey, you wanna come over for a while? I could ask my dad if I can borrow the car to take you home later."

She nods. "Yeah, sure. That would be good."

We're about halfway to my house when she blurts out, "I spent six months in a psychiatric hospital about a year ago. It was basically a lot of therapy sessions where we talked about impulsive behaviors and relaxation training, and the doctors packed me with pills to help with my stress and emotional outbursts. I think it was easier for my parents to stick me there than to have to deal with me. Parenting is not my mother's strong suit, in case you haven't noticed. Honestly, in some ways the psych ward was like a vacation. At least there people paid attention to me and I could count on a hot meal every day. Crazy, huh? Every pun intended, of course."

It's a lot to process. I kind of like that we know something about each other that no one else does. She trusts me with her secrets, and it makes me feel even closer to her. I want her to understand that I like being with her and this new information doesn't change anything, so I say, "Crazy is a relative term."

"True. So do you want to know why I was there?"

"Only if you want to tell me."

"I burned down a gardening shed."

"On purpose?"

"No." She digs her hands deep into her front pockets. "I don't know. My father and stepmonster said I did, and that's why they sent me there. I honestly don't remember. There are a lot of versions of this story depending on whom you talk to, and after a while they all sort of blur together."

"Did anyone get hurt?"

"No."

"Well, that's good. And you're feeling better now?"

"Better is a relative term too. Of all people, I'd expect you to understand that." She exhales loudly. "Anyhow, I'd rather not talk about it anymore."

"Okay."

So we don't.

When we get to my house, the lights are out, and it doesn't

look like anyone's home. Maybe Dad got the job and he's out drinking an advance on his first paycheck. At least he'd be working again. I prop my bike against the side of the house, and we head inside and upstairs to my room.

For the next three hours, I show her more *Freeze Frame* comics and we rank the worst villains and debate if DC is better than Marvel. Peyton tells me about this amazing photography exhibit she saw at a gallery in Boston with all these cool pictures of every major city at the turn of the century. She is so excited and animated when she talks about it that I can visualize each photograph from the way she describes it. It is really cool.

Then she yawns. "It's getting pretty late."

"Right, I should walk you home." I wish she didn't have to leave. It's been great to sit and talk with her like this.

Peyton stands, then reaches out to brace herself on my desk chair. "Whoa, I must have gotten up too fast. I feel dizzy."

"Why don't you lie down for a minute?" I suggest and she nods.

Then I yawn, and she scoots over. "You should lie down too. You're tired. You don't have to stand there like that."

"Okay," I say and lie down next to her. It's not like we're doing anything wrong that Nick needs to get all hopped up about; we're just waiting things out.

I ask her if she's feeling less dizzy, and she tells me that being still is definitely helping.

I turn off the light, because that might be part of what's making her dizzy. Now the room is completely dark. Peyton says that's better, and it is. It absolutely is better.

For a long time, we lie there, not talking. Eventually her breaths grow softer and steadier until I'm pretty sure she's fallen asleep. I suppose there's no harm, really, if she spends the night. I had friends sleep over when I was a kid. Of course, none of them were girls, let alone one that happened to be dating my friend. We're just two people lying on a bed in the dark, fully clothed. It's not like it means anything. Plus, it's late, and who knows what kind of situation she'd be going home to, so actually I *should* let her sleep, if I'm looking out for her. That's what friends do. Look out for each other.

Nothing wrong with that. In fact, right now, everything is perfect.

# 16

PEYTON LEAVES BEFORE I WAKE UP, AND WE NEVER discuss how she slept over at my house. When I see her at school, she simply acts like her usual self, and if Nick suspects anything, he doesn't let it show. In fact, he's hanging all over her, chatting her up and making her laugh, and she doesn't exactly look like that makes her miserable.

But what Nick doesn't know is that for the next three nights, when I get home from work, Peyton is waiting by the side of my house for me. Dad's been out a lot, still unemployed but apparently keeping the local bars in business, so I haven't had to explain. The truth is, he'd probably be psyched that I'm hanging out with a girl. He'd see it as confirmation I'm not gay, which would end years of speculative jabs. It isn't like that though.

Usually we just talk. Other times, I'll work on *Freeze Frame* while she reads the older issues I've made. I can tell she really likes them. She gets this intense look on her face when she's reading them, like she can't wait to see what will happen next. When we hang out at my house, it's as if she's a different person, relaxed and funny. Not someone who would deliberately set things on fire.

Sometimes, when she's not looking, I make silly drawings of her. I leave them rolled up in one of her Converse or tucked into her binder or on her pillow when she goes to brush her teeth before bed. I like how they make her laugh. Then we climb into my bed, shut off the lights, and go to sleep. In the morning, she's always gone before my alarm goes off.

Our relationship isn't sexual; more comforting, really. And after a few days, I can't imagine being able to fall asleep without her short, warm bursts of breath on my neck.

But by Friday, I honestly can't look at Nick without feeling like a total asshole. I know this thing with Peyton needs to stop, even though it's completely innocent, but I'm guessing he wouldn't be as understanding. Despite the fact that she's slept in my bed every night this week, they are still…well, whatever they are. I guess she could just as easily be hanging out at his house, but she's not. And I'm not exactly complaining.

I see Nick and Peyton across the quad between second and third period, and they both look pretty serious. With everything that's been happening, I feel awkward about just walking up to them and jumping into the conversation so I head to my next class. I'm not quite sure how to act around Peyton at school anymore. If I let something slip, the whole thing will blow up. It's easier to just avoid them both. I have no idea what I'd say if Nick confronted me. Even though there's nothing going on, I feel guilty, because truthfully I don't *want* it to stop.

I overhear the big news during history. Amanda has made her decision. The word is that she will announce the winner two periods from now during lunch. I'm not gonna lie. I've been so distracted with Peyton staying over that I'd almost forgotten about the contest. Hard to imagine that could be possible. The thing is, I feel like a different person than the guy who was at Amanda's house that night. So much has happened since then. The whole thing seems almost comical at this point.

As the bell rings for lunch and everyone spills into the halls, the buzz of excitement is audible, like the winning numbers for the Powerball are about to be read. Admittedly, I'm as curious as everyone else, so I join the crowd making its way to the quad.

Amanda is standing on the brick wall of one of the planter beds, holding court. She looks particularly amazing today in a tight, green cropped tee with a high-waisted floral skirt that appears to be dancing on the barbed-wire fence of passing the dress code. But no one cares; they're here for the show. This is probably the biggest thing to happen at Kennedy High since

they installed a vending machine that dispensed free candy if
you hit it in just the right spot. She's holding a handmade sign,
on which she has written *Prom?* in golden asterisks. I'm assuming the asterisks are meant to symbolize the letters lit up as
sparklers. She waves it at the crowd, getting everyone pumped.

Amanda calls out, "Are you ready to meet Prince Charming?
Because I know I am!"

The crowd goes insane. You'd think she asked if they were
ready to meet Justin Timberlake. My mind races. *What if she
actually calls my number?* I hadn't counted on having to stand
up on a stage next to her. I'm not even sure I'm wearing a clean
shirt. Plus, it's one thing if Amanda knows I set the fire, but
now everyone else will too, and only time will tell if that makes
me a total loser or the coolest guy in school. I've been riding the
wave of momentum like everyone else, but now I'm starting to
feel a little nervous and slightly pukish.

I scan the crowd and spot Peyton standing off to the side,
chewing the skin around her thumb like it's lunch. Between
seeing her and everything that's happened the last few days, I
wonder if I even want to win this thing anymore. As bizarre
as it may sound, my life is actually pretty good right now, and
I'm not sure I want anything to change. I make my way over
to her.

"Hey," I say.

"Moment of truth, huh?"

I shake my head. My palms begin to sweat. I can't tell if it's because I'm anxious about the outcome or how potentially winning might affect things between Peyton and me. I wipe my hands on my jeans. "I don't know about that. I'm thinking the truth is overrated."

"Well, how could she *not* choose you? You had to answer questions about that night, didn't you? Who else could have all the right answers?"

"Honestly, it's not much of a stretch. The news reported what happened. Anybody could make up the rest because there's no real proof."

"Did you tell her you had a witness?"

"Yup."

"Well, if she doesn't pick you, then I will lose all faith in humanity." She pats me on the arm, then turns back to watch Amanda. "Good luck, Hank. May the force be with you."

"Thanks." If the idea that Amanda could choose me upsets her, it doesn't show. Not that it *should* upset her. But for some reason, the fact that Peyton is totally unfazed by it after these last few days we've spent together bothers me.

Amanda waves her hands to quiet the crowd. "I had so

many people respond to the questionnaire on my website, and I have to say I am beyond flattered at some of the things you've said. Who said they would light the entire mall on fire if it meant they could take me to prom? That was beyond sweet. And saying I'm prettier than Emma Watson? Wow. Because she's like…stunning."

Peyton rolls her eyes. "Glad I didn't eat first."

Amanda continues, "But obviously, only one person *really* knows what happened that night. That person shared his story with me and let me know what was in his heart. His responses made me smile, and from everything he wrote, he's clearly sweet and romantic and funny—and I absolutely cannot wait to meet him."

The crowd "awwwww"s. It's like being on *The Bachelorette*. I smile and feel my adrenaline kick up a notch. The moment she said, "He made me smile," I knew it *has* to be me. Something big is about to happen. This is my before-and-after moment. Maybe, for once, the stars are about to align in my favor. Amanda will call my name, and I'll stand on that wall next to her and look down at Kyle Jonas and show him who's the worthless piece of shit now.

Someone from the band plays a drumroll on a snare. Amanda clears her throat and holds up her sign again and says,

"So, without further ado, *number two hundred eleven*, will you go to prom with me?"

The smile freezes on my face. Winner, winner, chicken dinner. Lucky number 211 has a date with destiny, or at least with Amanda Carlisle. The crowd roars. Everyone's looking around for who is moving toward the wall.

Peyton elbows me. "Go!"

It's over. "That's not my number."

"What? Shut up! It has to be you."

I shake my head. "It was never supposed to be me."

Peyton casts her gaze toward Amanda and says, "This is so wrong. She's an idiot."

I let the news sink in, wondering what bottom-feeder has the balls to stand in front of the entire school, take credit for my fucktastic fuckuppery, and smile pretty for the camera.

And then, as if this all wasn't insane enough, I am hurled off the diving board into a pool of pure batshit crazy as the crowd parts like the Red Sea and none other than frickin' Nick Giuliani swaggers toward her and climbs up on the wall, smiling like a walrus at a clam convention. He's even wearing his eye patch that makes him look like he's Johnny Depp in *Pirates of the Caribbean*. In less than two seconds, Nick goes from zero to hero.

*Well, I'll be damned.*

I turn to Peyton, and she is staring at the two of them, her jaw hanging slack.

"Are you kidding me?" I put my hand on the crook of her arm. "Are you okay?"

She bursts out laughing, which is completely not what I expected. Now I'm really confused as hell. We watch as Nick fist pumps the air for the cheering crowd as they snap pictures. The only person who looks slightly less enthusiastic is Amanda herself, who is probably realizing that her anonymous questionnaire, may have, in fact, been a terrible, terrible mistake. I'm betting none of the scenarios she ran in her head included Nick Giuliani. It would actually be pretty funny if I wasn't so confused about whether I should be elated I wasn't chosen or pissed off that he was.

Nick is clearly enjoying his fifteen minutes. He holds his hands up in his best Nixon "I am not a crook" pose and loops an arm around an under-enthusiastic Amanda's shoulders as they are immortalized for all time on Instagram, or at least in next week's issue of the *Kennedy High Gazette*.

I'm about to tell Peyton that Nick's a jerk and we should cut out and go somewhere, just her and me, but she shakes her head. "It's fine. I'm good."

"Are you kidding me? Are you watching the same thing I am? Because in case you haven't noticed, your boyfriend is kind of an asshole."

"I'm fine. In fact, this is perfect. I'm actually relieved." She really does seem relaxed. It makes me wonder if the reasons she might be are the same reasons I am.

I catch up with Nick in Mr. Vaughn's class. The kid practically radiates from his newfound celebrity. I can't even look at him.

"Can you believe this madness?" he says, leaning across the aisle as we wait for class to start. "Someone pinch me, right? Hey, you wanna go to Ziggy's after school and grab a burger to celebrate? My treat. I'm feeling generous."

*Is he kidding?* I lean in and whisper, "What the hell is going on, Nick?"

"What crawled up your ass and died? I'd think you of all people would be happy for me, man. Jesus." He frowns.

"*Happy* for you? Really?"

He seems as confused by my reaction as I am by his. "Hank, what's up? You're acting weird."

I shake my head. "What about Peyton?"

His brows knit together again. "What about her?"

"Well, she's kinda your *girlfriend*."

"Dude, we broke up three days ago. Keep up, man. I mean, Peyton's cool and all, but that girl has some serious issues. I'm not sure the chemistry is right. You know what I'm saying? We're better off as friends. Plus, every other word out of her mouth is about *you*. It was like you were there with us every time we hung out, even though you weren't actually there. So when she broke it off with me, I was honestly relieved. I didn't want to have to break her heart. She's pretty intense."

*Every word was about me? They broke up three days ago?*

Well, this is an interesting development. "Wow. I didn't know." I resist the urge to smile.

"I figured she told you. It wasn't like we were all that serious anyhow."

"That's cool," I say, trying to process all this new information. "I gotta ask you something though. Why'd you do it? You know…go up there with Amanda."

He looks at me, confused, and angles himself in his seat toward me. "What are you talking about? I got up there because I won."

Just like that, I'm back to feeling annoyed. I can feel the heat rising in my cheeks. He shouldn't have won. He bullshitted his way through those stupid questions on Amanda's website, just like everyone else. Now he's walking around like he's all that, and I'm the only one, aside from Peyton, that knows it's a load of crap. Plus, he was still dating Peyton while pursuing Amanda, which pisses me off even more. "Really? You set that fire?"

He looks around to see if anyone's listening, and then leans in and says, "You *know* I didn't set that fire, man. I wouldn't do something like that. I'm not a moron."

I ignore the moron bit. "So you're willing to lie on the chance it scores you a piece of ass? To climb the social ladder for a better view?"

He laughs, thinking I'm joking with him, but I'm not. I'm dead serious. His chuckle turns into a sputter. "When you put it that way…"

"What if I told you I know who set that fire? What if I told you there's evidence and a witness, and your story could be blown apart in two seconds?"

Nick just stares at me. "I guess I'd say to back me up, man. The girl chose me. This kind of crazy shit doesn't happen to guys like us every day, you know? So it would be cool if you kept what you knew to yourself and gave a guy a break."

With that, Mr. Vaughn enters the room, ready to get class rolling, although from the look of his pupils, he's already been rolling other things.

Ten minutes later, the fire alarm goes off. I'm theorizing that before this day is over, a male Ken doll with brown hair and a Sharpie-ed eye patch will be contorting over hot coals. Okay, so maybe Peyton lied. She's a little pissed.

As we're walking out of the classroom single file, Mr. Vaughn pats me on the back. "Hey, thinkin' good thoughts for you, Hank."

"Excuse me?"

"I'm glad to see you changed your mind."

I am thoroughly confused. "Changed my mind about what?"

Before I can thank him or ask him what he means, he gives me a thumbs-up and pushes ahead of the class to lead everyone outside.

This day just keeps getting more and more surreal.

✳

I sludge through the rest of the afternoon and show up ten minutes late for work, which sets O'Callaghan off on a rant. Tonight he has me checking the shelves for dented cans. He wants me to pull them all toward the front and angle them so unsuspecting customers buy them and he can unload the damaged stock. Apparently, people are scared of dented cans because they can, in rare cases, have contents with botulism.

But O'Callaghan is more concerned about lost profits than spreading a potentially fatal bacterial illness. The only thing that gets me through my shift is hoping that Peyton will be waiting for me when I get home.

Except she isn't.

Dad's watching the tail end of a ball game that's in extra innings when I walk in. He's wearing his lucky Red Sox shirt and a pair of blue Christmas boxers, which Monica bought him last year, with a big snowman's face that has a strategically placed carrot nose. Definitely a change from his interview outfit the other morning.

"Hey, Dad," I say, but he's too engrossed in the game to respond. My stomach growls with hunger, as it did nonstop during the last miserable hour of my shift, and I head into the kitchen to quest for food. I grab the last Stouffer's frozen dinner out of the otherwise empty freezer and throw it in the microwave.

There's a commotion in the crowd, and Dad yells at the TV, "Son of a bitch! That guy was safe!" He's on his feet. "This umpire is a piece of work. He don't know his ass from his elbow."

"Who's playing?"

"Sox and Angels. It's neck and neck at the bottom of the eleventh goddamn inning."

"Wow." I lean against the doorjamb, watching the end of the game with him while my food cooks. The Sox win and that puts Dad in a great mood. I take advantage of it and ask him, "I haven't seen you to ask. How'd that interview go the other day?"

"It didn't. Christ, everyone working there was half my age. A bunch of college pukes. They said I didn't have enough experience to be manager of a goddamned drugstore. Can you believe that? Because I'd never worked a friggin' register. It ain't exactly rocket science to ring up toilet paper and shampoo. You should know." I knew he'd have to get a jab in there somewhere, but I let it roll off me. He reaches for his beer. For once, there isn't a mountain of spent cans in front of him. He must be scaling back now that he's out of work. At least when Dad's drunk, I know what to expect from him.

"So you didn't get it, then?"

His eyes remain riveted to the TV. "I don't know. They said they'd call if they're interested."

"Well, once school ends, I'll be able to pick up more shifts at Shop 'n Save, so that'll be good," I tell him.

It's really starting to sink in that once I graduate, Shop 'n Save will pretty much be all I have. Wake up, go to work, face dented cans out, mop up spills, and ring up harried housewives with screaming toddlers on their hips. Go home. Sleep. Rinse. Repeat. Graduation is less than a month away, and the thought is depressing as hell.

Dad finally turns to me and says, "Looks like we're back to microwave dinners for a while, huh? I never thought I'd miss Monica's cooking, but you knew it was time to eat when the smoke alarm went off." He laughs but I know that he's lonely without her. If he hadn't been such an asshole and brought it on himself, I'd almost feel sorry for him.

"Have you talked to her?"

"Nah. I think I screwed that one up pretty good." He shakes his head and chuckles. "She could be such a pain in the ass, but I miss having her around."

He isn't the only one.

"I think she was good for you, Dad," I say. "You should call her."

"I don't know that there's anything I could say that she wants to hear." He winces slightly and I can tell he's been thinking about it. I offer a little encouragement, hoping that he does call her. She's good for him.

"You never know until you try."

"Maybe." He turns back to the TV.

The microwave beeps, and I pull out my steaming plastic

tray of semi-edible food, grab a fork, and head upstairs. After I finish eating, I lie on my bed and read the comic Peyton bought for me for the millionth time, but I'm distracted.

My thoughts keep drifting to what Nick said in class, about how she's always talking about me. I wonder if that's true. Honestly, I'm kind of relieved that whatever was going on between them is over. I can't really be pissed at Nick for liking Peyton, then going after Amanda, because it's not any different than what I've done, just the other way around.

I'm glad that Amanda didn't pick me. Because the truth is, I'm okay with no one knowing what I did. *Especially* Amanda Carlisle. From the get-go, that stupid promposal was a half-baked idea that went from bad to worse, and I was a coward. I started a frickin' fire, and I ran away. I didn't even try to warn her or call for help or even attempt to put it out. I was more worried that I'd get in trouble and prove I was the screwup Dad thinks I am. My actions weren't romantic or heroic, and I'm certainly no Prince Charming. It's downright embarrassing.

I shut off my light sometime around midnight, and I toss and turn trying to fall asleep. My room is cold and I can't seem to find a comfortable position. Eventually, I drift off into a light sleep.

Around 3:00 a.m., I startle awake at a sound at my window, only to find there really are such things as monsters.

# 17

THE PEBBLES HIT MY WINDOW HARD ENOUGH TO wake me but not enough to actually break the glass. I can make out someone standing in the shadows, and although I can't make out her face in the moonlight, I instantly recognize it's Peyton. She's dressed all wrong for how chilly it's been at night lately, wearing an oversize T-shirt and our school gym sweats, and rubbing her bare arms for warmth. She seems frantic. Something is wrong.

I jump out of bed and take the stairs two at a time, but I am ill prepared for what I find when I open the door. It's Peyton all right, but her hair is short, cut off at all sorts of crazy angles with long wisps sticking out here and there. Even in the low light, I can see the fresh, angry bruises on her left arm where someone grabbed hold and held on with force. The collar of her shirt is torn, and her left cheek is swollen and red. Her lower lip is split and covered in dried blood. She looks as if she will completely fall apart if I touch her.

"Holy *shit*, who did this to you?"

My mind runs with the possibilities. Because whoever could do a thing like this to another human being…

She steps toward me and folds herself into me, wrapping her arms around my neck. She holds on to me, shivering.

She lets out heaving sobs, gasping to catch her breath in between like she's about to hyperventilate, and I try to calm her down. I don't want to wake up Dad and have to answer a million questions. Not right now. I wrap my arm around her shoulders and lead her up to my bedroom in the darkness, stepping quietly and carefully to avoid the squeaky floorboards.

Once she's in my room, the rawness of seeing what's been done to her takes my breath away. She curls up fetal on my bed, crying and covering her eyes with her balled fists. I stand there frozen. I have no idea what the hell I'm supposed to do.

I watch her body quake and convulse with each round of fresh sobs, and I worry that Dad will hear. I make a little *shhhh* noise, which she must take as me trying to comfort her because she reaches for me. She leans on me and I wrap my arm around her so she can cry on my shoulder. Slowly I can feel her start to relax and eventually her crying subsides.

She seems calmer now, so I turn off the light and lie down on the bed next to her. She angles into me and puts her head on my chest. Her hair tickles my nose, and I try to push the spiky bits away, but they spring back into place. Stroking her hair seems to soothe her though.

"I'm sorry. I just…" she whispers and then her chest heaves with gasps. Snot pours out of her nose as new tears stream down her face, dampening my T-shirt.

When her breaths begin to normalize again and she stops shaking, I ask her quietly, "What happened?"

She shakes her head. "I can't talk about it."

I try to reposition myself since my arm, which is pinned beneath her head, is starting to fall asleep. "Hold up. You show up at my house in the middle of the night half dressed, your hair all hacked off, hysterically crying, and you won't tell me what happened?"

She sniffles and wipes at her nose. "No."

"But—"

"Please, Hank. Please just be here for me." She locks gazes with me in the dark. "You'll only hate me. I don't want you to hate me."

"Why would I hate you?"

"Because I know you. You'll feel responsible. But I brought this on myself."

I sit up. "Well, now you have to tell me what's going on."

She shakes her head and runs her fingers self-consciously over her hair. "I can't take it if you're mad at me, Hank."

I try to reason with her. "Listen to me. I'm not going to be mad at you, Peyton. Christ, are you kidding me? I need to know what happened. Who did this to you? Please. Tell me."

She's shaking like a leaf, her eyes wild. "I stole some money from my mother, okay? I found it in a jar in the back of a closet, and I figured she'd never notice it was gone. Or she'd think she was so fucked up one night that she forgot she spent it. But she found out. So I tried to cover my tracks and told her that Pete must have taken it."

Peyton shudders. "My mom confronted him, and he told her I'm a liar. Then she went completely ballistic, accusing me of trying to break them up. Yeah, I lied, but she always takes the word of some deadbeat loser over mine. She's never there for me."

Her lip starts to tremble so I take her hand, not really knowing what else to do except listen.

She says, "Of course, she's high, completely wasted, which is nothing new. They both are. So I go to my room to get away from them, and the next thing I know, she's in there, pulling down my records and smashing them, tearing my posters, calling me a whore and a thief, telling me I ruined her life and that she wishes I was never born." She shakes her head. The tears are flowing again.

I squeeze her hand, and she keeps talking. "So I tell her that makes two of us, and then she starts grabbing me, shaking me, slapping me, and I can't get her to stop."

My stomach twists. It's hard for me to even compute how her mother could do something like that to her, and how terrified Peyton must have been while it was happening.

She reaches for her hair again and looks at me with red-rimmed eyes, trembling as she says, "The next thing I know, she's got these scissors, and she pins me down and starts hacking off my hair. I just wanted her to stab me with the fucking scissors and put an end to it all."

"We have to tell somebody," I say, and she completely flips out.

"*No!* Please…you can't say anything. It'll only make it worse. Just…I can't go back there. I didn't know where else to go."

She starts crying again. I wrap my arms around her and pull her to me, rocking her back and forth like my mom used to when I was a little kid. Peyton buries her face in my shoulder.

"I'm glad you came," I whisper into her hair.

She looks up at me. "So you don't hate me?"

"Jesus, why would I hate you, Peyton? How could you even think that? Your mother and Pete should go to jail for what they did to you. Nobody deserves to be treated that way, no matter what." I'm so enraged and sickened I could put my hand through a goddamn wall.

And that's when I put the pieces together in my head. The comic. Of course. It's not like she had $275 sitting around.

I feel the blood drain from my face. "That's how you bought me that comic, isn't it?"

She turns from me, her voice quivering. "I wanted you to be happy, Hank. I wanted you to know how much you mean to me, and I wanted you to like me back."

My heart shatters like a piece of frickin' glass. The skin on her neck is so pale and white that it's practically translucent in the pale light from my window. I can even make out the blue highways of her veins. I fight the urge to trace them with my fingers.

Instead, I touch her hair. I run my hand gingerly over the jagged strands, and slowly she turns back to me. I lightly stroke her reddened cheek with the side of my hand and then run my fingertips down her arm to the purpling bruise.

I move my fingers across her leg and up her other arm, then trace her collarbone, moving up her neck to touch her lips. She closes her eyes and I wonder if she wants me to stop. And then I'm thinking that I probably *should* stop because it feels wrong to touch her when she's come here like this.

I pull back, and she opens her eyes. She must read my

hesitation because the next thing I know she inches forward, closing the gap between us and pressing her lips gently against mine. I can taste the dried blood, but I'm not exactly complaining. She kisses me softly at first, then with more urgency. Her hands reach up to cup both sides of my face. She slides her tongue between my lips and teases my mouth open, and then she lies back on my bed and pulls me down beside her.

She looks right into my eyes, like she can see through to my soul, and says, "I love you, Hank."

The words ripple through me like waves. I can *feel* that love, and it's amazing. From the way my heart is racing, how much I want to protect her and how everything makes more sense whenever she's with me, I must love her too. I don't know. I've never felt this way before. She's looking at me, waiting for me to say it back, and I want to, but I'm scared.

The truth is, I'm absolutely terrified of what will happen if I do. And I'm just as terrified of what might happen if I don't. I don't want to blow this or make her think I'm trying to take advantage of her in a vulnerable moment. I really care about her. In fact, I think I'm falling in love with her.

How could I have missed all the cues, the signs that she felt this way about me? I've been so caught up in my own crap that I've been completely oblivious to the way I feel about her.

The circumstances that bound me to Peyton when we first met are irrelevant now, and I could have easily cut ties, but I didn't want to. And then there was that annoying, twisty feeling in my gut when she and Nick were into each other and I thought I might lose her.

She turns on her side and laces her fingers through mine. I look at her in the moonlight, taking in how beautiful she actually is. Despite her hacked hair, bruised body, and broken spirit, she is absolutely radiant, and I know I can never let anyone hurt her again. I feel so connected to her, and I want her to feel safe with me. I want her to know that I'd do anything to make her happy. That the minute she walked into my world it became a brighter place and I don't ever want to stop feeling this way.

So I say it back.

# 18

I WAKE UP WITH THE SUN STREAMING IN THE window, hitting me full in the face. I blink a few times, adjusting to the light, and then smile, thinking about last night. The truth is, that might have been one of the best and the worst nights of my life.

I turn to Peyton, but the bed beside me is empty. My clock says it's 6:16 a.m. I sit up to look for her but all I see is two week's worth of laundry scattered across the floor like an obstacle course.

No Peyton.

Honestly, I'm not sure whether to be pissed or relieved. I know this is how it's gone all week, but somehow I thought after last night, things might be different. I guess it beats having to explain to Dad why there's a girl in the house.

I throw on my jeans and a T-shirt and head out into the hall. The door to the bathroom is closed and I can hear the shower running. Dad's up early. I start downstairs when I hear singing in the kitchen. Dad's crooning some off-key country song to himself while he bangs around making coffee.

*Crap.*

I retreat to my room before he can see me, hoping Dad doesn't decide to come back upstairs and take a piss because he'll be in for quite a surprise. I'm also praying he's wearing pants.

Somehow I've got to get Peyton out of here without him seeing her. I have no idea how to tell him about her or explain her unsettling appearance, and I'm guessing he won't buy that her bike jumped a curb.

Moments later, my door quietly opens and Peyton tiptoes in. She's wearing my Batman hoodie, which is way too big for her, and her sweats from last night. Her lip is definitely swollen and her cheek is still slightly pink. The sweatshirt hides the bruises on her arms, but her hair is even more devastating in the daylight. My stomach twists at the sight of it—forcing me to reimagine all she went through.

"Hey," she says. "I…uh…took a shower. I hope that's okay."

"Yeah, of course." I feel self-conscious around her in a way I never have. Awkward. Like I don't know what I'm supposed to do. I'm not sure if I should kiss her good morning or just act as if everything is normal. I don't know what *she* wants me to do.

"Is it okay if I borrow this for today? I don't have any other clothes," she says, gesturing to my hoodie she's wearing.

I nod vigorously. "Sure. Whatever you need."

"Thanks." She sits on the edge of my bed, inches from where we were lying semi-entwined only a few hours ago. "Thanks again for letting me stay here last night. I guess I need to figure out some kind of plan. I mean, obviously I can't go back home."

Before I can even think it through, I say, "You can stay here."

"Really? Are you sure?" She looks relieved, as if it's what she's been hoping to hear.

"Definitely."

"Is your dad going to be okay with that?"

"I'll talk to him."

"Because he seemed kind of surprised to see me this morning," she says.

*Shit. Fuck. Shit.*

"Did you say you saw my dad this morning?" I ask to make sure I heard her correctly.

"I was going into the bathroom as he was going downstairs. He was totally cool, but I don't think he expected to see a girl coming out of your room. In fact, he looked sort of amused."

"Fantastic. I guess he and I should probably have a chat."

"Probably." She puffs out her cheeks, sighing, then runs

her hand self-consciously over her hair. "I look pretty awful, don't I?"

I shake my head. "No. It's not that bad," I lie.

She bites nervously at her fingernail. "I'm hideous."

"I think you're beautiful," I tell her, and this time I'm not lying.

She smiles but I can see that she's feeling fragile. I walk over and kiss her, as if it proves what I said. Instantly, all the awkwardness washes away. We're just Hank and Peyton.

I tell her I'll be right back, because I should probably get things squared away with Dad as soon as possible.

I go downstairs and find Dad refilling his mug of coffee. He's dressed in that same nice button-down shirt and pants he wore the other day. Either he's run out of clean clothes or maybe he has another interview. I'm hoping for the latter, which would be good news and also mean he'll be leaving the house soon.

"I met your friend this morning." He gives me a knowing smile and raises his eyebrows, then lifts his mug as if he's toasting me. "It's about time someone popped your goddamned cherry. I was starting to wonder about you."

He chuckles and sips his coffee. Subtlety has never been his strong suit. I'm hoping Peyton can't hear him, but I don't bother to correct him because this information seems to put him in a good mood and I don't want to jinx it.

I try to laugh it off instead. "Yeah, about that. Listen, Dad. Peyton…the girl upstairs… I need to ask you a favor. She needs a place to crash for a while, and I was wondering if she could stay with us."

"For how long?"

"I don't know."

"What about her family?"

"Her family is *why* she's here, Dad."

"She a runaway?"

"No, not exactly."

His brow furrows with concern as he shakes his head. "I don't know, Hank. I don't want to get mixed up in any family drama. I don't need someone to come looking for her and start trouble."

"No one will come after her." *At least, I hope not.*

"I'm not blind, Hank. Someone knocked her around pretty good. I don't know her story, and it's none of my business, but I want to make sure that if I agree to this we're not putting ourselves in a bad position. I'm trying to get my life back on track and I don't need any setbacks."

"Dad, I swear, you'll hardly know she's here. I promise. It's only temporary, until she can figure things out."

He considers it and then nods reluctantly. "Okay. But I

mean it, Hank. Anyone comes nosing around for her, she has to go."

I bob my head. "Absolutely. Hey, you got another interview today or something?"

He glances at the clock on the wall, downs the rest of his coffee, and smooths his hair with his hands. "I'm going down to the factory to talk to my old boss about getting my job back. As much as I don't want to give those bastards the satisfaction of crawling back to them on my hands and knees, sometimes the devil you know is better than the one you don't."

"That's good, Dad. Good luck. And, um…thanks."

"Yeah, yeah. You keep chatting me up and I'm gonna be late."

We're not good with the sentimental shit, maybe because it doesn't happen too often, or like…ever, so that was as close to a father-son moment as any.

As soon as he leaves, I make the executive decision that given the circumstances, there will be no school or work today. First I call O'Callaghan and give him some bullshit excuse, but I need something legitimate for school in case I need to stretch it out for a while.

I call the attendance office and lower my voice two octaves, thickening my New England accent to play Dad. I go with the first thing that pops in my head. I tell the woman that my son, Hank, is very ill. It could be flu, but there's a possibility it could be encephalitis. The woman sounds shocked and concerned, so I know I've picked a good excuse. When I hang up, Peyton starts cracking up.

"What? What's so funny?"

"Encephalitis is brain inflammation."

"Shit, I overdid it. I meant bronchitis. All I know is, there's no way I can deal with school today."

"Definitely." She shakes her head. "What the hell am I gonna do, Hank? I need to figure out how to get my stuff from my house. I need to figure out the rest of my life. And I've got to find a way to fix this." She holds up a butchered strand of hair and then drops her hand into her lap. "I can't walk around like this."

And then it hits me.

"I think I know someone who can help."

✳

Mo's Boobie Barn is on the outskirts of town, sandwiched between a Motel 6 and a check-cashing shop that also offers bail bonds. Talk about knowing your target audience. The Boobie Barn is literally an old renovated barn, painted red with white trim, but the silo out back is bright pink, like a giant schlong. You can't miss it.

I gamble that Monica's there, even though it's early. I would've called first, but it's much easier to explain everything in person, and I'm hoping if I just show up with Peyton, Monica will be less likely to send me away. I see her piece-of-shit red Dodge Shadow parked on the side, and it makes me smile. It's been a few weeks since I've seen Monica, and I'd be lying if I didn't say I missed her.

I remind myself that I am here to help Peyton so my mind doesn't wander to all the hot girls wearing next to nothing. I've never actually been inside Mo's because I'm underage, but I'm hoping that since it's lunchtime and there aren't many cars in the parking lot, I might be able to convince someone to at least get Monica a message.

"You're taking me to a strip club?" Peyton shakes her head as she climbs off the handlebars of my bike. "I'm not taking off my clothes for money. No way. I'm not that desperate."

"You don't have to take off your clothes. Just follow my lead." I prop my bike against the side of the building and make my way to the front, past the first blinking neon sign that says "Open 24 hours / Live DJ" and the second that says "Live naked girls."

When I open the front door, I'm greeted by pulsating music and a bouncer built like a sumo wrestler. He doesn't look like the sort of person who would take pity on a not-quite eighteen-year-old trying to get into a strip club with his equally under-age girlfriend. He positions himself squarely in front of the purple velvet curtain that separates the entrance from the actual lounge.

"Can I help you?" he asks.

"Uh…yeah. I'm here to see Monica."

He narrows his eyes. "Can I see some ID?"

"Um…I don't actually have it on me. If you could just tell her that Hank is here, she can totally vouch for me."

He doesn't budge. "Uh-huh. You need an ID to get in. No ID, no access."

The man clearly takes his job very seriously. I'm betting he's been Employee of the Month more than once.

"Here's the thing. I really need to talk to Monica. It's sort of a life-and-death situation." I can feel Peyton staring at me, and I silently plead for her to roll with it.

The bouncer dude crosses his arms over his four-foot-wide chest and says, "Life and death, huh?"

"Yes, life and death," I assure him. "You see…I've just found out that someone we both know and care about is sick, dying actually. And I know she'd want to know about this. He's like a father to her, and she'd be devastated if something happened and she didn't get a chance to say good-bye."

"It's really rough when someone passes and you don't get to say good-bye. You never get any closure," Peyton chimes in, and I bite my lip to keep from completely losing my shit.

"Never. It's like an open wound," I say as Peyton gives a sorrowful shake of her head.

The guy shifts uneasily. "Dying, huh?"

"Could be a matter of hours. So touch and go," I say.

"The worst part is he's so young, like a brother," Peyton says.

Bouncer Dude's brow creases with confusion. "I thought you said he was like a father to her."

I nod. "Yes, he's like a father *and* a brother. I don't know which is worse."

"I lost my father," the bouncer tells us. "Two years ago next Sunday."

"That's awful. I'm so sorry," Peyton commiserates.

"Then you know how it is," I say, sensing his weakening resolve. "She's gonna be wrecked. Like a total head case. So I'm hoping we can break this to her in person. You know, in private."

The guy hesitates. We're as good as in. He shoots a glance over his shoulder. "Okay, there's practically no one here so be cool. Monica's dressing room is in the back, although around here she's called Fantasia."

"Thank you," I say before he can change his mind, but the bouncer sticks out a beefy arm the size of a small tree trunk.

He leans in and says in a voice that's all business, "Walk like you know where you're going, because if anyone asks where you came from, I'm going to say I was on a piss break and you two snuck in. So be cool."

"Like frickin' ice cream," I assure him.

He parts the purple velvet curtain for us and we're in.

"Nice work. I'm not even going to ask why you're on a first-name basis with a stripper," Peyton says as she looks around, all wide-eyed.

"Monica used to date my dad," I explain. "Don't worry. She's cool."

"And how exactly is she going to help me? Because call me crazy, but I don't think I can pole dance myself out of this situation."

"Would you please trust me?" I say, which seems to pacify her.

Jesus, this place is everything I imagined it would be. There is a smattering of tables and bar stools around the edge of the stage where a few early-afternoon diehards are guzzling drinks and watching a bored-looking brunette with a cheetah G-string and black tassels grind a pole.

The DJ is in the corner, jamming to the beat of the house music and wearing giant headphones and sunglasses despite the fact that he's inside. He can probably stare all he wants and no one would even know. It's like my dream job. There are seminude girls every-frickin'-where, and it's like naked Disneyland.

A cocktail waitress wearing a sexy maid apron and not much else checks me out, then notices Peyton, who stands out like a sore thumb in my Batman hoodie and sweats, and looks the other way. It figures that the one time I actually get to be in a place like this I can't even enjoy it. I grab Peyton's hand, and we wind our way through the maze of tables toward the back like we mean business.

*Be cool, Hank. Just be cool, keep it together, and find Monica. Or Fantasia.* Whatever.

At the back, a narrow hallway leads to a series of black doors, which I'm figuring are the dressing rooms. There's a piece of paper taped to each one, and the names of the dancers are scrawled on them in Sharpie. This is obviously not a big-budget operation. I find the one that says Fantasia and knock.

"Who is it?" a voice calls.

"It's…um…Hank."

"Hank...*Kirby*?"

"Yeah," I say and dig my hands in my pockets.

The door flies open, and Monica is suddenly all over me, throwing her arms around my neck and pressing her perfect body up against mine. Thankfully, she's wearing clothes. I'd forgotten how completely intoxicating she smells. I try to shift my thoughts to incredibly unsexy, un-hot things—like senior citizens without their dentures and people with excessive body hair—so I don't get too excited about this reunion.

She pulls back, still holding on to my shoulders and says, "Oh my *God*! Hank! How are you? I've been thinking about you. I'm so glad to see you. How did you get in here?"

"It wasn't easy, but if anyone asks, we have a mutual friend who's dying."

"Hi, I'm Peyton." Peyton shoves her hand into the space between our bodies, forcing Monica to let go of me. Christ, I'd almost forgotten Peyton was standing there.

Monica responds with her name and grins. Then her gaze travels to Peyton's hair and her expression turns to confusion.

"Listen, I need to ask you a favor. Is there somewhere we can maybe talk in private?" I ask.

Monica invites us upstairs where she is renting a small room above the club. She listens intently as I tell her Peyton's story, and how I thought she might be able to help Peyton get fixed up since she's studying to be a beautician. The next thing I know, Monica's putting her arms around Peyton and telling her she'll do whatever she can.

Peyton looks uncomfortable with the attention, with a stranger knowing her story, but honestly, I don't know who else to turn to. I'd ask my mom, because she always knew what to do no matter the situation, but that's not an option. Ironically, Monica's probably the closest substitute I have.

Monica settles me in front of the TV while she digs through her closet to find Peyton some clothes and then takes Peyton into the bathroom and sits her on a chair in front of the sink. She starts rooting through a bag and pulling out scissors, combs, and all sorts of crap. I catch the occasional sentence here and there over the sounds of the TV, and I presume that Monica is sharing her own story with Peyton. A good half hour later, they emerge from the bathroom. My jaw drops.

Peyton's Peyton, but transformed.

This girl is wearing jeans that hug her in all the right places and a skintight long-sleeved top that shows the curves I didn't even know she had until last night. Monica has cut Peyton's hair into a short pixie style that's sexy as hell. For the first time, she's not hiding under all that hair or a hoodie. She's also wearing just enough makeup to even out her skin and hide her bruising.

Peyton's smokin' hot.

I'm guessing my slack-jawed speechlessness confuses her, because Peyton runs her hand self-consciously over her hair and folds her arms over her chest, holding on to her elbows.

"Wow," I manage to say.

"Better?"

"You look amazing," I tell her. She visibly relaxes, hints at a smile even.

As I'm hugging Monica good-bye, she asks if Dad ever talks about her. It's as if the floodgates open. I share how lonely he's been since she left and how he's not the type of guy to admit when he's wrong, but I think he knows he screwed up. I even mention that he misses her cooking, but I leave out the "almost" part.

"You should come by and say hi."

"I don't know. Maybe." From the distracted way she twists the fabric at the bottom of her shirt I know she's considering it.

I seize the opening. "You said it yourself. My dad isn't the easiest guy to live with. When my mom and brother died, it messed him up pretty good. You're the first person he's cared about since then."

Even though their relationship has its fair share of what-the-fuckery, Monica makes my dad happy, and I believe she genuinely cares about him too. If only I could get her to come back to the house, I bet they could work it out and things might start inching back to normal.

Monica smiles and nods in Peyton's direction. "Everybody needs somebody who gets their kind of crazy, right? That doesn't come along every day."

I glance at Peyton. She's staring out the window, lost in thought, and I am grateful that Nick Giuliani won Amanda's damn contest and bailed, because he doesn't deserve her.

As Peyton climbs onto the handlebars of my bike and we ride back toward town, it occurs to me that I have no idea what normal is anymore. Normalcy is elusive, redefining itself on a daily, if not hourly basis.

But when Peyton glances back at me, the breeze ruffling her short hair, I know there is nowhere I'd rather be than with this girl and all her baggage. I want to freeze-frame this moment—her on my bike with her face to the sun, looking free and happy—because deep in my gut, I know it won't last.

# 19

WE CAN'T GO BACK TO MY HOUSE YET IN CASE
Dad is home, because I don't want him to start in on me for
missing school, so we go to Ziggy's for burgers and fries. Now that
the adrenaline and tension have worn off, I'm starving. I haven't
eaten anything since yesterday's nuked TV dinner, and so much
has happened since then.

It's weird to be at Ziggy's with Peyton and not Nick. I haven't
talked to him in a couple of days—since Amanda chose him to go
to prom. I don't really know what to say to him, especially since
things have ramped up between Peyton and me. We both kind
of messed up, and the truth is, I miss hanging out with him. The
only thing greasier than this burger is Nick Giuliani's hair, but
right now I don't care because the burger is the best damn thing
I've ever tasted.

While I practically shove the whole burger into my mouth in
two bites, Peyton deconstructs hers with precision. First she lifts
off the slice of lettuce and sets it aside, then peels the thick layer of

cheese from the top of the bun and tears it into strips, eating it in small pieces. I stop chewing and smile as she carefully puts the fluffy top of the bun back on her burger and smashes it flat with her palm before tentatively taking a bite. I used to find all her food quirks to be weird as hell, but now they're actually sort of endearing.

We spend the rest of the afternoon hiding out at Crescent Park and talking. We sit at the edge of the woods and Peyton lights leaf after leaf on fire, then stamps them out with a battered Converse. Even though it scares me a little, I act like this is perfectly normal.

I googled "pyromania" the other day. It literally means "fire madness." The article was wicked long and confusing, but the gist of it was that it's an impulse-control disorder. A person sets fires to relieve built-up tension. The behavior can be triggered by extreme stress, neglect, abuse, or because the person is seeking attention. I'm no shrink, but with what I know about Peyton's home life, it's not a stretch to see the links here.

She seems calmer as she watches the flame from her lighter eat through each leaf, though I wish I could get her to stop. I'm worried that sometime she'll be careless and get in trouble, or maybe the fire will get out of control and she—or someone else—will get hurt. At least now I'm there to keep an eye on her and make sure that she's safe.

Around four we head back home. Dad's car is in the driveway and he's inside, planted in his usual spot on the couch, watching TV.

"Hey, Dad," I say, making for the stairs with Peyton.

"Whoa, slow it down. I wanna talk to you."

I motion for Peyton to go up without me, and then I sit down in the chair across from Dad. A small puff of dust rises from the cushions, and the particles shimmer in the sunlight. Sadly, my mom was probably the last one who dusted around here.

"What's up? Did you get your job back?" I ask, hoping that's what this heart-to-heart is about.

"Yeah, I did."

"That's great! I told you if you talked to them they'd listen to reason."

"Don't pat yourself on the back too hard. They put me on probation. I have to go to AA meetings twice a week, and if they catch me drinking again, I'm out. It's a bunch of bullshit, but it's a paycheck, so there's that." He locks eyes with me and crosses his arms. "But that's not what I wanna talk about. I got a strange call from the school today. You know anything about that?"

So many ways to play this… I swallow and shake my head. "No," I say. "Strange how?"

"I mean, they called to see how you were feeling."

I try to play it cool so I don't go off at the mouth like I usually do. "How I'm feeling? That's weird. What's up with that?"

"Apparently they were concerned, because they seemed to think you might have encephalitis."

"Encephalitis? That's like…a brain inflammation, right?" I let out an exaggerated laugh. "That's crazy. You know how big the high school is. They must have me mixed up with some other kid with a similar name."

"That's what I said, but here's the kicker. I asked the lady how she'd heard that, and she told me *I* called you in sick this morning."

As if on cue, my diarrhea of the mouth kicks in. "That's ridiculous. You'd think they'd keep better records of whose parents called in. Clearly somebody at the attendance office was hitting the sauce this morning. Man, you could totally freak out a parent by saying shit like that. They'd think their kid is really sick."

"That's what I said. I told her you were at school today, so it had to be a mistake. But she tells me it's no friggin' mistake. That you were most definitely *not* in school today."

He's not amused anymore. In fact, his face is piss serious and I know I'm screwed.

"Dad, I—"

"I won't tolerate lies, Hank. I won't be disrespected like that. I won't be made a fool of when the school calls and you aren't where you're supposed to be."

"I'm sorry, Dad." The words come out just above a whisper.

"Don't think I haven't noticed you coming and going at crazy hours. I found a matchbook for a hookah lounge in the laundry. *I* certainly haven't been to a hookah lounge. What are you getting mixed up in, Hank?"

*Jesus, the matches.* I'd forgotten I'd shoved them in my pocket each time Peyton dropped them on the ground. "Nothing, Dad. I swear. I can explain everything."

"What, you're going to tell me more lies?" He points upstairs in the direction of my room. "Does this have to do with that girl upstairs, Hank? Because I told you, I don't want any trouble. And I can assure you that's all that girl is going to bring you."

I shake my head. "You don't even know her, Dad. You don't know the situation."

"Something's not right. Those bruises, that hair… That ain't normal. She may have gotten cleaned up, but whatever she's going through is beyond anything you and I can fix."

Like he's ever tried to fix anything or anyone in his entire life. His comment pisses me off, but I hold it together. "Well, it doesn't mean I'm not going to try to." He raises an eyebrow, but before he can launch into another lecture, I say, "I took Peyton to see Monica."

Now he looks wicked confused. "Monica? What the hell for?"

"I thought she could help her. You know, even out her hair, make it look better. Monica is going to beauty school. She knows about that kind of stuff."

Dad nods. He doesn't even question where we went to find Monica. "She help her?"

"Yup. She did."

His stern expression gives way, and he rakes his hands through his hair. "How's she doing?"

"She's okay. She asked about you."

"Yeah?"

"Yeah. I told her she should come by."

"What'd she say?" he asks tentatively.

"She said maybe." His expression brightens momentarily as that sinks in, and then he snaps out of his reverie, remembering he was in the middle of ripping me a new one.

"I mean it, Hank. I'm as serious as a goddamn heart attack. You go to school and you keep your nose clean. I don't know who this girl is, but the minute her problems become my problems, I will not be as understanding. Be careful. You get me?"

"Got it." This is going better than I anticipated. He's actually looking out for me and is so distracted by my mention of Monica that he seems to be letting the missed school thing slide with little more than a reprimand. I'll take it.

"If you really want to help her, we should call the friggin' cops on whoever did that to her."

"*NO!*" There're thumping footsteps behind us as Peyton takes the stairs two at a time, making her way to the front door. She's obviously heard everything. "I'm so sorry. I'll leave. This is all my fault."

She bounces her teary gaze between my dad and me, and before we can say anything, she's out the door and down the driveway.

I don't even think; I just react. I leave Dad sitting there slack-jawed on the couch as I bolt out the door after her. Peyton's already halfway down the street, and I'm thinking maybe she wasn't bullshitting about the whole early-morning jogging routine, because when she wants to, this girl can run like a cheetah. I curse myself for not being more in shape as I struggle to keep up with her. I call her name, but she ignores me and keeps running. I can hear my pulse in my ears, boxing at my eardrums, and there's a stitch in my side. I never was very good at the track unit in gym.

"Jesus, Peyton! Hold on!" I yell after her, but she abruptly veers to the left, cutting through someone's yard.

By the time I reach where she peeled away, there is absolutely no sign of her and I have no damn clue where she might have gone. I panic. What if she does something stupid? I spin in circles in the middle of the street, silently willing her to appear. Wherever she's going, she doesn't want me with her.

✳

I visit every place I can think of looking for her, but she's not at any of them and I can't call her because she doesn't own a cell phone. I can barely piece together what to do next because my brain is so jacked, worrying about what may have happened to her. Dad even lets me borrow the car to drive around looking for her, but she's nowhere to be found.

I want to call the police, file a missing person report, something—anything. But doing so will open a whole other can of worms, and Peyton didn't want that. I don't know what the right thing to do is except simply wait and have faith that she'll send some sign that she's all right. She always does. This isn't the first time she's gone off the radar only to reemerge.

She has to, because the idea that I might not see her again is too much.

I spend the weekend stocking shelves at Shop 'n Save, hoping she'll show up, loudly asking for condoms or lubricant, so we can laugh and pretend none of this shit ever happened. Then we'll both sit down with Dad and explain everything so he'll chill. As I corral the carts in the parking lot, I decide I'll talk to O'Callaghan about giving her a job too.

Peyton once mentioned that she'd be eighteen by the start of summer. Which means she'll be an adult in the eyes of the law; she can legally vote, be drafted, and get a tattoo. I'm pretty sure it also means she can live wherever she wants and no one can stop her. If we both work a ton of shifts, we might even be able to save up to find a place together.

The idea gets my heart pumping. I want to time travel so we can be there already, just us, away from all the bullshit. Safe. If only she would show up so I can tell her my idea.

Instead, I get a very different visitor.

I'm extracting a cart that wound up in a hedge beside the building rather than the cart roundup, which is a mere three feet away, when a car pulls in next to me. The driver cuts the stereo, and I turn as the door to a white Honda opens and out steps Amanda Carlisle. Seeing Amanda instantly takes me back to my misguided promposal, which started this whole mess.

"Hey, I thought it might be harder to track you down," she says. She smiles, and her teeth are all white and shiny, like in a toothpaste commercial.

I look over my shoulder because frankly, I can't imagine she's actually talking to me, but there's no one else around except for a homeless guy talking to a pigeon at the far end of the parking lot. When I turn back to her, she's still smiling. She tugs at the hem of her light-pink Abercrombie tee and kicks absently at the concrete curb in front of her car with her matching pink flats.

"You mean me?"

"Yeah, you. Got a minute?"

Why the hell does Amanda need to talk to *me*? I tell her I need to bring the carts back to the front of the store, but then I can take my break. She seems cool with waiting, so I go through the motions, and when I return, she's sitting in her car playing music with the engine off. She motions for me to get in. Her car smells like vanilla air freshener and about six different types of scented hand lotion, all competing for first place—sort of what I'd imagine it would smell like if Bath & Body Works exploded.

"I'm sure you're wondering why I'm here," she starts off.

"You were out of eggs?" I offer.

She giggles. "It's so typical that you would say something funny like that."

My brow knots in confusion, and I wonder how the hell she'd know what's typical about me. "So this isn't about eggs?"

"No." She angles herself in the driver's seat and lowers the music, then says, "I know Nick Giuliani didn't set the fire. I had my doubts once we started talking after I chose him."

I swallow. "Oh yeah?"

"I mean, the truth is, the website was a dumb idea. Anyone could figure out the right answers, really."

"Wow. You don't say." I'm uncomfortable, like I can't get enough air. At any previous time in my personal history, the small space between our bodies would be enough to send me over the edge, but now it's just stifling.

"I thought I'd never find out who was there on my lawn that night. I know the fire was accidental, and I know from the evidence that those sparklers spelled *Prom*. And I felt bad that the person who went to all that trouble to ask me out disappeared when it turned into this big disaster, probably thinking I was mad or he would get in trouble, you know?"

I'm pretty sure I can see where this is going. I roll down the window.

"You okay?" she asks.

"I'm fine, just a little stuffy in here," I say.

"You know how I know Nick lied?" She doesn't wait for me to answer. "Because I had one final question to ask in person. A question I knew the answer to because it was the only detail I could make out in the dark that night. I wanted to know how he was able to leave the scene so quickly. Nick said he drove away, that he was parked down the block. But I saw the person ride away on a bike. Kind of like the bike you were riding that day when it was raining and we were talking in front of my house."

I swallow hard and wipe my palms on my fashionably challenged yellow Shop 'n Save polo. I'm starting to sweat bullets. Clearly not too many people, given the choice, buy a bike the color of a Cheeto. "Why are you telling me all this?"

"Because I wanted you to know that *I* know, Hank. I know *everything*. I know it was you." She reaches out and squeezes my hand. "And I want you to know that I think it's super sweet. You're a really nice guy, Hank."

Here it is: my chance to be with Amanda. Except everything's different now. That's not what I want anymore. "Why would you think that?"

"That you're a nice guy?"

"No, that I did it."

"Because that weird girl who lives across the street told me everything."

"Peyton?" My heart races just saying her name, and I grip the door handle, ready to dash if Amanda knows where she is and how to find her. "When did you talk to her? Is she okay?"

"Jeez, excitable much? She left me a note. She was your witness, right? That's what you said in your entry; that you had a witness. And even though she's strange, what she said added up. It would've been nice if maybe she'd come forward *sooner* so I hadn't made an ass out of myself picking the wrong guy, but better late than never, right?"

"*When* did she leave you the note?"

Amanda twists a strand of hair around her finger and shrugs. Clearly she didn't expect me to focus on this part of the story. "Why are you, like, freaking out? Why does that matter?"

"It just does."

"It was on my car window this morning. She said she wanted me to know the truth because you're a great guy and deserve to be happy. She said she was telling me because she knew you wouldn't, and she was trying to put everything back together the way it was supposed to be. She said you'd probably under-stand what that meant." She tucks her hair behind her ear and narrows her eyes. "And what do you mean, is she okay? What's wrong with her?"

If she left the note this morning, she must be all right. But why would she tell Amanda the truth? Doesn't she get that I'm not interested in Amanda Carlisle, prom, or this stupid frickin' contest anymore? Because even if our situation is all mixed up and insane right now, the one thing I know for sure in my gut is that we're *exactly* the way we're supposed to be when we're together. I had hoped Peyton felt that too.

Amanda's sitting there, waiting for me to answer. To say something. Anything at all. She prompts, "So it *was* you, right?"

I take a deep breath and look her right in the eye. I can't believe I'm about to say what I'm about to say. But I do. "Look, Amanda. I'm really sorry. If you actually knew me, you'd know that I pretty much make a mess of everything. I don't mean to; it just happens. It was stupid of me to think you'd want to go to prom with me in the first place, and when the mulch and the tree and everything caught on fire, I chickened the hell out. I'm not proud of that. The whole thing was a mistake. And I'll pay you and your parents back for the damage. I promise."

"I'm not here for money, Hank. You went to a lot of trouble to invite me to prom, and I want you to know I appreciate what you tried to do. It was very sweet and romantic. I'm here because I feel badly about the way it turned out, and I want to make it right. And besides, I think you're really cute."

I shake my head, my mind still on Peyton. "You don't need to do that."

"So are you saying you *don't* want to take me to prom?" She looks a little hurt, and I'd be lying if I didn't say I savor that power for a few seconds before letting her down easy.

"I can't."

She raises her eyebrows in surprise. "Wow." She was most definitely not expecting this reaction. I'm guessing nobody turns down Amanda Carlisle. Except, of course, me. "May I ask why not?"

"It's nothing personal. It's just…there's someone else."

She nods. "Okay… Well, this is awkward."

"It doesn't have to be. And I really am sorry about the fire."

Christ, only a few weeks ago I would have given anything to sit and talk with Amanda Carlisle, let alone take her out on a date. But it's different now.

I ask her, "So does everybody know? That it wasn't Nick?"

She shakes her head. "No. I wasn't going to say anything until I talked to you."

I picture Nick, how frickin' crushed he's going to be when she kicks him to the curb. I kinda feel sorry for him.

"Can I say something then? I mean, I know this is going to sound crazy, but I think you should still go to prom with Nick Giuliani."

She raises both her eyebrows. "Why?"

"Because he likes you and he wants to take you out. He probably never imagined you'd go for a guy like him otherwise. Being vulnerable like he was in front of the whole school takes a lot more guts than lighting a few sparklers and running away. When the truth gets out, he's going to feel pretty shitty, so maybe we could keep this between us. Go to prom with the guy. It's one night. It'll probably be the best night of his entire high school existence. Then let him down easy. Consider it... community service." I can't believe I'm saying this, but Nick is my friend. He doesn't deserve that kind of public humiliation.

She lets that marinate for a minute, then her face lights up. "Oh! I nearly forgot. In her letter, Peyton said that if we talked, I should give this to you."

Amanda reaches in her purse, extracting a small, white envelope, the kind with the plastic window you use to pay bills, and hands it to me. It's folded in half and secured with a rubber band. And my name is scrawled on it in Peyton's writing.

I take it from her and tear open the envelope. Inside is a book of matches from Mo's Boobie Barn. The *o*'s are white with red dots in the center that look like nipples. I burst out laughing. Amanda stares at me like I'm nutter, and then she starts laughing in that way people do when they don't get what's funny but think they're supposed to, which makes me laugh even harder.

"What's that?" she asks.

I smile and curl my fingers around the matchbook. I can't even begin to explain. "It's a sign," I tell her.

She has no idea what the hell I'm talking about, of course, and there really isn't a whole lot to say after that. My break is over anyway, so I thank her for stopping by and get out of her car. I imagine most people would swear I am out of my mind for walking away from Amanda for Peyton. But then again, I'm not most people.

# 20

NOW THAT I KNOW WHERE PEYTON IS, I HAVE TO see her.

It's going to be a lot harder to get past Bouncer Dude since it's already dark outside and more customers will be there. I try to imagine what Freeze Frame would do in this situation. In each episode, after he freezes time, he only has a finite window to search for his love, Rowena, before time resumes, so his movements must be precise. Every second counts. Essentially, he has to create a diversion so that he can save her undetected.

And that's how I come up with a plan so screwy it just might work.

I stop at home to ditch my Shop 'n Save uniform, changing into all black, and I purposely don't shave. I can't swing a five-o'clock shadow like Nick's, so it adds maybe a year at best. I spike my hair with some gel and find an old, black eyeliner of Monica's in the bathroom and draw a soul patch on my chin. The result is pretty damn hilarious, but I should pass for older.

I borrow Dad's aviator shades to complete the look and grab an empty duffel bag from the hall closet. I fill it to capacity with whatever will fit from my CD collection, my old headphones that only work in one ear, and a bunch of wires from behind the stereo so that everything looks official. And then I'm off.

Mo's Boobie Barn is definitely a lot busier at night. The parking lot is jammed when I arrive, and the music is so loud I can hear it from the street. I park my bike on the side of the building, don the aviator shades, extract the headphones from my bag, and put them on. They're giant and metal and make me look like an air traffic controller, but it's all good.

I carry the bag with a firm grip and walk to the door like I mean business. I try to ignore the signs plastered everywhere that say "No admittance under age 21. Violators will be prosecuted," because I get one chance at this. Dad's made it clear he's not going to bail me out, so I'll pretty much end up as someone's prison wife if I screw this up.

Yes, technically I'm breaking the law, but I'm not hurting anyone or putting someone in danger. As far as I know, no one ever died from exposure to major boobage. And it's not like I'm trying to sneak in and watch the show for free. Plus, really, nudity is natural, so what's the big deal? If anything, I'm trying to help someone I really care about, so hopefully the big guy upstairs will look the other way on this one.

A bunch of college guys are jamming up the entrance, and the bouncer from the other day is scrutinizing their IDs with his penlight. Clearly none of these kids are old enough to get in, and they're all scoffing and protesting, which makes it even more obvious that they're underage. Bouncer Dude has his hands full. It's perfect.

I take a deep breath to calm my nerves, stare straight ahead, and then stride toward that purple velvet curtain. I'm a man on a mission.

Bouncer Dude sees me. His hand, which is the size of a personal pan pizza, comes down on my shoulder, stopping me in place.

"Hold up, man. Where do you think you're going?"

The lines in his forehead form a capital *V*. But I'm ready for him. "Dude, it's cool. I'm with the DJ."

Confidence is key. I look at him over the tops of my aviator shades, and I unzip the bag to show him all the CDs and wires. I bop my head along to the music like I saw the DJ do when Peyton and I were here and rezip the bag before he can ask any questions. If he recognizes me from the other day, he doesn't show it.

One of the college guys slips the bouncer a twenty and tries to push inside, which pisses him the hell off. Like he can be bought and sold! He turns to the kid and starts ripping him a new one as he pockets the twenty, and in what may be the single greatest break of all time, he waves me through the curtain.

I'm in!

This place is off the hook. Every table is taken. The chick onstage runs her tongue down the pole as she twists one leg around it and spins. Holy crap. I'm guessing that's highly unsanitary. The dancer runs her hands through her hair and shakes her ass. The crowd goes wild. I'm not gonna lie: I'm kinda hypnotized.

"You the guy covering for Jake tonight?" a voice shouts. It's male, and I have no idea what the hell he is talking about. I turn. It's the DJ dude.

"Huh?"

"You're the guy Jake sent, right? I gotta take a piss, man, and I should have had a break a half hour ago. Where the hell you been? The playlist is on top of the CD player." He slaps me on the arm, dragging me to the DJ booth, and then takes off, presumably toward the bathroom.

Okay, this is definitely *not* part of the plan. I try not to panic, hoping that the equipment is straightforward and nobody notices that I'm seriously underage and not actually a DJ. How hard could this be, right?

I quickly look over the setup in the booth. There are a playlist of songs, two CD players side by side, and some kind of receiver to toggle back and forth between them. Pretty basic. I scan the list to find the title of the song currently playing and load the next CD into the other player, keeping my hand on the switch so it's ready to go. I can do this.

I glance at the stage. The tongue chick is still up there dancing, and the audience is going bananas for her. I bend my knees, dancing in place, trying to get a groove going to keep in character. This place is sensory overload.

The song ends and I start the next one. Some other girl crawls across the floor like a cat. She's even wearing pointy ears and a tail. She begins to do this thing with the pole like it's a scratching post, and I am so mesmerized I do not even notice that the song has ended until Catwoman is staring at me along with everyone else in the room.

*Shit. Fuck. Shit.*

I gotta say, few things are sadder than a nearly naked girl crawling on the floor pretending to be a seductive cat with no music to pull it all together. It's like when Dorothy discovers that the Great and Powerful Oz is just a man sitting behind the curtain. The illusion is broken, which is actually useful because it helps me refocus. Folks start getting restless and annoyed.

I scramble to find the next CD and get it playing before the audience and the dancer lash out at me, but I send half a stack of cases clattering to the floor first. When I stand up, DJ Dude has magically reappeared, and he doesn't look happy. I quickly get the next song going.

"What the hell, man? You some kind of moron? You wanna get us both fired?" he asks. That word does seem to be coming up a lot lately.

"Sorry," I say, hastily grabbing my duffel bag.

"What'd you say your name was again?" he asks me.

I say the first thing that comes to my mind. "Peter Parker." If he's ever read a single issue of Spider-Man, it doesn't show.

"Well, where do you think you're going, Peter? You just got here."

"Now *I* gotta take a piss."

"Why do you need your bag?"

I think fast. "I always travel with my own toilet paper. Germophobe."

He narrows his eyes. His look is one of pure disgust. "Don't take too long." He waves me away, and I'm out of there like a shot, winding my way toward the back dressing rooms to find

Monica. After a few songs play and I don't return, it's only a matter of time before the DJ realizes I'm not, in fact, the guy Jake sent and signals the bouncer, and they start looking for me. The clock is ticking. I've only got one shot, and there's no room for error.

It doesn't take me long to find Fantasia's dressing room door. I give a quick knock, looking over my shoulder nervously.

"Yeah, yeah. Relax… I've still got ten minutes," she yells from inside.

She opens the door, and she's wearing nothing but a G-string and those red tassels. I try to keep my eyes focused above her neck and on the reason I'm actually here. "Monica, I need—"

She pulls me into the room.

"Holy shit, Hank! What are you doing? They'll arrest you if they catch you in here!" she tells me as she reaches for a robe that's draped over the back of her chair and wraps it around herself. "Not to mention your father is going to kill me if he finds out."

"Then don't tell him."

"Interesting look for you," she says, raising an eyebrow.

"Where's Peyton?" She stiffens and I can tell she wants to protect Peyton, but so do I. "Look, Monica. I need to know that she's okay."

"I don't know if she wants to be found right now, Hank. I get the feeling she'd like to stay lost for a while."

"She sent me a matchbook from here, and I know that won't make any sense, but it's her sign that she wants me to find her. She *is* here with you, right?"

Monica sits down in her chair and begins applying her makeup for the show. "She came here after she heard you and your father fighting about her. She didn't want you to get in trouble. I guess she didn't know where else to go. She was pretty upset. I felt bad for her so I let her crash with me, but I told her it could only be temporary. I had to tell the manager she was my sister."

I shake my head. "It was a big misunderstanding. Dad didn't know what was going on, and I didn't have a chance to explain before she bolted out of there. But I talked to him, and everything is okay now so she can come back."

"You stormed the castle to save the princess, huh?" She smiles as she brushes bright-purple eye shadow on the creases of both lids. "That's very chivalrous, Hank."

"So does she hate me?" The words just flood out of my mouth. "You said she was upset, and then she left this note for Amanda Carlisle, like she *wanted* me to go out with her or something. But then she gave me the matches. She had to know I'd come looking for her, and I can't help but believe that's what she wanted. So I'm really confused."

"So am I. I have no idea what the heck you're talking about. Who's Amanda Carlisle?" she asks.

"It doesn't even matter."

Monica draws her eyeliner carefully on each eye, making it fan out at the corners like she's from ancient Egypt. "She doesn't hate you, Hank. Just the opposite. And I think that scares her as much as anything else right now."

"I need to see her."

"She's lucky, Hank. You know why? Because she matters to you. It would have made all the difference to me at her age to know I mattered to someone like that. It can be a lonely friggin' road, Hank. But knowing you're not alone can carry you through some pretty dark places."

I shift the weight of the duffel bag to my other hand and tell her, "Look, I figure I've got about another thirty seconds until someone comes knocking on this door looking for me. Is she upstairs in your room?"

She smiles and nods. I breathe a sigh of relief. "Thank you."

"She can't really stay here, Hank. I could get in big trouble if anyone finds out that she's not really my sister and she's under-age. She doesn't belong in a place like this."

"Yeah, well…neither do you." It's the truth. Monica deserves much better. She stands and pulls me into a hug, then motions to the door.

"Go get her."

I sneak out of Monica's dressing room and make my way up the back stairwell undetected. I can hear the sounds of a muffled TV on the other side of the door and I knock gingerly.

A few seconds later, Peyton is standing in front of me. I have about five million things I want to say to her, but all I really want to do is hug her because it's so damn good to see her.

I thought she'd be equally excited to see me, but instead she bursts out with a single laugh, then covers her mouth. Not quite the reaction I expected. That's when I realize I still have the frickin' headphones around my neck and aviator shades on my head, and I'm carrying the duffel bag. "Is that eyeliner on your chin?"

"Nice to see you too. Laugh it up all you want. You have *no* idea what I went through to get to you."

"So, I'm guessing you must have talked with Amanda Carlisle," she says, her smile fading. Her mouth turns down slightly as she says Amanda's name.

"Can we discuss this on our way back to my house? Because I'm positive the DJ has figured out by now that I'm not here as his backup." I motion with my thumbs in the direction of the exit, but she just stands there.

"Amanda wasted no time tracking you down, did she? Well, I'm glad it all worked out. I know this is what you wanted, and you deserve it. I'm happy for you guys."

"Why would you do that?"

"I made such a mess of things between you and your dad. The least I could do was make sure Amanda knew the truth and set things right."

I step into the room and shut the door behind me. "Seriously? I just snuck into a strip club, which, according to the signage outside, is highly illegal and impersonated a DJ. So please, can you grab your stuff? We can hash out all the details somewhere less sketchy."

She's still not moving. I lean back against the door and sigh.

"Jesus, Peyton, why'd you run away like that? I didn't know where you were or if something happened to you."

"I didn't want to make things more complicated for you than I already have. I thought it would be easier if I left. It wasn't fair to you." She bites at her lip. "That night, when I saw the fire you set on Amanda's lawn, I thought you were a kindred spirit. *Finally, someone who understands me!* Why I do what I do, what I think, how I feel. Someone who wouldn't judge me. But I was wrong. I got so caught up in spending time with you that I forgot you actually wanted to be with *Amanda*. The whole reason we started hanging out was because you showed up that night to invite *her* to prom. Well, now you have a chance to finish what you started. Take it. I want you to be happy, Hank."

I step into the room toward her and tell her, "I *am* happy, Peyton. Don't you get that?"

She folds her arms across her chest and avoids looking at me. "You guys can go to prom, boy gets girl, and the story has a happy ending after all."

"I'm not taking Amanda to prom. Do I honestly look like the kind of guy that gives a crap about a dance?"

"You should go, Hank. I won't hold it against you. Amanda Carlisle is pretty, popular, and uncomplicated. Everything I'm not. I'm sure that would make your dad super happy."

"I'm not interested in prom or Amanda Carlisle or what my dad thinks about who I like. For the first time in my life, I can't wait to wake up every day. I can't wait to see what crazy thing you're gonna do, or what completely inappropriate thing you will say to make me laugh, or what long-haired seventies rock band will be on your shirt. I like that you're unpredictable and complicated. Because I like *you*, Peyton. When I'm around you, I feel like I can do anything. You helped me let go, feel free, and give myself permission to move forward. For the first time in my life, I'm not scared of anything."

I move a little closer. I want her to see I'm telling the truth.

Peyton cracks half a smile. "I'm sorry. I know we're having a poignant moment here, but it's very hard to take you seriously with that thing on your chin." She rests her hand on my shoulder, laughs again, and pulls me into a hug. I breathe her in.

I whisper into her hair, "I mean it, Peyton." I run my hand down the small of her back and press my cheek against hers. "I'm not going to let anything bad happen to you ever again. I promise."

Her body is warm and soft, and I can feel her heart beating as she leans into me. She buries her head in my shoulder, and I whisper, "Please just come home with me."

After what seems like an eternity, she replies in a voice so quiet I can barely hear it. "Okay."

I'm smiling from ear to ear as I help her gather what few things she has lying around and shove them in an empty, plastic drugstore bag. She scribbles a quick note to Monica and leaves it on her pillow. As we're leaving, I say, "We can't let anyone see us. We could get in trouble."

"No kidding. That's why we take the back exit," she says as

she leads me down the hall to a separate stairwell that empties out by the giant, pink phallic silo. "You could have just come in that way in the first place, you know."

Who knew?

# 21

I'M BACK AT SCHOOL. PEYTON IS BACK TOO, AND
I swear everyone thinks she's a transfer student because no one
recognizes her with her new hair.

I'm going through the motions the best I can, like nothing ever
happened, but I can sense something is off. Life in general seems
too calm and I don't trust it. It's like we're in a frickin' snow globe
that someone's about to give a good shake.

So when Peyton is paged to the front office during last period, I
get a weird feeling. It's probably because she was MIA for a week.
There must be rules about extended absences, but she knows how
to work the system because in the time I've known her, Peyton has
pretty much come and gone as she pleases. I have to be at work
by four, but I wait for her after school by her locker to see what
that's all about.

She doesn't show. I'm not gonna lie; this makes me anxious.
A million scenarios compete in my head. Did she get detention?
Could they have found evidence she was responsible for the fires

and kicked her out? Or something worse? I unlock my bike from the rack in front of the school and climb on, about to leave, when I spot her walking down the front steps of the school with some woman. I can't make out their words, but the body language between them is tense and the woman seems agitated. I ride toward them slowly, wanting to make sure Peyton is okay.

The woman looks vaguely familiar with curly, shoulder-length hair, tight clothes with cleavage spilling out, cheap shoes, and too much makeup. She reaches for Peyton's arm, but Peyton pulls it out of her grasp, falling two paces behind her. Each time the woman speaks, Peyton flinches as if she's been slapped. In between sentences, the woman's mouth is an angry, straight line.

They walk in the direction of an old yellow car with oxidized paint and rimless tires. The woman opens the door to the driver's side and Peyton begrudgingly opens the passenger's, her head down.

That's when I officially flip out, because I know why this woman seems so familiar to me. I've seen her picture on the walls in Peyton's house. It's her mom, the same woman who took scissors to Peyton's hair and gave her those bruises. My stomach lurches. I yell, "Peyton!" and pedal faster until I'm practically on top of them.

Both train their eyes on me at the same time. Peyton shakes her head slightly, as if she's willing me to go away, but I can't *not* get involved. That ship sailed a long frickin' time ago.

"Peyton, are you okay? What's happening? Where are you going?" I'm on edge, and it feels as if everything is spinning out of control.

"Who are *you*?" her mother asks before Peyton can answer me. Her tone is clipped and cautious. Up close, she could easily be mistaken for Peyton's older sister. She is young but battle-weary.

"I'm Hank Kirby."

Her mother gives me the once-over, assessing me. Her eyes are cold.

She says, "So *you're* Hank. The boy she was staying with, right? You have no idea what you put me through. It would have been nice if you or your family had called and let me know she was all right."

*Is this lady frickin' serious?*

"The school kept leaving messages that she was absent, and I figured she'd turn up eventually. She always does. It's not like she has anywhere else to go. But when she didn't come home after two or three days, I started to worry. I only find out she's okay and back at school because the principal calls me in for a meeting to discuss all the time she's missed, and now I have no choice but to deal with it. I had to take off work today to clean up this mess."

The inconvenience of losing a day's pay is more important than learning that her daughter—who hasn't been home in a week—is alive and safe? I feel my temper rising.

I pull myself up to my full height as my adrenaline surges. "*You* were worried about her? Concerned for her safety? Are you kidding me?"

"Hank, what are you doing?" Peyton interrupts, but I keep going.

"I'm sure that you were up each night, wondering where she was. Putting up flyers, crying yourself to sleep, filing a missing person report with the police." I nod my head in the direction of the school. "I'm sure you probably have them convinced this was all some big misunderstanding, but it still doesn't explain why you never called them, does it?"

"Excuse me?" Her eyes narrow to slits. "Is there some sort of problem here?"

I'm not sure where this bravado is coming from, but I run with it. "Oh, I think there is most definitely some sort of problem here. When Peyton went missing, why didn't you call the school? You said the principal called *you* after she'd been out for several days. Wouldn't you think you should let the school know in case she shows up here? I mean, since you are such a concerned parent and all."

She's pissed now, and frankly I don't give a crap. Peyton deserves to have someone defend her, and I refuse to let her mom intimidate me. Mrs. Breedlove takes a step closer. "I don't know who you think you are, talking to me like that. You should mind your own business."

My parents had an issue of *Time* magazine that was in the bathroom for, like, three years when I was growing up. I read the articles over and over until I'd practically memorized the text. In one of them, there was a quote by this social rights activist dude from South Africa named Desmond Tutu. He said, "If you are neutral in situations of injustice, you have chosen the side of the oppressor." It always struck me as something a superhero might say, but I never fully understood it until right this moment.

"Peyton *is* my business," I say. I shoot a glance at Peyton, who looks absolutely terrified. "There's no way in hell she is getting in that car with you and going back to that house. I can't let that happen."

Mrs. Breedlove raises her eyebrows at Peyton. "Well, Peyton, you certainly did quite a number on this boy. That's very noble and all, Hank, but you don't have the right to tell me what my daughter can and can't do."

Something in the way she speaks, as if each word is as sharp as a razor blade, reminds me of my dad when he was drunk, and I reflexively ball my hands into fists. "I think Peyton should stay with me."

Mrs. Breedlove smirks. "Oh, you think that, huh?"

"Yes." I made Peyton a promise. I'm not going to back down.

"And why is that?"

"Because I know what happened that night. I know what I saw. You can't do that to her."

Peyton's eyes go wide. "Hank, don't—" But her mother cuts her off.

"And what exactly do you think you saw?" Her mother scoffs, and before I can answer, she says, "You are *so* out of bounds, kid. I'm sure you both had a wonderful time playing house, but Peyton's seventeen. She's not a legal adult. And neither are you. So as I see it, our family matters don't concern you." She narrows her eyes at me and then says, "Get in the car, Peyton."

"Don't, Peyton," I say, standing my ground. If she gets in that car, who knows what might happen. Her mother's jaw tenses.

"Hank, please don't," Peyton pleads. "It's fine, okay?"

"It's *not* fine. Look what she did to you."

Her mother locks eyes with me. "What *I* did to—"

Peyton's voice cracks. "Don't get involved, okay?"

I don't understand why she's trying to get me to back off. It doesn't make sense. Not after everything that's happened.

Mrs. Breedlove's voice is low and intense. "Look, if I were you, I'd shut my mouth and quit throwing around accusations, especially when you don't have the first clue what's really going on." And then, without ever taking her eyes off me, she says, "Get in the *car*, Peyton."

Peyton gives me one last pleading look to leave her alone before opening the door and climbing in.

I practically spit words at her mother. "I know *exactly* what's going on. She told me you came at her with scissors, that you cut off her hair, told her you wished she'd never been born, slapped her across the face. I should probably call the cops right now." I reach for my cell phone in my back pocket just to show her I'm serious. It doesn't seem to faze her a bit.

"Is that what she told you?" Her mother calmly shakes her head. "Peyton has always had quite an imagination."

"It's pretty hard to make that kind of stuff up when there's physical evidence," I say. I figure I'm already way past the point of making a good impression on her mother so I don't give a crap anymore.

Mrs. Breedlove adjusts her purse strap over her shoulder and gets right in my face. Her tone is terse. "You may think you know a lot about my daughter, Hank, but I assure you, there's more to the story than whatever she's told you. Everything isn't always as it seems. Let's leave it at that."

"Why would she make something like that up?"

"That girl will do whatever she has to do to get attention. She always has. And it certainly looks like she got yours." She turns her back on me and gets into her car, putting an end to our conversation. Peyton doesn't even look back at me.

After everything that's happened, I can't believe that she'd just go with her mom like that. Or that the school wouldn't intervene. Mrs. Breedlove must've put on a helluva show in there. It seems like I should tell someone, but what can I say? I don't have any *actual* evidence, only my word against her mother's, since Peyton isn't speaking up, which I don't get.

I consider following them home because I'm worried about what might happen to Peyton, but if I do, there's a good chance O'Callaghan will call Dad looking for me, and everything could unravel if Dad pieces together why. I'm gonna be a good ten minutes late for my shift as it is, and I can't get canned.

During the whole ride to Shop 'n Save I replay what her mother said. What a bitch. Trying to cover up what she did to Peyton by implying that what Peyton said wasn't true. Why would anyone lie about a thing like that? I know what she looked like when she came to my door—the bruises, her hair, the blood. What assurance do I have that it won't happen again? And what the hell did her mother mean that there's more to the story than I know?

＊

The night is a blur. O'Callaghan has me inventorying pet food, and it makes me want to pull out my eyebrows, hair by hair, knowing I'm here doing this petty crap while Peyton is dealing with who knows what. It drives me crazy that she doesn't have a frickin' cell phone. At least then I could try to text her. God, I hope she's all right.

I get home around ten thirty. On my way upstairs, I catch sight of the mail sitting on the table. Nestled in between the bills and the supermarket flyers, a big, fat envelope from the School of the Museum of Fine Arts in Boston is sticking out. Another one of those useless college solicitations. I'm not in the mood for thinking about everything I can't have right now, but I grab it anyway, along with the latest Victoria's Secret catalog addressed to Monica, and head upstairs.

I flop down on my bed and flip mindlessly through

the catalog. Even totally hot, half-naked, perfectly tanned models in lacy lingerie can't do the job in taking my mind off this afternoon. Not even the chick in the bra with the real diamonds.

I feel so completely impotent, and not in that can't-get-your-jock-up kind of way. I mean, after everything that happened, I just stood there and watched Peyton leave. Short of throwing myself across the hood, I don't know what I should have done. Peyton didn't make a move. And what if she *had*? What then? Ride off into the sunset with her on the handlebars of my frickin' bike?

I can't sleep. All night I toss and turn, listening for her at the window. Every noise I hear outside I think maybe could be her. I consider riding over to her house to make sure she's okay, but I worry what might happen if her mother or Pete sees me, and the position that might put her in. I finally fall asleep, but I swear I hear a girl's voice downstairs as I drift off.

I wake up to the distinct smell of overcooked eggs and burned bacon. I'm halfway down the stairs when I notice the green suitcase with the rainbow-colored ribbons propped neatly by the door, like Mary Poppins has come back to visit. I smile and groggily stagger into the kitchen, following the smell of cremated food. Sure enough, there's Monica, standing at the stove wearing my dad's lucky Red Sox tee and a pair of pink fuzzy socks, and cracking more eggs into the pan.

"Good morning," she says and grins, nibbling on a slice of semi-burned toast while she scrambles the eggs, like it's no big deal that she's in the kitchen making breakfast at six thirty in the morning.

"Hey," I say. "You're back."

She smiles as she pours herself a cup of coffee. "I am."

"That's great," I say. "I'm glad."

"We talked last night. Like…really talked. Your dad's trying to get his shit together, and it's about time I got mine together too. So we're gonna try to help each other, you know? Make a few changes. He's quittin' the drinking, and I've decided to quit dancing." She plates some eggs, hands them to me, and adds, "Actually, I have you to thank for that."

"Me? How so?" I ask, taking a bite of eggs. They're crunchy. I subtly extract a piece of eggshell from my mouth and place it in my napkin.

"That day when you brought Peyton to see me? You know, to fix her hair? It felt so good to help someone, to know that what I did was making a difference in how they felt about themselves. It made me realize I want to do something that makes me feel like that every day. I don't want my past to hold me back."

She reaches for her mug of coffee, takes a sip, and says, "Then I bumped into your dad as he was coming out of his AA meeting downtown. That's how we started talking about how he was making some changes too, and I thought to myself, 'Monica, this definitely is some kind of sign.' And you know I'm into signs."

"Can't ignore the signs," I say. I bite into the bacon. It makes the eggs suddenly seem delicious by comparison.

"You really can't." She smiles, then asks, "So where's Peyton?"

I shake my head and tell her about what happened yesterday.

She refills her mug, grabs the milk from the fridge, and adds a splash, stirring it with her spoon as she says, "Wow, that's rough. It sounds as if you need to lay low for a while. It's not like they have her chained there, so if she were really in some sort of danger, she'd run away again, right? Maybe there is more to the story. Peyton knows how to reach you. I'd let it sort itself out."

I shovel another bite of eggs in my mouth. They're terrible, but I appreciate that she's here and that she made it for me. "That doesn't feel like much of a solution."

"This is real life, Hank, not some movie. Every problem doesn't necessarily have a solution."

That might actually be the first thing anyone has said in the last eighteen hours that makes any sense.

# 22

THE WARNING BELL RINGS FOR FIRST PERIOD, and I begin to worry that Peyton isn't going to show up, but then she emerges from behind a pack of shaggy-haired skateboarders, her backpack slung low over her shoulder, her eyes cast down. As soon as I see her, it makes me smile and I breathe a sigh of relief. She seems okay. Now that she's home and has access to her stuff, she's back to wearing an oversize Stones tee and ripped jeans. She looks like Peyton again.

She doesn't see me standing there, so for a minute I watch her: how she self-consciously keeps trying to tuck her hair behind her ears, though there isn't much of it left to tuck, the way her Converse scuff the ground as she walks.

As she's about to head inside, I pop in front of her. "Hey!"

"Hey," she says coolly and reaches around me to open the door to the school. She heads down the main corridor, and I follow her.

"That was pretty off the rails yesterday. Your mother scares the shit out of me."

"She has that effect on people." The most she'll give me is half a smile, and she keeps walking.

I move to keep up with her. I'm unsettled by her greeting or lack thereof, so I launch right into the verbal diarrhea. "I wanted to come by and check on you, but I was nervous that it might get you in trouble. I kept hoping maybe you'd sneak out, you know, to let me know what's happening. Because I gotta be honest—I have no frickin' idea what's going on." I rake my hands through my hair, reliving all the anxiety. "Christ, I was so worried, Peyton. I didn't know what to do. I'm just so glad to see you and that you're okay. I mean, you seem okay. Are you okay?"

She turns on her heel and looks me in the eye.

"Are you kidding? Everything is so completely *not* okay." She shakes her head at me. "And the worst part is, you don't even understand why."

She turns the corner toward her first-period class. It's not that far from mine so I walk with her since there's no way I'm letting her get away without explaining what she means. "What don't I understand? Your mother shows up, puts on a big act for the school, and because you're under eighteen, she's legally allowed to force you to go back home. And I couldn't do a damn thing about it. I spent half the night wondering what she might do to you. You have to tell someone what happened, Peyton. The authorities won't make you stay there."

She seems agitated, shifting her backpack from one shoulder to the other. "And go where? I'm sure as hell not going into some foster home, and I have a short list of other options." She stops short and lets out a loud sigh. "I'm just saying that the situation is what it is. I appreciate all you've done for me, Hank. I really do. But you should probably walk away. I won't hold it against you."

"Why would I walk away? Jesus, Peyton, what's going on?"

She shakes her head and focuses somewhere over my left shoulder. "Look, there's a lot you don't understand."

"Well, I *want* to understand, so tell me." I move into her line of sight, forcing her to look at me. "Seriously, you're freaking me out."

She stands there not saying anything as people push past us to get to class.

"I am definitely missing something here." I search her face for answers but she's unyielding. Her lip quivers and I glance at the clock in the hallway. I'm running out of time. "Can we, like, go somewhere and talk after school? My shift doesn't start until eight tonight, and then I'm stuck there until midnight."

She shakes her head. "I can't. I'm supposed to go straight home."

"Well, that's a new one. Since when does Peyton Breedlove follow the rules?"

"Since I'm not looking for any new trouble." Then she relents and says, "Look, meet me by the science labs at lunch, okay? We can sneak out to the park and be back in time for fifth period. I have something I need to tell you."

She skitters down the hall, and I have to hustle it double time to avoid getting marked tardy myself.

*I have something I need to tell you.* In movies and novels, when someone says they have something to tell someone, it is rarely good news. It usually means "I have six days to live" or "I met someone else" or "I thought you should know I have a raging case of gonorrhea." I'm seriously hoping it's not number three. Not like one and two would exactly be kick-ass options either.

What the hell is going on?

The morning couldn't move any slower if it were tied to a tortoise's shell. I swear some of my teachers are even talking in slow motion, like the whole world is trying to torture me.

At lunch, I book it to the science labs. Peyton's there waiting for me, but she's not alone. She's chatting up Nick Giuliani. I'm hoping he is not part of the reason we need to talk. I don't think I could deal if they're getting back together or something shittastical like that. But frankly, if there's one thing I've learned these past couple of months, it's that anything can happen. In fact, the less logical, the more likely it is.

I cautiously move toward them.

"Nick," I say.

"Hank," he replies. His jaw tenses.

"Well, now that we've all established who we are," Peyton says. Nobody laughs.

Nick bobs his head in Peyton's direction and says, "Well, I'll see ya." He hightails it out of there in a hurry, but not before giving me a look that implies *I'm* the asshat for hooking up with Peyton after he decided to jump ship for the Amanda Express. Of course, he has no clue how I saved him from some potentially epic public humiliation.

"Okay, see ya," Peyton says and pops the tab on a can of soda, taking a big sip.

"What was that about?" I ask as we make our way to the back gate.

"Why, are you jealous?"

"Of Nick? Absolutely. Who wouldn't be jealous of a guy who can wax a car and shine a pair of shoes with his frickin' hair?"

"He actually came over to apologize about the whole Amanda Carlisle thing. He was hoping we could all hang out again like we used to and not have it be weird or whatever."

"Don't kid yourself. He probably didn't recognize you and thought you were a new girl he could hit on."

We slip through the opening in the gate and walk down the parking ramp toward Walter Reed Park. Most people actually call it Walter Weed Park because it's where all the stoners hang out after school.

"Are you still mad at him?" Peyton asks.

"Sort of. What he did was shitty." I take a shortcut down a grassy slope that leads to the park.

"Sometimes people make mistakes," she says as she follows me.

"I don't really want to talk about Nick Giuliani."

"Neither do I."

The park is empty except for a mom with her toddler over by the merry-go-round. We each take a seat on a swing, side by side, and Peyton takes a deep breath.

Here we go.

"So what's up?" I ask her.

She hesitates and sighs. "Sorry, this is really hard."

"Just say it." I brace myself, not sure what the heck is coming.

"I really like you, Hank. I mean, *really, really* like you."

"I really like you too. I'm not sure that's a problem though." I smile and lean into her with my swing playfully, but she shakes her head.

"You're the best friend I've ever had. In fact, you might be the *only* friend I've ever had, and I'm truly sorry. I don't expect you to understand, but please know that everything I'm about to tell you I did because I genuinely care about you. Being with you is just about the best feeling there is, and I wanted to do whatever I could to make sure I never stopped feeling that."

My heart starts pounding faster. I realize I've been holding my breath, and I let it out. "Why would that have to stop? It's not like I'm going anywhere."

She digs her fingernails into her arm, leaving little red, indented crescents. She won't look at me. "I didn't tell you the whole truth about that night. In fact, I haven't told you the whole truth about a lot of things."

"Like what? Are you in the witness protection program or something? Because if you are, it's totally cool. I won't tell."

"I'm trying to be serious." She doesn't even crack a smile. "You sent me all these mixed signals, Hank. You filled out the questionnaire on Amanda's website, and it seemed like you were pushing Nick and me together. But then I started staying at your house. It felt like this connection was growing between us, and I hoped you'd forget all about Amanda. But then you showed up in the courtyard for her announcement. You looked nervous, as if you were still hoping you had a shot. Even if she didn't choose you, I knew she was bound to discover sooner or later that you set the fire. I was worried that if she found out what a great guy you are, maybe she'd actually be interested. I felt really confused."

"You shouldn't have been confused, because I told you, I don't care about Amanda."

Her eyes cast downward as she digs the tips of her shoes into the sand. She bends her knees, rocking herself on the swing. "That night, when I came to your door a total mess…my mother didn't do that to me."

"Then who did?" I feel anger building inside me as I say, "Was it Pete? Because I'm not scared of him. I swear I will kick his ass if he laid a finger on you."

"Pete would never lay a hand on me. He wouldn't want to risk losing the free rent." She faces me as tears start spilling down her cheeks. "I did it to myself."

Her voice is so quiet I have to strain to hear her, and even then I'm sure I've heard her wrong because that doesn't even remotely make sense. "What are you talking about?"

She takes another deep breath and lets it out. Her hands are shaking. "That night, after my mother found out I stole her money, she *did* fly into a rage. She *did* say all those hateful things. And when I blamed Pete, she *did* accuse me of trying to break them up and make her life miserable. That's all true.

"But it was like she pressed this button inside me and I snapped. I knew I'd pushed her too far this time, and I couldn't deal with the fact that you might still have feelings for Amanda. I locked myself in the bathroom, and the scissors were in the drawer. I just started cutting. I hated myself so much. I wanted to disappear."

It feels like someone has punched me in the stomach. I start to feel sick. Peyton is speaking, but the words aren't registering. "I don't understand."

Her voice begins to catch in her throat as the tears start streaming down her face. She goes on. "After I'd cut off my hair, I started banging my face against the wall, because even though it hurt like hell, at least when I hurt myself I *feel* something. I didn't even want to try to hide it like I usually do. I *wanted* to hurt. I *deserved* it. It's like my mom said, I always screw up, and I was scared I'd screw everything up with you too."

She really starts crying now. Guttural, chest-heaving sobs. I just sit there dumbfounded, not knowing what the hell to say. Because what exactly *do* you say when your girlfriend tells you that she went off the deep end and beat herself up? I shake my head in disbelief, blindsided by her lack of faith in me. "So...you basically lied to me so I'd be sympathetic? Because you assumed I wouldn't be otherwise. Because I'm an insensitive asshole."

She reaches out for my arm but I jerk it away. I lean forward, creating distance between our bodies, and grip my head in my hands. "I didn't *want* to lie to you, Hank. But I didn't know how you'd react and if you'd think I was just disgusting or crazy. I didn't want to lose you, but I knew I probably would anyway once you found out what I'd done. I was so ashamed. I'd messed up. I decided to tell Amanda about you and what really happened that night because you deserve to be happy, even if I can't be the one who makes you feel that way. I owe you that. I swear you are everything to me at this point, Hank. In my whole life, no one ever cared where I was, and you actually came looking for me."

She turns her body toward me, but I'm having trouble looking at her right now. I don't know the truth about anything between us anymore. I feel numb.

Her tone is urgent and high-pitched. "Mom was so angry, saying all these horrible things, threatening to send me back to my dad or, worse, to that awful hospital. I can't go back to either one, Hank. I can't. I wouldn't be able to see you anymore. There was only one place where I knew I would feel safe, and that was with you."

I can't keep sitting here like this. I abruptly stand up and start walking, trying to get my bearings and process everything I've just heard—most of all, how she could have hurt herself like that. Pebbles on the path go skittering in all directions as she races to fall into step beside me. "Wait… What do you mean, send you back to your dad? I thought he left when you were a baby."

"He did. He lives in California. But my mother sent me to live with him and his new wife and baby a couple of years ago because she couldn't deal with me. My dad didn't want me there, and his wife wanted me even less. They had a perfect new family and I was this screwed-up kid who ruined it. They ignored me. That's when I began setting stuff on fire. I started with little things—a random baby toy, one of my dad's ties, an expensive scarf that belonged to my stepmother. Stupid stuff. It made me feel powerful. Until things got out of control."

Despite the fact that it's about seventy degrees, a chill goes down my spine. "What do you mean?"

"They have these winds in California. They call them the Santa Anas, and when they blow, they can be like forty to fifty miles an hour. I was in the backyard while my dad was still at work and my stepmother was trying to put the baby down for a nap. I was lonesome and bored, so I started burning a stack of her stupid fashion magazines, when this big gust of wind came out of nowhere. It carried the embers, which were really beautiful actually, these glowing orange specks that just flew everywhere in the wind, and they landed on the roof of the old gardening shed. It was basically kindling, and the next thing I knew, the whole shed was on fire."

"Holy shit," I say softly.

I steal a glance at her. Peyton's eyes are a million miles away, as if she's reliving the moment. "I couldn't stop watching it burn. My stepmother noticed it from the house and came outside, screaming and carrying on. She accused me of deliberately setting the fire and trying to harm her and the baby. She told my dad I was going to light the house on fire some night while they slept, and that I had to leave. I suppose I'm lucky because they could have sent me to some juvenile detention center, but instead they put me in the psych ward." She wipes her nose with her fist and shakes her head. "I would never hurt anyone on purpose, Hank. You have to know that."

"Except yourself, apparently."

She stares down at her shoe and kicks at the dirt. "It wasn't like I meant to burn down the shed any more than you meant to light Amanda Carlisle's yard on fire. It just happened. In a way, it was the same kind of thing. We wanted to be noticed, to stop being invisible in plain sight for once."

She steals a glance at me as I let that sink in for a minute. In a completely bizarre and messed-up way, I get what she means. And then I remember what she said that night she gave me the comic—about how we tell ourselves stories to survive, but that doesn't mean they're the truth. I wonder how many other things she's lied about.

"So what happened after that?"

"After I was released from the hospital, I was sent back to my mother. She wasn't too happy about it because I got in the way of partying with her steady stream of loser boyfriends. But then she realized it meant she'd be getting child support again, plus more welfare money until I'm eighteen, as long as I'm living with her. Suddenly she's more than willing to have me come home. Not because she gives a crap about me, but because for the first time, having me around actually holds value for her. But trust me when I say that's where it ends."

I don't say anything. I don't even know where to start.

"You know what it is to have people care about you, Hank. To have a family who loves you. I never had that, not for a single day, until I met you. You became my family. And because of that, despite all the evidence to the contrary, my life was pretty amazing." She breathes in deeply and then blows out. "You hate me."

"I don't hate you," I tell her.

"You're mad. You have every right to be."

"I do. But weirdly enough, I'm not angry. I'm just unbelievably sad." We reach a picnic table that is metal and covered in graffiti. She straddles the bench. I can't sit. My body and brain are too amped up so I stand. "Why didn't you tell me the truth, Peyton? Did you think I couldn't handle it? That I would think less of you? Is that what you think of me? Because I gotta say, that makes me feel like a giant load of crap."

"No. I don't know." She reaches for a rock on the ground and rubs it between her thumb and index finger.

"It's not like you asked for any of this," I say. "You didn't pick your mother. Or your dad. Of all the people in the frickin' universe, Peyton, you should know that I understand shit happens to us that we don't ask for."

"I'm sorry, Hank." She screws up her face and starts crying again. "I'm so sorry. I know I've made a mess of everything."

There's this pang in my chest when I look at her, this deep ache that radiates through me. I'm sad about what happened to her, sad about how she doesn't know me as well as I'd expected. "Funny thing is—I used to be the kind of guy who got scared and bailed when things got messy. But I'm not anymore, and you're the one that helped me be that way. I guess I thought you knew that."

She opens her mouth to speak and then stops herself.

My brain is firing on all cylinders. "Look, can we talk later? I need to go."

She nods. "I don't blame you for walking away from me."

"I'm not walking away from you, Peyton. I just need space to clear my head. There's a difference."

I turn and head back toward school. Despite the fact that we're outside, I suddenly can't get enough air in my lungs.

# 23

I SHOULD HAVE LISTENED TO MONICA. SHE TOLD me to stay out of other people's shit. That the better you know someone, the more likely you are to create expectations, and life and people never live up to those. She was spot on.

I don't know what I expected from Peyton, really. I think the problem is that I started to expect anything at all.

With every step I take away from her, I can feel myself putting up a wall. I don't usually allow myself to get close to people, because it generally ends up biting me in the ass. I'm usually much more guarded than that, but I left myself wide open with Peyton. It's confusing as fuck because now I'm questioning everything, sifting through what I thought we had together and trying to figure what's real.

I feel for her and her craptastic life; I really do. I wish I could fix it. In fact, I was trying to, because I thought I knew who I was protecting her from. I feel like an idiot.

Despite everything, a part of me wants to go back and put my arms around her, to tell her I understand and that it's okay.

But the truth is, I don't.

And it isn't.

And I'm not sure if it ever can be.

It's not that I don't want to be with her anymore. The thing is, I do. But I just can't be around her right now. I know she needs help, more than I can give her.

I head back toward the school, but there's no way I'm staying. Instead, I grab my backpack from my locker and walk right out the front door of the school and get on my bike. Nobody even notices. I don't care if they call my dad. I'll deal with it. I just have to get out of here.

I don't want to go home. I can't. So I start pedaling, slowly at first and then faster until the muscles in my thighs and calves burn. I push through it. As long as I concentrate on the pain in my legs, I don't have to focus on the raw ache in my heart.

I cycle through town, out to the country roads that lead toward the woods and the organic farms with their roadside stands for freshly picked lettuce and squash. When I was younger, my mom would drive out here in the summers to get fresh sweet corn and blueberries. She said everything was fresher in the country. I'm hoping that applies to perspectives too, not merely the food and the air.

I ride through three neighboring towns, out past where the

houses are spread so far apart you can't even see them from the road. Despite the fact that my legs are screaming, I feel like I could ride forever.

I must have ridden a good ten or fifteen miles when I hone in on what hurts so damn bad. When Peyton came along, it was like Monica said. She made me feel like I mattered. I haven't felt that way in a long time. It was as if somebody was finally on my side. She understood me and all my bullshit and liked me anyway. It felt honest and real, like the moments she captured in her photographs. So when she didn't think I could handle the truth, *her* truth, after everything we'd been through, it was as if I didn't matter at all.

I'm no stranger to feeling irrelevant. I've pretty much felt that way since Mom and Mickey died. I just didn't expect *she* would ever make me feel that way. Peyton made me believe that I was talented. Not just that I could be somebody special, but that I already was. I'm afraid if I let her go, I might never feel that again.

I guess that's the crap love does to you. It turns your brain to mush. It sneaks up on you and turns everything upside down and inside out. Honestly, it's kind of a pain in the ass.

Admittedly, when I first met Peyton, I thought she was a little crazy. Now that it turns out she might be, I'm not sure what the hell I'm supposed to do. Because only someone who is crazy would engage in self-destructive behaviors like setting fires and cutting off her hair, right? But she'd said it herself; those actions were sort of a release.

I understand feeling like no one gives a damn about you. Feeling alone, and in the way, and believing that maybe things would be easier if you weren't around. We simply have different ways of dealing with it. So maybe she *isn't* really *crazy*; maybe she's just lonely. She might not have acted that way if she'd thought someone genuinely cared about her. She didn't know how deeply I cared about her until after she showed up at my house that night, bruised and broken. And the truth is, neither did I.

Maybe when we're together, we help each other find a way out of the darkness and feel a little less alone.

I pass a box of matches tossed on the side of the road. It's a big box, for the kind you'd use to light a fire in a woodstove. It's smashed flat where a car has run over it and kicked it into the weeds. Slightly farther down the road is a Zippo lighter, dented and tarnished with its lid hanging open. I stop to look at it, resting my legs for a minute. It's engraved with "Love you like a house on fire." It makes me smile. Monica would probably say it's a sign.

The sky is turning the color of a tangerine as the sun moves lower in the sky, and I figure I should probably head toward home since I have no idea how long it's going to take me to get there. My skin is taut and red, and my T-shirt is soaked through like I'm competing in the Tour de France.

By the time I get home, I feel a million times better even though I'm pretty positive I'm not going to be able to walk tomorrow. I take a long shower, enjoying the hot water pounding on my sore muscles and the sting on my face and neck where I got sunburned. Afterward, I lie back on my bed and let the weight of the day settle.

When I open my eyes, I'm staring at the envelope I'd tossed on my nightstand the day before, the one from the School of the Museum of Fine Arts in Boston. I pick it up, ready to pitch it in the trash, but there's a giant red "Congratulations!" stamped on the outside. It looks all official, like I've won a contest or something.

I tear open the envelope and skim the enclosed letter. It says my application materials have been received and reviewed by their Graphic Arts program. The letter goes on to say that my work samples and recommendations have "convinced the faculty that I have the aptitude, talent, and imagination needed to make valuable contributions to their diverse community and thrive in their rich artistic environment." And to top it all off, they would like to invite me to Boston to tour their state-of-the-art facilities and meet with faculty for an interview. I read it two more times until the words sink in.

Clearly, this is a mistake.

I never applied, so how could they have seen my stuff? I flip through the rest of the envelope's contents: financial aid forms and a few informational pamphlets, all of which seem pretty legit.

Suddenly everything clicks into place. Peyton keeping my drawings. Mr. Vaughn's comment the day of the fire alarm about how he was thinking good thoughts for me.

Peyton must have sent the application and asked Mr. Vaughn to write the recommendation. I swear, sometimes it seems like *Freeze Frame* means as much to her as it does to me. She knew I would never have the confidence to do it on my own, because honestly, going to college is a dream, kind of like winning the lottery or finding out that doughnuts are healthy. The odds of spending my life doing what I love rather than saying "Would you like ketchup or ranch?" or "Cat food is in aisle six" are not exactly stacked in my favor.

Until maybe now.

Not gonna lie: it's a little overwhelming to allow myself to think like that. When you're used to falling down over and over again, it's hard to believe life could ever be any different. In fact, I can come up with lots of reasons I shouldn't even consider going to this college, but it all boils down to this: I'm scared. Like crap-my-pants, what-if-I-go-for-it-and-find-out-I-completely-suck-ass-and-this-is-as-good-as-it-gets scared. I'm so convinced I'm gonna fail that I find a way to sabotage the situation before it can happen. Honestly, the biggest thing standing in my way is me.

I picture Peyton sitting in the park, scared and ashamed. I'm a total jerk for letting her feel that way. After all she's been through, even though she lied, she meant to protect me. In the end, the person she was trying to protect me from the most was herself.

Somehow, that makes me love her all the more.

I decide that tomorrow I'm going to tell her I'm sorry, that we'll figure it all out as we go.

I make it until about 2:00 a.m. Tomorrow, even if it is technically now today, is too far away. I have to tell her right now. So I grab the envelope and get on my bike, despite my legs' protests, and ride to her house. I'm not surprised to find her walking down the street, even though it's the middle of the night. It's like she was waiting for me, as if she knew I'd come.

Of course she knew I'd come.

I slow my bike and ride alongside her as she walks. She digs her hands in her pockets and steals a glance at me before returning her gaze to the full moon overhead.

"What do you want, Hank? I told you that you could walk away. I'd understand. And I meant it. You didn't need to come here to tell me I'm crazy and need help or that I'm some horrible person. Let me save you the trouble. I figured all that out on my own."

"I wanted to talk to you," I say.

"Seriously, I'll be fine. Things are looking up. My mother finally kicked Pete to the curb. Turns out he really had stolen money from her too. On the downside, the new wallpaper and pool are a no-go. But, I'll be eighteen in less than three weeks. Then I can get the hell out of here and none of this will matter anyway. So what I'm saying is, you don't have to worry about me. I can take care of myself. I always have."

When she's done talking, I reach behind me to pull the envelope from the back pocket of my jeans and hand it to her. She stops walking, and I straddle my bike as she eyes it curiously. "What's this?"

"Open it."

She does, and her eyes fly over the words. Then she half smiles. "Not a surprise. Congratulations."

"I can't believe you did that."

She hands me back the letter and her smile fades. "I'm sorry. I thought it would make you happy. I should have asked." She takes off walking again, and I hop off my bike, holding the handlebars and keeping pace with her.

"Jesus, Peyton. I'm not mad. I'm about as opposite of mad as it gets. You probably know better than anybody how much I dream of this kind of opportunity—to write and illustrate comics. I didn't know what I was supposed to say or feel this afternoon. I was confused. I biked halfway across the state of Massachusetts, trying to make sense of what you told me. But when I opened that envelope, it was like everything crystal-lized. The first thing that went through my mind was I couldn't wait to show you. You're the one person in the whole damn universe who knows what this means to me."

She smiles weakly and says, "I'm really proud of you, Hank. I never doubted you'd get in."

"It's only an interview. I'm not in yet. And even then, I'm not sure if I could go."

"Of course you're going to go. You *have* to go," she says.

"I don't know. I haven't even talked to Dad yet."

"He'll miss you."

"Yeah, right." I snort a laugh. "He'll miss my paycheck, microscopic as it may be."

"Okay then, *I'll* miss you."

"So come with me."

She raises an eyebrow, clearly amused. "Yeah, right."

"I'm serious."

She smiles. I stop walking, reach for her arm, and pull her toward me. "I've never meant anything more, Peyton. The minute you came into my life, everything went batshit crazy. Good batshit crazy. It's like it went from black and white to color. I'm not just giving up and walking away because you're the best thing that ever happened to me."

I move a little closer to her. "You may have a seriously messed-up family and some major issues with olives and tomatoes and who knows how many other foods I don't even know about yet. You may walk around at four o'clock in the frickin' morning, and you may burn Barbies and set shit on fire, and some people may not understand any of that. But I do. I *get* you. I get you *and* all your crazy. And I think you get me."

She ponders what I've said for a minute, then holds my gaze steadily. "What would I do? If I went with you, I mean?"

"Anything you want."

"Anything?"

"Anything. Maybe you could get a job at that gallery you told me about in Boston, the one where you saw those cool photos of the cities. It doesn't matter. It's a fresh start. Just come with me." That makes her smile.

"That would be like a dream."

"You can make it a reality." She puts a finger thoughtfully to her lips. I lean over and kiss her. "So you'll think about it?"

She nods. That's good enough for now.

Peyton invites me back to her house. Her mother's out late and may not come home at all. She's on a date with a new guy. A mechanic. Peyton jokes that he's probably rotating her tires and giving her a lube job, so we're blissfully alone.

I'm ecstatic there will be no potential late-night reunion with Mrs. Breedlove. She's not exactly the president of my fan club, and I'm guessing that discovering me in their house wouldn't change that.

We go back to Peyton's room. Her forty-fives are still suspended from the ceiling and the posters are still intact, as they were when I was last here, but I don't want to focus on her lies.

Peyton lights a small candle and puts it on her bookshelf so the room is bathed in a gentle, warm light. I'll spare the details, but mood lighting and makeup sex really is "a thing." It couldn't have been more perfect. Afterward, we're both so relaxed that we fall asleep.

When I begin to come to, I think I'm at home. The smell is reminiscent of Monica's cooking. I open my eyes and they burn in the haze. The room is filling with smoke, and there's a crackling noise like a campfire. I start to cough and shake Peyton awake. She winces as her eyes begin to water.

She sits up. "Shit! The candle!" We fell asleep with it burning, and now the bookcase is on fire and it's spreading fast.

# 24

I LEAP OUT OF BED AND TRY TO TAMP DOWN
the flames with a T-shirt that's on the floor, but that only seems
to make it worse. The flames defiantly snap, spreading from book
to book, leaping higher, consuming whatever is in their path, and
making it almost impossible to reach the door without becoming
a human torch. The room is as hot as Miami in July, and the
smoke is getting thicker. I cover my mouth with the bottom half
of my T-shirt. I yell at Peyton to open the window.

She tugs and pulls on it, but it does not budge an inch. "It's
stuck again!" she yells frantically.

Panicked, I look around for the heaviest thing I can find, which
happens to be a lamp, and I smash it through the window. Now
there's an opening, but with all the jagged edges of glass, we would
impale ourselves trying to climb out.

I grab a shoe from the floor and set to work shattering the
remaining pieces to minimize the danger and then order Peyton to
climb out the window. There's a rushing noise and the flames kick

higher, licking at the posters and slowly climbing the wall. I'm about to give her a boost so she can crawl out the window when she turns to look behind her and her jaw hangs open.

"Look," she says and points up toward the ceiling, transfixed. One by one, the forty-fives warp and spin as the vinyl mutates and melts in the heat. It would be kind of cool if it wasn't so completely terrifying.

"Go! We've gotta get out of here!" I shout.

She leverages herself and starts to shimmy out the window, but her hand catches on a shard of glass I missed. She cries out in pain. There's no time to waste though; she's got to get out of this room—and so do I—or we're both going to be crispy.

I can hear the sirens wailing in the distance as she falls to the grass outside, coughing and catching her breath. The trucks come barreling down the street, and the sirens become shriller. It's like déjà vu from the night I lit the sparklers on Amanda's lawn. I begin to feel light-headed and nauseous.

"Come on, Hank! Hurry!" Peyton yells, but her voice is muffled over the roar and hiss of the fire, and the air is so smoky I can barely see.

I stumble to the window, my lungs gasping at the fresh air. I trip over something and go down. My brain is commanding me to move, that I have to get out of here, but my body won't respond.

I lift my head, and I can make out the fireman climbing in the window. He's reaching for me with his hand, but I don't have the strength to reach back. My lungs are screaming.

The fireman is in my face now, but it's like I'm seeing him in double. He's all blurred and his features are fuzzy. He keeps saying my name over and over, and that I need to stay with him. Maybe it's the shortage of oxygen to my brain, but I swear his voice sounds exactly like Mickey's. "Hold on, buddy," he says.

That's what Mickey used to call me. I try to focus, to see Mickey's face, but I can't see through my tears and his mask. I hear my brother's voice again. It's so distinct I'd recognize it anywhere. He says, "Everything's gonna be okay, Hank. Just keep breathing."

As I slowly feel myself losing consciousness, I try to ask Mickey how I can hear him so clearly through his mask and over the roaring, rushing noise from the fire itself. But that's the last thing I remember as his arms encircle me and everything goes black.

✳

I wake up to the sound of someone crying. It's not loud, hysterical crying, but quieter, pained sobs. I open my eyes slowly to adjust to the light. I don't recognize where I am. There is a big, fluorescent light fixture overhead with two long, rod-shaped bulbs, one of which is brighter than the other. A TV is suspended from the ceiling in the corner. My eyes drift to the walls, which are painted a soft robin's-egg blue. Wires connect me to the machines next to my bed. It feels like tubes are jutting into my nostrils. I grip one of the metal rails that run alongside my arms. I must be in a hospital.

I hear the noise again, the crying. Someone is hunched over in the chair next to me, their body heaving up and down slowly. It takes my eyes a moment to focus on who it is.

"Dad?" My voice comes out all raspy, and my throat feels parched and sore. My mouth has an awful taste to it, as if I've eaten the contents of an ashtray.

He looks up at me, and his face is a mix of deep grief and joy. He reaches for my hand and clutches it in his own. I don't remember my dad ever holding my hand, not even when I was little. His skin is calloused and rough.

"Hank, you're okay. You're going to be okay," he assures me, then calls to the nurse, letting her know I'm awake. This must be a big deal because she's in there like a shot, taking my vitals, letting me know I've given them all a scare. Apparently I inhaled quite a bit of smoke, and by the time the fireman got to me, I was about to lose consciousness. I'll be fine, but my lungs will need time to recover.

Just hearing the story again sets off my dad, and when the nurse leaves, he squeezes my hand again and says to me, "I was so scared. First your mom and Mickey, and when this happened... You're all I've got left in this world, Hank. You and me. You're my flesh and blood. I swear to God, I don't know what I would have done if I had lost you too."

"Mickey was there, Dad," I say. "I heard him."

Dad smiles and wipes at his eyes. "I believe he was, Hank. I believe he was."

Slowly the night starts to come back to me. "Is Peyton okay? Is she here?" I try to sit up, but it's uncomfortable.

"She's fine. Don't worry. She'll be back in a few hours. I sent her back to our house to get some rest. She's been here all night with you, and she refused to leave until the doctors assured her you would be all right."

"Her mother will think she started the fire. She'll send her away," I say, panic rising in my chest.

"No one is sending her away."

"No, Dad, you don't understand—"

"Actually, I do. Peyton told us everything, and Monica and I spoke to her mother. Because of the fire and Peyton's allegations about her mother's neglect and abuse, we convinced her mother it was best for everyone if Peyton stayed with us right now. It was that or call Child Protective Services, and I think her mother liked that idea even less. With a short list of options, she relented pretty quick."

"Thanks, Dad."

"It's the right thing to do." He pats my arm, and his face brightens. "Peyton told me you have an interview at a fancy art school in Boston. I'm real proud of you."

I let those words sink in. He's never said he's proud of me before. But then I get paranoid that he's baiting me to tell me all the reasons I can't go.

"I'm sorry I didn't get a chance to tell you, Dad. But don't worry, I don't need to go to art school. I mean, I know you need me here too."

He shakes his head. "You're going. You have to take opportunities like that when they come your way. If you never take a single chance in life, you know what you'll get? Nothing. You've got talent, Hank. Somebody is going to notice that. Clearly they already have. Hell, I've seen your stuff. It's great."

"How have you seen my drawings?"

"You leave it lying around that room of yours all the time. You think I haven't noticed? I may have been out of it after your mother died, but I'm not blind. I especially liked that one you made where your superhero guy—"

"Freeze Frame. His name is Freeze Frame," I say, not even caring that my dad has probably riffled through stuff in my room if he's seen my comics. He's seen my drawings. He likes them. That means more than I could ever explain to him.

"Yeah, Freeze Frame. I liked that one where he tries to stop that mad scientist from turning people into life-size ants because the scientist was plotting to make Earth into a giant colony and enslave everyone as workers. Except, of course, him and that other scientist guy."

"Dr. Kingsley," I tell him.

"He was pure evil. But it was great how Freeze Frame defeats them by stopping time and putting the ant formula into their coffee so the scientists drink their own poison and turn into giant ants that then get squished." Dad chuckles and he gets all these lines at the corners of his eyes.

"Yeah, that was a fun one," I say. "So you really liked it?"

"I loved it," he says, and he seems genuine. "When you're given a talent like that, you don't waste it. That's something even money can't buy."

"I won't," I tell him.

"Maybe someday they'll sell *Freeze Frame* at that shop where I bought you that Captain America comic. Then I'll go there and tell everyone you're my kid."

He *does* remember. I smile and say, "That would be pretty awesome, Dad."

"You're like a real-life superhero, Hank," Dad tells me. "You saved Peyton's life. Probably in more ways than one. If you hadn't helped her get out of there when you did, she'd be lying here too, or worse."

"It wasn't anything anyone else wouldn't have done. I just made sure she got out."

"You did good, Son." His face gets serious again, and tears well up in the corners of his eyes. "You've put up with a lot these last few years, especially from me. I was just so angry—angry with them for dying and angry with myself for living. It never occurred to me you might have those same damn feelings. I let you down. And when I got the call that you were here and I thought you might die…"

He takes a deep breath, trying to compose himself. I know this kind of stuff is not easy for him. He shakes his head and says, "I had no right to call you chickenshit all those times, because the truth is, you have more courage than anyone I know."

"Thanks, Dad." I know this is his form of an apology, and even though it can't erase years of hurt, it's a start.

My eyes begin to feel heavy again, like there are weights beneath the lids. Whatever the nurse shot into my IV when she was here is making me groggy.

"I think I need to take a little nap, Dad. I'm feeling sort of tired," I tell him.

Maybe it's the drugs, but I swear before I drift off again I hear him say, "I love you."

The next time I open my eyes, Dad is gone and Peyton's asleep in the chair next to me, her body curled in a ball, her mouth hanging open. She's snoring lightly, and she looks so peaceful that I don't want to wake her, but given how medicated I feel, I have to seize these moments of clarity while I can.

"Hey," I whisper. She stirs. "Peyton, hey, wake up."

Her eyes flutter open and then she excitedly leans forward, grabbing my hand. "Hey, you're finally awake."

"I am. It's kind of hard to sleep too long when they wake you up every few hours to poke you and take your blood. I'm not entirely convinced that they're not secretly vampires."

"They're just making sure you're okay. You inhaled a lot of smoke."

"Is that why the inside of my mouth tastes like I smoked a carton of cigarettes?"

"Pretty much."

I try to scoot to the side and pat the space beside me in the bed. "Come lie next to me."

"You must be feeling better. You're up for thirty seconds, and already you're trying to get me into bed with you," she says. "There're all these wires. We might set off an alarm."

"I don't care," I say, gathering the tubing to the side to make room for her.

She glances at the door, then grins, gingerly lying down beside me. She puts her head on my chest, and I wrap my arm around her. I run my fingers through her hair and down her cheek, and kiss the top of her head.

My lungs hurt. I cough. It makes her jump. "I'm fine," I assure her and she curls back into me.

"I don't know what I would have done if you hadn't made it, Hank," she says. "This was all my fault. All of it. I lit the candle. I'm the one who fell asleep before putting it out. When the paramedics got to you, you were barely breathing—"

I silence her. "It's not your fault, Peyton. I could have blown out the candle too, but I didn't. Accidents happen. I'm still here. And so are you."

"I'm glad."

"Me too," I say. "My dad says you told him about the whole art school thing. He thinks I should go."

"Of course you should go," she says.

"Well, that depends," I tell her.

She looks up at me. "On what? You just said he told you that you should go."

"On you."

She hesitates. "I don't know about the whole gallery thing. Why would they hire me? I don't have any experience."

"You could always be an entrepreneur," I suggest. "Like sell your photographs. Or open a market where you sell only foods that have no skin or pits. You could call it Pitskinno's."

She laughs. "Now you're really thinking out of the box."

"So does this mean you'll go?"

She repositions herself, and then she leans down and kisses me. Her mouth is warm and soft against my cracked, dry lips, and I imagine she must feel as if she's kissing a piece of sandpaper. If she minds, she doesn't show it.

It would be incredibly romantic, us lying in a hospital bed making out, except for the fact that I have tubes sticking out of my nose and an IV in my arm, and they are completely getting in the way. If only we could get away with hospital sex. That would be totally frickin' hot.

# 25

IRONICALLY, I MISS PROM BECAUSE I'M IN THE hospital, having nearly bit the dust in a totally different fire. What are the odds?

Nearly dying makes you realize who and what really matters. By the end of the following week when I finally get to go home, I know there's something I need to do.

I show up at Nick's house unannounced, and lucky for me the gate is open. There are a bunch of cars in the driveway. I'm hesitating, thinking I've probably come at a bad time if the Giulianis have company, when Nick drives up behind me in his dad's black Mercedes, music blaring. To say he's surprised to see me is an understatement.

He climbs out and heads toward me. "Hey. What are you doing here?" he asks.

"I wanted to talk to you," I say. "Actually, I've wanted to for a while, but I was kind of in the hospital."

"I heard about that. Jesus, you okay?"

"Yeah, I'll be fine," I say. "Worked out in my favor, really, because I didn't get stuck going to prom."

"Lucky you." Nick pops the trunk. It's filled with ice.

"You need a hand with that?"

"Sure. Good timing. You saved me from frostbite carrying these things," he says and hands me a bag of ice to carry and grabs the other bag for himself. "I would've stopped by, but I wasn't sure if you'd want to see me."

"I know things have been weird lately. But that's why I'm here. I'm hoping we can put all this crazy shit behind us, you know? Keep moving forward."

"Forward is good. Listen, I'm sorry, man."

"I'm sorry too. Things got a little out of hand."

"So we're good?"

"Definitely." I follow him into the house. "So what's all this ice for?"

"Giovanna's engagement is back on so my parents are throwing a party. And false alarm on the pregnancy thing. Turns out the wedding jitters made her late for her monthly bill, so at least we won't have to be looking for a place to hide her fiancé's body anytime soon."

We bring the ice into the kitchen, and as soon as Mrs. Giuliani catches sight of me, her face lights up like she's won the Publishers Clearing House sweepstakes. "Hank! Oh my God!" She rushes over to give me a hug. Same as the first time we met, she enfolds me into her ample bosom, but it's extra awkward because I'm still holding the bags of ice. Nick pulls me to safety.

"Ma! Seriously, give the guy some air."

The next thing I know, Mr. Giuliani is shaking my hand and pulling me into the living room, telling everyone about the fire and how I was in the hospital. Suddenly, the party guests are fanning out in a circle around us, wanting to hear all the details. Unfortunately, I don't really remember most of them. But I'm overwhelmed by how genuinely glad Nick's family is to see me and their concern.

They offer me a drink and plates of food, and I glance at Giovanna because I'm sure she's pissed that I've diverted all the attention from her special occasion, but she's sitting there as rapt as the rest of them. I'm not used to being the center of attention in a good way, and it feels pretty amazing. Then Nick's mom says the capper.

"It's so wonderful to see you, Hank. Nicky would give us updates, of course, but we were all so worried. You just take things slow, and if there's ever anything we can do, you don't hesitate to ask, you hear me?"

I turn to look at Nick, but he's busy stacking a cracker with salami and cheese, completely avoiding eye contact. "Thank you, I will."

Nick tells his parents we're going to go hang out in his room, and on the way up the stairs, I say, "So you got updates?"

"It was no big deal. I asked Peyton to keep me in the loop and let me know what was happening. Like I said, I didn't think you'd want to see me."

"For the record, I would have, but I get it. No hard feelings," I say.

"So are hospital nurses as hot as they are on TV?"

Same old Nick. I laugh even though it still hurts to do so. "Not even close."

Upstairs, Nick tells me about prom. He took Amanda, and at first things seemed to be going well, until sometime between the main course and dessert, she excused herself from the table to go to the bathroom, where she apparently hooked up with Clay Kimball, who was having a hetero moment, and they took off. As in, left the dance. It took Nick nearly an hour to realize she wasn't coming back. It's a pretty awful story, and I feel bad, especially since I was the one who encouraged Amanda to go with him, so I tell him the truth.

When I share that I was actually the one who started the

fire, he's practically rolling in the aisle. He thinks it's all pretty funny, and looking back on it, I guess it kind of is.

Graduation blows by, and then it's the beginning of summer, and with it, Peyton's eighteenth birthday. It's truly a celebration because she's finally free to make decisions for herself. Monica even bakes her some cupcakes, which turn out exactly as you'd expect, but it's about the gesture and people showing up for her, celebrating her.

Peyton's been staying with us, and Monica helped find her a counselor who she talks to once a week. She's doing so much better, says she feels more in control of her emotions. She's even mentioned reaching out to her dad at some point and perhaps trying to work things out with her mom, but that's all way down the line. The main thing is that she's hopeful again and working to try to heal as best she can. It will be a long road, but at least she's not traveling it alone anymore.

Before I know it, it's August, and I'm packing my life into a bunch of brown cardboard boxes I snagged from the recycler at Shop 'n Save, getting ready to move to Boston.

On our last night together for the foreseeable future, Nick, Peyton, and I are driving around in Nick's dad's Mercedes trying to figure out something special to do to mark the moment. Nick suggests bowling, but we all agree that's lame and anticlimactic.

Peyton suggests a movie, but it defeats the purpose of spending the evening together if we sit in the dark and don't talk for two and a half hours. We come up with several other equally lackluster ideas, and then, as we loop down Main Street for the fourth time in a row, it hits us. It is so obvious it's crazy we didn't think of it right from the get-go.

Ziggy's.

It's on.

The three of us sit at a corner table, and when the waitress comes by and asks if we're ready to order, we most definitely are. We order three How High burgers (no tomatoes for Peyton), a large order of fries, and three Cokes. The waitress rings the giant bell by the register and announces to the kitchen in a booming voice, "We got three How Highs!"

Nick points to a blank spot in the row of pictures of those who have successfully finished their burgers. "That's where mine is going. Right there."

"If you can finish it without puking," Peyton tells him.

"The rules merely say you have to finish. It doesn't say anything about puking afterward," I point out.

"Truth," Nick says and pulls a stack of about fifteen napkins from the metal dispenser on the table. He notices us both watching him with great interest. "What? I'm getting prepared."

"Clearly," I say. He grabs another just to piss me off.

Nick turns to Peyton and asks, "So what's the story with you two? I mean, now that Hank's going to be in Boston, are you guys gonna live together or something?"

"Or something," I say as the waitress brings our Cokes. I pull the wrapper off my straw, jam it into the iceberg floating on top, and take a long sip.

Peyton explains, "Actually, Hank's going to go and get settled, and I'm going to stay here with his dad and Monica for a while. Hank talked to his old boss at Shop 'n Save, and he hired me to pick up some of Hank's old shifts, so at least I'll have that going on until I figure out what's next."

"I've gotta assess the roommate situation," I add. "He sounds totally chill and says he's completely down with Peyton staying there so it shouldn't be a problem. He has a girlfriend who goes to Boston University, so he said he'll probably be at her place most of the time anyway."

"I've been talking to this woman at this gallery on Newbury Street, and she said she might be looking for a gallery assistant," Peyton says. "I'd love to do that and save up to take some photography classes next semester." She lights up like a candle as she tells Nick about it. She seems so hopeful and excited.

"Nice. Sounds like you have a good plan." Nick leans back

to take a sip of his Coke, only to have the block of ice crash forward with the liquid and hit him in the mouth. Smooth.

I hand him one of the sixteen napkins from his pile. "So how about you? You're gonna be freezing your balls off in Chicago, huh?"

"I can't wait to blow this clambake," he says. "Plus, those Midwestern girls are smokin' hot."

It's funny the things you talk about when you're hungry. Our conversation slowly degenerates into a discussion of where would be the safest place to survive a zombie apocalypse. (Our answer: one of those wholesale club warehouses. Not only do they have all the food and supplies you could ever need, but you can't get in without a membership card.)

And then the moment of truth arrives. The bell rings again, and seconds later, amid a chant of "How High, How High!" from the entire kitchen and waitstaff, three beauteous fifteen-dollar burgers the size of our heads are delivered to our table in all their greasy glory. They are a true culinary masterpiece. I'm not even sure I can get my mouth around the thing.

"Let's do this," Nick says. We raise our burgers as if we are making a toast, and then we all take our first bite at the same time.

The rush of flavors hits my mouth all at once: the melty

cheesiness of the mozzarella sticks, the spice of the jalapeño poppers, and the lukewarm, runny egg yolk are balanced by the coolness of the secret sauce, lettuce, and tomatoes. It all perfectly meshes with the ground beef and salty strips of bacon. It's pretty much the best thing I've ever tasted in my entire life.

Nearly thirty minutes later, we finish the damn things and the waitress snaps a picture of the three of us for the wall with an ancient Polaroid camera. Before she can put the camera down, Nick bolts from the table and heads to the bathroom, looking slightly ill. They put our picture up on the wall, and as I look at it, I know that we're savoring the final moments of something special. We may remain friends, but as time progresses, there will be new experiences, a loss of common ground, and inevitably, the connection will never be quite the same again. Not because we don't care about each other, but because you can't hold on to the past forever. That photo on the wall is already a memory.

We drive around in Nick's car for a while after that, laughing and talking, with no particular destination in mind. It feels good to be together, and for the first time in a long time, I feel a sense of belonging and family. Family isn't about sharing the same blood in your veins; it's about the people who come into your life and see how completely messed up and nutter you are and then stick around anyway. I wish I could freeze-frame this moment because I don't ever want to forget it.

I gotta be honest. I have no idea what the hell is going to happen next. I don't know if my relationship with Peyton will work out and be great forever, or if it's just great right now. I don't know when I'll see Nick again.

That's the amazing thing about life: you can be sure you know what's going to happen next, but you never really do. Anything can happen, and amazingly, that doesn't scare me.

In fact, it's pretty frickin' cool.

# ACKNOWLEDGMENTS

Although writing a book may be a solitary venture involving copious amounts of caffeine and cupcakes, it takes many wonderful people to bring a book to life, and I cannot thank them enough.

First, confetti drops, sparkles, and never-ending gratitude to my amazing editor, Annette Pollert-Morgan, whose incredibly thoughtful comments, brainstorming sessions, and genuine love for these characters helped make this story so much richer. I still owe you an "I Heart Hank" tee. Thank you for giving a home to the book of my heart.

To my incredible, hilarious, rock star agent Leigh Feldman. Thank you for believing in me and this story from the very beginning. I am so grateful for your invaluable advice, wisdom, and laugh-out-loud emails. I feel so lucky to have you in my corner.

To Dominique Raccah, Todd Stocke, Elissa Erwin, Alex Yeadon, Kathryn Lynch, Nicole Komasinski, Elizabeth Boyer, and the rest of the incredible team at Sourcebooks Fire, for that kickass cover, for making me look like I can grammar and English like a pro (I kept you on your toes!), and for being part of helping me hold my lifelong dream in the palm of my hand.

To Jessica Brody, mentor/friend/soul sister: there are not enough words to express what your friendship and support mean to me. Whether we are dreaming up book titles and apps over pancakes, eating our weight in sushi while sharing sage advice, or playing Mall Madness and baking cookies, you keep me smiling. Thank you for being that friend that always seems to bring perspective and sunshine.

To Gae Polisner: my partner-in-crime. This novel is what it is in huge part because of you, and I thank you for your spot-on, brilliant insight, your grounded reality checks, and your equally twisted sense of humor that so perfectly matches my own.

To Jessi Kirby: between your book touching my heart at a time when I needed it most, introducing me to Leigh, and lending your last name to Hank, you have helped change my life. Thanks for all your kindness. You are one of the most genuine souls I have ever met.

To Alex: thanks for being my light in the darkness when I needed it most. I miss you every day.

If ever there were a profession where one needs people who get his/her crazy, it's writing, and I am so grateful for some fabulous friends in my life who do just that. All the squeezy hugs and gratitude to Demetra Brodsky, Tracy Holczer, Shelli Cornelison, Michelle Levy, Jessica Love, Ara Grigorian, Jennifer Bosworth, Gretchen McNeil, Nadine Nettman, Julia Collard, Jennifer Olson, James Raney, Lisa Marnell, Anne Tibbetts, Meredith Glickman, Eileen Cook, Beth Navarro, Claire Di Liscia Baird, Nicole Maggi, Dana Elmendorf, Cindy Pon, Shaun Hutchinson, Karen Grencik, my fellow Sweet Sixteeners, SCBWI, and all my SoCal writer peeps! And to Laurie Halse Anderson, who gave me my first manuscript critique and made me swear I would never stop writing.

Additional thanks to my nonwriter cheerleading squad: Jill Freeman, Rachel Greenwald, Lisa Fragner, Julie Hallowell, Susan Wolf, Marcus Ryle, Nancy Walker, Martha Green, Niki Ross, Melissa Beal, Mike Gangemi, Jacob Walker, Arun Burra, Michelle Choi, Ilene Bobrowsky, Cori Henry, Debbie Blander, and all my WHS Regiment moms! Please know that your encouragement and support has meant the world to me.

And last but not least, to my incredible family, who never stopped believing in me, who reorganized their lives around my writing time, who put up with my crazy way beyond the call of duty. John, Ethan, Katie, Mom, Dad, Ben, Bonnie, Lee, Scott, Lily, Sasha, Joy, Jason, Roberta, and Nan—you are my heart, and this book is for you. "The delay is never the denial."

# ABOUT THE AUTHOR

Robin Reul has been writing stories since she was old enough to hold a pen. Though she grew up on movie sets and worked for years in the film and television industry, she ultimately decided to focus her attention on writing young adult novels. And unlike Hank, she does not know how to ride a bike. She lives in Los Angeles with her husband, son, and daughter. *My Kind Of Crazy* is her first novel.